www.haseleyhinton.com

Fiction by Haseley Hinton

Novels

Shadow of the Seacrow
Song of the Seacrow

Short Story

Curio of the Seacrow

HASELEY HINTON

Song of the Seacrow

Book Two of the Sacred Mountain Trilogy

SECOND BORN BOOKS
Edinburgh

Published by Second Born Books 2012

All rights reserved
Copyright © Haseley Hinton 2012

Haseley Hinton is hereby identified as the author of this work in accordance with section 77 of the Copyright, Designs and Patents Act 1988

No part of this publication may be reproduced, stored in a database or retrieval system, or transmitted, in any form or by any means, electronic, mechanical, photocopying, recording or otherwise, without the prior written permission of the publisher, nor otherwise be circulated in any form or binding or cover, other than that in which it is published and without a similar condition including this condition being imposed on the subsequent purchaser.

Second Born Books
c/o Starbit Limited
The Caretaker's Cottage
Edinburgh Technopole EH26 0BA.

ISBN 9780956113528

Typeset by Starbit Ltd, Edinburgh.
Printed and bound in Great Britain by Inky Little Fingers Ltd, Gloucester
using 100% recycled paper.

For Jonathan

With grateful thanks to Chris and Rosemary
and all those who helped.

Chapter 1

Maina stood at the window of her room staring steadily northwards. She could see the sea on the horizon and to the right a line of mountains just catching the last of the afternoon sun. She felt in her pocket for a parchment envelope, grubby now with too much handling. She took out of it the coil of hair that she had picked up many moons ago from the floor of the kitchen on the Sacred Mountain. Somewhere beyond those distant sunlit peaks was the man whose hair had been cut and shaved that night. But, though she longed to see Kesh once again, she could not think of a way of persuading her father to let her travel to Morth, much less to allow her to invite Kesh to visit the palace at Zoradetra.

There was a knock at the door, and Maina quickly put the hair back into its envelope. Her nurse-sister came in as she was pushing it into her pocket.

"Greetings, sister. How goes the world today?" asked Wyn. "Still dreaming of a certain Morthern monk, I see. Don't go thinking I don't know what you keep in that envelope."

Maina coloured a little. "Well," she said. "I like to think back now and again."

"Now and again! Maina, you are forever brooding over him."

"It is not without reason. Brooding over him, as you put it, stops me brooding over something worse."

"You are worrying about Calim Bradmutt?"

Maina turned towards the window again.

"Oh, Wyn, what did I do?" she fretted. "How could I have abandoned my own child? How could I have left him to the care of others when I can't know if they will show him love and kindness or bring him up with cruel discipline and too much punishment?"

"Maina, Maina," Wyn chided her. "Kesh is there to supervise. He will take him away from any carers who do not measure up to his standards. Don't you trust him?"

"Of course I trust him. But what if Calim's carers hide their faults from him?"

"That will not happen. Calim is a lucky boy. He has two fathers and two mothers to worry over him. But worrying does *you* no good. You should try to concentrate on your life here. We are very busy at the temple. I have had to take some of the classes for first round girls because priestess

Vanoula has just had her baby, and the priestess at Brinay is too ill to lead the prayers so the temple has had to be closed. I know you are committed to helping your father, but if you took on some of the temple duties here in Zoradetra, priestess Finna would be free to go to Brinay to take over."

"I'm sorry," Maina answered quickly. "I am too busy at the palace. I have so very much to learn. After managing to stop the war by persuading my father to make peace with Morth, I felt empowered. It gave me the confidence to contemplate becoming a ruler in my own right, but I have since discovered that the day to day administration of an empire is extremely complex and requires a great deal of knowledge and attention to detail."

"But you already have many rounds of studying behind you. You should use the training that you strove all that time to complete. We could really do with your help, even if it is just now and again."

"I am sorry. I am failing in my duties as priestess but the truth is ..." Maina drew in a long breath before confiding, "My faith is not as strong as it once was."

"Oh, Maina!" Wyn made a restrained exclamation, as if she was afraid of being overheard. "Why? Whatever happened?"

"Perhaps I spent too long in the company of a Mortherner. Kesh seemed so sure of his beliefs that I began to doubt my own. After all, we can't both be right." Maina searched Wyn's face for a glimmer of understanding, but saw only puzzlement. "Surely you had the same problem with Ahbrem? How did you reconcile your beliefs with his?"

Wyn shrugged and smiled.

"There is no conflict between our beliefs. Tarn is the god of the sky, Gorlan is the god of the sea and Harg is the god of Morth. Where is the difficulty?"

"So if you went to Morth, you would pray to Harg?"

"Certainly I would hope for his protection while I was in Morth, especially if I was married to a son of Morth."

Wyn could not repress the joyful grin that spread across her face as she gave out this last sentence.

"Oh, Wyn! Are you going to be married?"

"Ahbrem has proposed to me, yes. But I have told him I must stay with my mother for at least another round of seasons yet. I must be sure she has recovered from the shock of my father's death before I can think of leaving her."

"So he has managed to keep in touch?"

"He sends me messages now and again. Salwell knows a fishing captain who calls into the port at Fullabish about once a moon and collects any letters waiting there for me. Then Salwell takes my letters back to him. Has Kesh not kept in touch with you?"

"No," said Maina sadly. "I have not heard any news since the peace treaty was signed.

"Oh," said Wyn. "I'm sorry. I didn't mean to gloat."

"No, of course not," said Maina. "But Wyn, why do you have to stay with your mother? Surely Salwell is there to look after her?"

"Er ... yes. But what if Salwell marries?"

"Salwell? Your little brother?" Maina laughed at this possibility. "So, do you expect him to be married soon? Does he already have someone in mind?"

"Someone in mind, yes, but that's about as far as it goes."

"Salwell married! Now there's a thought. I still think of him as a child."

"Oh, he is quite grown up, I can assure you."

"So, is she pretty?"

"She? Oh, yes. Beautiful. At least, Salwell thinks so."

"Well, that's what counts, after all," Maina laughed lightly. "Is she a local girl?"

"Oh, er … yes."

"He is lucky to have someone close." Maina sighed. "I sometimes wish I had fallen in love with someone from nearby. At least I would get to see him now and again, even if it had to be in secret. Kesh seems to be so very far away."

"Maina ..." Wyn began.

"What is it, Wyn?"

"Oh, nothing," she said, and then immediately began again. "It's just that ..."

"Yes?"

"It's not that I see Kesh as a bad man. I don't think that. He is taking his responsibilities as a father very seriously. He can't be faulted on that score, but he is ... impetuous. He lacks self-control. I mean, if, when you were drunk, he couldn't resist the temptation of taking advantage of you ..."

"Oh!" Maina breathed, a little shocked. "I don't think it happened like that at all ... "

But Wyn went on.

"And Ahbrem tells all sorts of stories about him."

Maina's curiosity was aroused despite her dread. "Such as?"

"Such as, when Kesh had climbed the waterfall and was getting dressed in the robing room, he heard the cry of a maiden, and Kesh was going to open the door back to the waterfall, even though he knew the maiden would be naked. Ahbrem had to step in front of him to stop him."

"Oh!"

"And Ahbrem has told me innumerable tales about the scrapes Kesh got him into as a boy. They were the best of friends, so Ahbrem wasn't trying to make me think less of Kesh. He was just telling me about his childhood. He is genuinely fond of Kesh, after all, but he knows his friend has ... limitations. I am not at all surprised that Kesh caused you so much trouble, now I have this insight into his character. So, I think perhaps ... all things considered ..."

"Yes?" Maina's face had lost all its joy. She was staring bleakly at her friend, wondering whatever could be coming next.

"Maina, is it not time you thought of moving on? Perhaps you should consider a different suitor?"

"A different suitor? Wyn, I thought that you, of all people, would understand that I am sick of suitors. I am not marrying any man my father chooses for me. Now that I have known love, I cannot go back to the idea of marrying simply out of duty."

"But you could still marry for love. It does not have to be one your father's choices. You have admirers. It could be your choice."

"I have made my choice. My choice is to marry the man I love or to remain unwed. So I am resigned to not marrying, at least until my circumstances change."

"You mean until your father dies?" Wyn asked. "Maina, that might not happen for many, many years."

"No, I don't mean that!" cried Maina sharply. "I am not *waiting* for my father to die."

She frowned and turned away. Wyn could see that she had upset her.

"I'm sorry. I didn't mean to cause you pain."

Maina did not answer, so she said, "I'd better go."

As Wyn backed silently out of the room Maina was once again left staring through the window, with her fingertips on the envelope in her pocket. She felt as if Wyn had just reached in and torn at part of her innermost core. Her love for Kesh had been challenged and, by implication, his love for her. The prop she leaned on in every difficult moment had been attacked by her closest friend. She felt shaken and distraught.

***

Meanwhile at Khoulan, the sun had disappeared behind the Sacred Mountain and the sky was tinged with the colours of the sunset. Kesh looked up from his notes. He had been preparing to deliver a lesson the next day on the culture of the Enahet people but he caught sight of the mountain silhouetted against a blaze of golden clouds and paused to admire it. He wished that he could be there on the mountain, where the sun still shone and where he would be able to look southwards over Xoutha. He took from his pocket a folded piece of parchment and read once again the words in ink that had been black but were now faded to a muddy brown.

> *To the most honourable Kesh of Khoulan*
> *Revered Mattouk*
>
> *I most respectfully request that you appoint a suitable escort to accompany this messenger to the capital in order to safely deliver the accompanying offer of peace from His Highness the Emperor of Xoutha to the most esteemed King of Morth.*
>
> *I cannot speak freely, as I have to assume that this letter could be read by eyes other than those for which it is intended. Suffice it to say that good fortune has created the possibility that the accompanying offer of peace can be made whilst also releasing the emperor's daughter from her betrothal vows.*
>
> *I must now take Bradmutt's place, as far as I am able, in assisting my father with the empire's administration. I look forward to better times when I might be released from these duties long enough to visit the Sacred Mountain Community and, perhaps, to travel even further afield.*
>
> *I trust this finds you and all your family in good health. I fervently wish you and all your kin lasting peace and blissful long life, and look forwards to future opportunities to further our acquaintance.*
>
> *Thanking you in anticipation for your help in finding an escort for this important messenger.*
>
> *Yours sincerely*
> *Maina, Priestess of the Temple of Tarn at Zoradetra.*

Kesh looked once more towards the mountains and, in his head, he tried again to translate the stilted words on the page into the message that was to be read behind them. 'All your family' and 'all your kin' both referred, of course, to their son Calim Bradmutt. Kesh had just taken Calim back to his nurse family after a day's visit to the monastery. Perhaps that was why he was feeling a little low. Calim was walking now and able to toddle around after his father, but he seemed to prefer the view from higher up. He was forever holding up his little arms to Kesh to be picked up and carried. This silent request for closeness was one Kesh usually found impossible to resist. He considered it a gift from Harg that this child remembered him from one visit to the next and always seemed pleased to see him. In fact, the infant spent most of his visit in his father's arms whilst Kesh was consulted by his colleagues about this or that in the normal way, so that Kesh ended up making some of the most important decisions about the running of the Khoulan community with the little boy watching solemnly over him.

Then there were Calim's early attempts at communication, both loveable and a source of amusement. He said 'orter' in place of water and called his friend Ahbrem 'Brembum'. Kesh always spoke to Calim in the Sacred Language so that he would be able to communicate easily with his birth mother, if ever the day should come. That meant the child had to cope with speaking two different languages, as his Morthern nurse-family only spoke their native tongue.

Kesh had taught Calim to address him by his first name, as it was impossible to acknowledge his fatherhood within the Khoulan community. He felt it was especially important that their true relationship was hidden from the students. He did not want Calim to have to explain his position to his fellows when he came to Khoulan permanently. It was only Ahbrem who knew the truth.

But Kesh was not comfortable with being secretive, and it was difficult, sometimes, not to blame Maina for this state of affairs. He had worked so hard to achieve the dispensation that allowed Khoulan monks to marry. They could have been living in newly designated rooms at the monastery by now, all together, as a family. But, although Maina had seemed to return his love, she could not be persuaded to marry him. He struggled to remember how she had convinced him, before returning to Xoutha, that there were more important considerations than their happiness together. She had convinced him that it was necessary for them to part in order to end the war but it all seemed so long ago now and he couldn't help thinking, looking back, that there might have been another way.

Taking Calim back to his nurse-family after his visits got more and more difficult, but Kesh would have to wait for several more years before

Calim would be old enough to stay permanently at the monastery and become a student. Kesh lowered his eyes from the colours of the sunset and looked again at the well-worn letter. Maina's wishes for lasting peace and blissful long life were a much appreciated tribute to Kesh's predecessor, Mattouk Calim, whose name Kesh had passed on to his son. The mattouk's favourite parting words had always been a wish for his fellows to enjoy peace and long life.

The reference to 'future opportunities to further their acquaintance' remained a mystery. Kesh thought back to how his heart had leapt when he had first read that Maina had been released from her betrothal. During the early days when he had returned to the monastery without her and given up his son into the care of the nurse family, his soul had languished for a long while in despair. There had followed a colourless period when he had carried out the functions of the mattouk mechanically, without the pleasure or pride he surely should have felt at his promotion. The ray of hope that Maina had given him, by suggesting in this letter that she might not have to marry the Prince of Benethan after all, had put a little light back into his life. Kesh's soul had begun to sing for joy when the news that had subsequently come from Wyn, via her letters to Ahbrem, that Benethan had been banished from the palace in disgrace. He had eagerly awaited word from Maina, expecting her soon to announce that she was now free and able to take up residence at Khoulan. But Maina had not written to him again and, as far as he knew, she had not visited the Sacred Mountain Community recently, much less travelled any further north. Excerpts of Ahbrem's letters from Wyn were all the news Kesh ever got of Maina.

Was Maina's failure to communicate a result of her father's strict supervision, or did Maina now regret her friendship with him and wish to bring an end to their relationship? He was aware that Wyn did not fully approve of him, and in her latest missive she had hinted to Ahbrem that she planned to suggest a new prospective suitor for Maina. This was truly dismal news to Kesh but he had no idea what to do about it. He was the mattouk of a Morthern monastery. He had to maintain the appearance of respectability. He could not write a personal letter to a Xouthan priestess. The letter might be intercepted. If the true nature of their relationship were to be revealed his position as mattouk would become untenable.

Nor could he visit her in Zoradetra. He could not even travel safely over the border into Xoutha. He did not speak the language and, despite the recent peace treaty, Mortherners were not likely to be the most welcomed strangers in that country. Perhaps he should learn to speak Xouthan. If he could become sufficiently fluent in the language, he could leave Ahbrem in charge at Khoulan for a while and take the path down the south side of the Sacred Mountain. Then perhaps he would see again the object of his deep devotion. He so admired the grace and dignity with which she held herself when she was in the role of Xouthan priestess but most of all he had loved that breathless flush and carefree laughter that had come on the day she had chased the sheep. For that precious moment in time she had forgotten that she was an emperor's daughter.

He let out a silent sigh as these images faded to reveal his lonely study once again, and resolved that, on his next official visit to the Sacred Mountain, he would ask the principal priestess trainer, Hannala, if she could spare some time to instruct him in the Xouthan language. He knew he would find the pronunciation so much more difficult than either Enahet or the Sacred Language and that he would need expert help. Then he could perhaps go to Zoradetra and ask Wyn to arrange a secret meeting so that he could find out if Maina still had feelings for him.

He got out his astronomical calendar and found that the next lunar eclipse was only a half a moon away. He took a piece of clean blank parchment and began a letter to the Prophet of the Burning Ship, to tell him that he intended to visit the Sacred Mountain to celebrate the eclipse and asking if they could accommodate him for a visit of five days duration. That should give him time to start on his study of the Xouthan language.

Chapter 2

On the Sacred Mountain, preparations were underway for a visit by the second of the four kings. Nathan, the member of Ship's crew who had set up a Christian community in the Land of the Four Kings, was coming to see his old captain. Ship was dreading the visit, as he knew from Kevin, the first of the four kings to visit him, that Nathan would disapprove of the fact that he had allowed his Penethellan friends to think of him as a prophet. Ship had spent the preceding day nervously tidying his study. One of the trainee priestesses had helped him to clean and polish the desk, the map table and the bookcases. Ship somehow hoped that being clean and tidy would temper Nathan's disapproval. He carefully hid his handwritten copies of the first versions, in the Sacred Language, of the Xouthan 'Book of Sacred Texts' and the Morthern 'Histories of Harg'.

A knock came at the study door. It was a trainee priestess announcing that figures had been seen climbing the path on the Xouthan side of the Sacred Mountain. Ship took his cloak from its hook on the door. Although spring was approaching, the weather was still chilly and his old bones were sensitive to the cold. He found Hannala, the principal, already waiting outside the Xouthan gate along with two of the maidens. The visitor was going to get the best welcome that the Sacred Mountain Community could possibly offer.

"Nathan!" Ship called out as soon as he saw figures rounding the last bend. "How wonderful to see you!"

He embraced his former crewman and patted him on the back while the maidens took his luggage from the Xouthan bearers who were allowed no further.

"Hello, Ship," Nathan returned more reservedly. "Kevin told us that you preferred to be called Ship. I hope that's right."

"Yes, yes, absolutely. You haven't aged a day, I see."

"Oh, I don't know about that. You're looking pretty good yourself."

"Oh, I'm feeling my age these days. Always getting aches and pains, and I tire so quickly. But never mind me. How was your journey? Was the sea voyage rough?"

"Not too bad, but it seemed to take a good while to get across."

"It's a long way. You must be exhausted. Let's get you settled in. One of the maidens will show you to your room, and then we'll have some tea."

Later that afternoon, Ship and Nathan were sitting either side of the fire in Ship's study. They had drunk tea and eaten cakes but it would be some while before the maidens on kitchen duty would ring the bell for dinner. Ship had already run out of trivial conversation topics and they now sat in silence. Nathan was turning his teacup over and over in his hands, absent-mindedly following the patterns around the cup. Ship would have liked to show him the view from the balcony, but the sun had already set and it was too cold for standing out of doors. He searched in vain for a new subject to discuss, but eventually decided that the best policy would be to get the awkward topics out of the way first.

He cleared his throat and said "Kevin told me that you wouldn't approve of the fact that Xouthans and Mortherners refer to me as a prophet."

Nathan shifted in his seat slightly. "I must admit I'm not at all comfortable with that title."

"It wasn't through choice, I can assure you, but it was better than them thinking of me as a god."

Nathan drew in a long breath and spoke as if he was restraining his anger. "You are allowing them to think of you as something you are not."

"They don't mean it in the religious sense. They just seemed to think I was predicting events before they happened. In reality, anyone with a bit of common sense could have seen what was coming, but they would insist ... "

Nathan's restraint was overcome. He interrupted Ship. "It really is unforgivable. It is blasphemous, in fact. If you had religious convictions of your own and you mistakenly believed yourself to be a prophet, I could forgive it. I would even feel a little sorry for you, but Kevin says you don't actually believe in anything."

"No. That's true. I lost my faith a long, long time ago."

"So there's no excuse," Kevin said curtly. "These beings need to know the truth. They need to prepare themselves. We have a duty to pass on our knowledge to them, to enable them to come to Christ as we humans can."

"My feelings are that we should not interfere. Their beliefs are important to them. We should respect their religions and leave them to worship their god or gods as they see fit."

"I am afraid I can't agree with you. I believe God's purpose in putting us on this planet was to bring His message to them. I had hoped you would not oppose me in this endeavour."

"I will not oppose you. I respect your beliefs as much as I respect theirs. Probably more, in fact, as I was brought up in a predominantly Christian country. But I do ask that you limit yourself to telling them about what you believe, and refrain from telling them that they must believe it too. Don't go criticising their beliefs, and don't try frightening them with tales of hell-fire and damnation. Let them choose for themselves. If your message is powerful enough, I'm sure it will get through."

"So you won't object to me preaching here?"

"Preaching? Here on the Sacred Mountain?"

"It seems as good a place to start as any."

"You must ask Hannala's permission. She is the principal here."

"There is another thing. This mountain would be the perfect site for an etherium."

"What's an etherium?"

"It's just my name for an elevated enclosed space set aside for prayer and worship. Any secluded roof space or hilltop garden could be converted. It's important to me that, when we pray, we are as close as we can be to God, so I've been creating rooftop courtyards and enclosed mountain gardens. Private spaces for undisturbed contemplation. It can take years, you see, to build a church, but you can put up a wicker fence and plant a few trees in an afternoon. Would you have any objections to me looking for a suitable area on the mountain?"

"Personally, I would have no objection to the creation of such a space, as long as it can be used by anybody. I wouldn't want you trying to claim part of the Sacred Mountain exclusively for Christian use."

"Oh," Nathan paused. "I don't know if that would work. I wouldn't be comfortable with heathen prayers being said in my etherium."

"Well anyway, it isn't up to me. The Sacred Mountain is on Xouthan land, so you must again ask Hannala for permission to use any place that is part of it."

"Perhaps it would be alright," Nathan muttered to himself, "as long as we could have an altar and a cross at the eastern end, to mark it out as Christian."

"So you're thinking of staying on quite while, then?" Ship asked.

"If you'll have me. I mean to leave behind at least one Christian convert to start the movement on this side of the ocean. I won't go before that happens."

"I see," said Ship, not entirely happy.

"My dear friend, if you would only open your heart up to the Lord, it could be you." Nathan forced a little laugh, "Your soul would be saved and my mission would be accomplished. You could send me home and you could carry on my work yourself."

"I'm afraid the Lord might find the hinges of my heart have gone a little rusty after all this time. I really can't imagine me finding God at this late stage."

"Clever words. Perhaps you will not find Him," Nathan said smoothly. "You put up these defences - but He might still find you." He slid one hand inside his jacket. "Captain, I have brought you a little gift."

Nathan pulled out a sizeable book bound in dark leather.

"My Penethellans have set up a primitive printing press in our community," he said. "We print and bind about a hundred copies a moon these days. I didn't know if you had brought a bible with you, so this one is for you."

"Thank you. Very thoughtful."

Ship took it from him and opened it up. He attempted to move Nathan on from the subject of his own salvation. "The quality of the printing is quite good. What's the paper made from?"

"Straw," Nathan answered proudly. "We experimented with several sources. Wood was the hardest to extract useful fibres from, but we found that certain crops yield strong straw fibres that work really well."

"You must tell the Morthern monks about this," said Ship, genuinely impressed. "And the Xouthans, too. They'll all be interested in ways of making more books without needing to copy out each one by hand."

Nathan's face broke into a genuine smile for the first time since his arrival. "I'd be happy to."

***

Maina was in the stateroom, a frown across her brow as she worked at her father's desk while he peered over her shoulder.

"You have made an error," the emperor said coldly. "I don't know why you bother to keep on trying, if you can't do any better than that."

Maina hid the hurt she felt.

"Surely it's possible to leave your accountants to deal with these figures." She suggested defiantly.

"Of course, but how do you gain trust in your officials, if you can't follow what they're doing? You have to understand every action and operation if you want to maintain a position of strength. I cannot emphasise enough the importance of keeping abreast with the machinations of the empire. If you want me to change the law so that you can take over when I'm gone, you must first convince me that you will be able to lead your court with wisdom and authority."

"I understand," Maina sighed. "Only I think I need a short rest. My head is spinning."

"We'll say that lessons are over for today, then. We'll tackle it again tomorrow."

As her father moved away, Maina stood up and stretched her back. Wyn had been sitting near one of the windows, embroidering a wall hanging for the temple, and Maina went over to her.

"This is going to look magnificent," she said, stretching out the part of it that Wyn had already completed. "It's the burning ship falling into the sea, isn't it?"

"Yes," said Wyn. "We are updating our stories about the Ship Prophet in the light of recent revelations."

"Doesn't that trouble you?"

"Why should it?" Wyn asked. "We misunderstood but now we understand a little better. The ways of the gods are always going to be mysterious to us. The truth will be revealed a little at a time, just as fast as we grow in our ability to assimilate it."

"Perhaps."

"Maina, we all have doubts now and again. Come to temple, and those doubts will start to fade. Come and help us train the maidens."

"Maybe next full moon I'll come. It's the festival of friendship then, isn't it? I must admit that I miss the celebrations - all the festivals that mark the passing seasons. But I'll just be there to watch, not to teach."

"It will be good to have you there." Wyn looked around and dropped her voice. "By the way, Salwell wants me to give you a message."

"Oh?"

"Yes. He says that if you want to write to Kesh, he will take the letter to his sea captain friend along with mine."

"Oh," said Maina. "That's very kind. I'd better think of something to write, then."

"He said he will come to collect the letter here tomorrow. He will meet you in the palace garden at mid-day."

"Couldn't you just take it to him?"

"Um, I think he perhaps thought," Wyn started hesitatingly, "that you'd want to hand it over personally. After all, it's a rather special letter if it's the first in such a long time."

"I trust you to hand it to him, Wyn."

"Perhaps Salwell's going to offer to travel to Morth to deliver it personally."

"That won't be necessary. I won't write anything that must be kept secret. Just let it go with your next letter to Ahbrem."

"Oh," said Wyn hesitating. "Alright. So you don't want to see Salwell, then?"

"No, no need. Don't trouble him."

"Very well."

Chapter 3

Ship and Nathan were sitting at the little table on the balcony of the Great Hall. Kesh, who had only been on the Sacred Mountain since the previous day, was standing with his hands on the balustrade enjoying the views west across the sea and southwards over Xoutha. Occasionally white columns of spray dashed soundlessly against distant rocks and a single seacrow circled, gliding on the updraughts.

It was the first warm day since Nathan's arrival and Ship sucked in the balmy breeze as though he had not dared to fill his lungs to capacity all winter.

"So you spoke to Hannala about setting up a printing press?" he asked Nathan.

"I did. It seems that it would have to be set up somewhere down in Xoutha because it would involve the employment of men. They'd need trained craftsmen to construct the machinery, even if it could be operated by women thereafter. I wish she'd change the rules but that doesn't seem to be possible."

"And will it be for Xouthan books or will you hijack it for bible printing?"

"I would hope some bibles could be printed there but the press will be free to print any kind of book. That does remind me of another problem that has come to light, though."

"Oh? What's that?"

"Well, I didn't realise that so few of your Penethellans speak the 'Sacred Language' as they call it. For the bible to be read by the layman, I'm going to have to have it translated into Xouthan. I'm assuming that goes for Mortherners, too."

"I don't think you should call them *my* Penethellans. Do you mean to tell me all the Penethellans in your country speak our language?"

"Most of them do, now. There are a few areas where the people are sticking to their local languages. The mountain tribe, for example, although, strictly speaking, their land is not yet part of our country."

Kesh had been day-dreaming about Maina, but pricked up his ears at hearing mention of a mountain tribe.

"Not yet?" repeated Ship. "Does that mean Doug retrieved the radioactive power unit in time?"

"Um ... it was retrieved, but apparently the tribal chief looks very sick.

He is expected to die quite soon, I'm afraid."

Kesh frowned, listening intently now, without understanding.

"I am very sorry to hear that," said Ship.

"Yes," Nathan said with some regret. "I wish I'd spoken against the idea at the time, but I didn't see the mountain tribes then as I see them now. I regarded them as the enemy. I thought of them as little better than savages. I didn't see them as intelligent creatures with souls that needed saving every bit as much as those of the more cultured Penethellans, the civilised ones who had been living with us for generations. I realise now that my mission must be to all Penethellans, not just the ones we happened to come across first."

Ship huffed under his breath, agreeing with the sentiment but not with the conclusion drawn from it.

"So," Nathan continued, "I'm looking for someone to translate the bible into the Xouthan and Morthern languages."

"Well, Kesh here is very fluent in what they call the 'sacred language' (apostrophes added) and is just starting to study Xouthan. Perhaps he could translate it for you." Ship turned to Kesh and asked, "Would you be willing to help my friend?"

"I am afraid I have not yet begun a proper study of Xouthan," Kesh said, "And, anyway, nearly all my time is taken up with my duties at Khoulan. Ahbrem would be the man for the task. His language skills are excellent. I believe he learned a good deal about the Xouthan language from the trainee priestesses during the round that he was stationed here."

"Could you spare him from his duties at Khoulan?" Ship asked.

"Once I get back, he could be spared for a little while. How long do you think it will take? Is it a long document, this bible?"

"It is rather long," said Nathan.

"What kind of document is it?"

As Nathan drew in the deep breath he needed to power a sufficiently worthy answer, Ship cut in,

"It's the equivalent in Nathan's religion to the 'Histories of Harg' or to the 'Xouthan book of Sacred Texts.'"

"I see," said Kesh. "But why ... ?"

"It is the one true religion," Nathan told him, scowling at Ship. "Everyone should hear its message."

"Oh," Kesh hesitated, not sure now that he could justify donating a Morthern monk's labours to the translation of the sacred text of another religion.

"You couldn't possibly spare Ahbrem for such a lengthy project," suggested Ship. "Perhaps we should find someone else. The problem is that nearly everyone here who is fluent in the sacred language is also involved in the administration of one or other of the existing religions."

Kesh paused for thought before saying, "I will tell Ahbrem about the task and let him decide for himself."

"Thank you," Nathan said gushingly. "I would be so grateful if you would put the proposition to him."

"I am returning to Khoulan in four days' time. I will tell him about it then."

"That is very good of you. Thank you."

"The mountain tribe you spoke of," Kesh ventured. "That wouldn't be the Ahn Dehar, would it?"

"I believe that is what they call themselves," Nathan answered. "Do you know of them?"

"Yes. We met chief Ackhart on our way to your country. The Ahn Dehar provided us with accommodation for a night. The chief was not well then."

"Um ... no. I regret what we did. I am afraid it's impossible now to put things right. It's too late."

"So what exactly did you do?" asked Kesh.

Nathan stared silently at the floor. Ship answered for him.

"They put a power unit in the chief's mattress. It contained ... well, a kind of slow-acting poison."

"We thought it might avoid a war," said Nathan by way of excuse. "His son was willing to sell us the coal we needed, you see."

"Ah, yes. I remember that Hernst felt differently about mining the land."

"Water under the bridge," said Ship. "Nathan's friends tried to retrieve the unit but it had already done its work by the sound of it. No use fretting over it now."

"I suppose not," said Kesh, hiding his discomfort.

That evening, Kesh witnessed the lunar eclipse from the balcony of the Sacred Mountain with the two humans and the rest of the community. He had seen a lunar eclipse before but the clear weather they enjoyed that night made this the best he had ever witnessed. The once full moon seemed to disappear slowly behind a dark disc but then reappeared as a dim but clearly spherical object, softly illuminated by a rosy glow.

"I didn't realise your Penethellans were interested in astronomy," Nathan said to Ship. "Doug made a telescope using the lenses from a broken gun scope. I'll tell him to bring it over when he comes."

Kesh spent the mornings of each of the following days listening to Hannala emphatically pronouncing the guttural sounds of the Xouthan language while he tried to imitate them. She praised his efforts sweetly, but Kesh doubted that his attempts were very accurate. Nevertheless, he felt it was important to pronounce the words correctly in order to hide his Morthern accent whilst in Xoutha. When he left a few days later, Hannala gave him an armful of papers that she had prepared to help him with his studies. He was touched to realise that she must have spent a great deal of time preparing these notes but he was also dismayed at how much of his own time it would take to go through them.

Once back at Khoulan, he told Ahbrem about the translation task that Nathan had proposed.

"How would you feel about taking on such a task? Would you be willing to undertake the translation of a sacred text of an alien religion?" Kesh asked.

"I am eager to learn about all religions," Ahbrem answered. "But I am surprised that Nathan and Ship have different religions. I assumed all humans had the same beliefs."

"I am not sure that Ship has a religion. He is the Prophet of the Burning Ship to both Xouthans and Mortherners and yet he does not seem to share the beliefs of either."

"Well, I cannot be opposed to Nathan's religion and yet be considering marriage to a Xouthan. If I can accomodate Wyn's beliefs, I must be open to hearing about all religions. Tell him that I would be happy to help."

"He will be very grateful, I am sure," said Kesh. "So has Wyn accepted your proposal?"

"Praise Harg, she has, although she says she has to stay with her mother for at least another round to be sure that she is over Bradmutt's death. But the first moon has passed already. If I keep myself busy, I am confident that the time will seem to fly by."

"I am very happy for you. You will probably be the first Khoulan monk to marry. It is a special honour but it could not happen to a better man."

Again, Kesh refrained from voicing his real feelings. It should have been him! He should have been the first Khoulan monk to marry. All the effort he had gone to in order to get the dispensation to make it possible for him to marry Maina would now benefit the man for whom sticking to the rules came naturally, to whom celibacy had never seemed to pose a problem. Soon Ahbrem was to enjoy marriage while Kesh suffered in silent anguish, unable even to contact the woman who constantly haunted all his waking thoughts. He found it hard to imagine that Ahbrem could have half the strength of feeling for Wyn that he felt for Maina.

***

After a few more days of getting used to the ways of the Sacred Mountain community, Nathan plucked up the courage to ask Hannala about creating an etherium. He was careful to describe it simply as a place for worship, prayer and contemplation and had managed, for now, to curb his desire to spread the Word to the Xouthan priestesses, saving that for a later, more appropriate juncture. When Hannala asked him why the Great Hall would not serve his purposes, he tried to explain his need to be as close as possible to his god, to explain that he felt closer in a space that was open to the sky and that he liked to be as high above the surrounding countryside as he could get. This was just a personal preference, of course, but he didn't emphasise that to Hannala. Better to let her think that it was a requirement for worship in his religion. He felt she was more likely to help him if she thought that.

Hannala took a walk with him around the buildings on the Sacred Mountain, looking at the courtyards and roof spaces, gardens and walkways, even considering the balcony of the Great Hall as a site possibly suitable for Nathan's requirements. As they walked, Hannala sought a deeper understanding of his philosophy.

"So your religion is of another world?" asked Hannala. "I still find it hard to believe that it is possible to cross the heavens to a different world."

"It is possible no longer. We can't travel back."

"And on this other world they worship just a single god?"

"Mostly, yes. Those who are blessed with knowledge of the truth know that there is but one God."

"Ah, that is what the Mortherners would tell us. For myself, I would never risk ignoring any of the gods of nature. We need the help of all."

"But God has dominion over all of nature. You need only pray to Him."

"When Ship tried explaining your religion to me he told me that some humans think of your god as divided into three and that, in addition, some pray to the mother of your god. He made it sound very similar to the Xouthan system of belief."

"It is true that the mother of God is a very important figure to a large section of believers. She is very special. She was chosen by God to bear his son, because of her purity and innocence."

"Ah, innocence," nodded Hannala. "We also value innocence. Our prophet Sandbert said 'a child born in innocence will save the world.'"

"You have a prophecy of a virgin birth?"

"A virgin birth?" repeated Hannala. She smiled, thinking he was joking. "If I understand anything of biology that has proved to be impossible."

"With God anything is possible. That a virgin gave birth to the son of God was truly a miracle but it was not impossible."

"We take Sandbert's words to mean that we should preserve the innocence of children for as long as we are able. All children are born in innocence and we need our children to remain pure of heart for as long as possible if their goodness is to survive the trials and tribulations of this life."

Nathan did not answer her. He was staring at the building ahead of him.

"What a pity that building doesn't have a flat roof. It is so much taller than the ones around it. An etherium up there would almost be in Heaven."

"Could you make a platform on the top?" Hannala asked.

"Not without the help of workmen to construct it."

"Well, if you could purchase the necessary timber and tools and also sufficient supplies of food and drink and so on, we could employ Morthern monks again, now the war is over. Some of them are very skilful carpenters."

"I thought you didn't allow men on the mountain."

"Only Xouthan men are banned. They can't take holy vows. Morthern monks are always welcomed here, as long as we are not at war. You remember Kesh's visit?"

"Ah!" said Nathan. "And his friend Ahbrem, the one who is going to translate for me, he is also allowed on the mountain?"

"Absolutely."

"Well, I'm very pleased to hear it. That will make the task a little simpler."

Ahbrem reached the mountain just a few days later. He arrived with Grenholt, one of the younger monks, and a packhorse laden with gifts for the community of the Sacred Mountain from the monks of Khoulan, together with a monetary donation from the king that had been sent via the administration at Khoulan.

Nathan showed Ahbrem his own printed bible that he had brought from overseas. The monk was very impressed and asked Nathan to explain exactly how it had been made. It was only after he had spent some minutes marvelling at the workmanship that he realised what a task he had let himself in for. It was an exceedingly long document and he was expected to translate it into not one, but two, other languages. The Morthern translation would be easy enough, he thought, but even that could take him many moons, perhaps several rounds. The translation into Xouthan was a completely different matter.

"I could help you in my spare moments," Hannala offered, after Ahbrem had confided his fears to her.

"Would translation involving another religion not conflict with Xouthan teachings?"

Hannala shrugged. "We are all still learning here. How will you reconcile your translation work with your religious duties?"

"I like to think that I can be open-minded and show respect for the beliefs of other cultures without it demeaning my own religion."

"Exactly! We mountain priestesses are used to exposure to your Morthern traditions, so I doubt that exposure to a third religion will have much effect. A woman of my maturity is hardly likely be corrupted by exposure to an alien belief. I am not suddenly going to change my faith just because I translate a few words of human text."

Nathan was made very happy. Two Penethellans were about to start on the translations and Grenholt was travelling back to Khoulan with a request from Hannala to seek, amongst those monks who were trained carpenters, volunteers who would be willing to come to the mountain to build a platform for his etherium. Everything was suddenly progressing rather well.

Ahbrem had given a letter to Grenholt in which he warned Kesh that the translation was going to be an enormous task and likely to take a very long time. He was allocated the empty room at the top of the north tower to use as his study. He liked the view of Morth. He felt content to begin his labours there. He had extra tables carried up, on which he could spread out his papers, and also three chairs, one for each of them, in case they should all need to work together. Finally, when all was ready, he and Nathan solemnly climbed the steps to begin their first translation session.

"As Hannala can't be with us today, we'll concentrate on the Morthern translation to begin with. I think we'll start with the New Testament," said

Nathan, opening his great book at a point nearer to the end than to the beginning.

"I don't understand," said Ahbrem. "Does it come first?"

"No, but some people regard it as the most important."

So they began with St Matthew and the story of the birth. Ahbrem became very confused over whether the translation should state that Joseph was, or was not, the father, and, if not, why Ahbrem was obliged to copy out the long section describing his lineage. Nathan found that it took all his patience to explain the circumstances to the monk. It was a difficult enough concept to explain to ordinary folk but this celibate follower of another religion who was working in a second language did not seem to have any of the right pegs in his head for Nathan to hang the story on.

They took a break for tea on the Great Hall balcony. One of the trainee priestesses had made cakes and they drank and ate with the sun on their faces and the sea in their view. It was a good counterpoint to their academic struggles.

A seacrow came and begged crumbs, landing near their feet and then skipping away shyly to consume them on the balustrade. It wasn't Sakki, but it made Ahbrem think of him, and he began to tell Nathan how Sakki had saved Kesh's life. He retold the stories as Kesh had related them to him: the story of the near-drowning in the night at Hittan and the story of the scaring-away of the islander marauders on the battlefield near Larkat. He mentioned the size of Maina's belly as part of the story, as it had made it difficult for her to conceal the bird under her cloak, so Ahbrem found himself confessing that Maina had been expecting Calim Bradmutt at the time. He did not go so far as to say that his own mattouk was the father, although that was hardly a secret on the Sacred Mountain.

"Yes, I remember Kevin telling us a version of that story. The Xouthan lady had got herself into trouble, then?" asked Nathan disparagingly.

"Yes, I am afraid she was not married when she conceived the child nor, indeed, when he was born," Ahbrem was looking at the flag-stones, shame faced, but then he laughed lightly as he added, "A bit like your Mary, I suppose."

Nathan felt a rush of anger and indignation but then he remembered that the creature before him was an ignorant and innocent Penethellan, on whose help he was dependant.

"I find that comparison offensive," he said with restraint. "Please do not repeat it."

"Oh," said Ahbrem. "I am so very sorry. I did not mean ..."

"No, no. Of course you didn't. Let's get back to work then, shall we?"

Chapter 4

The winter had seemed long to Sakki. He had only left the monastery once when his crumbdropper had travelled to the mountains. There the weather had been mild with a gentle breeze blowing in from the warmer south, but that balmy air had taken a long time to reach Khoulan. When spring finally came and the buds started to burst on the trees, Sakki stretched his wings and found that his new primaries were now fully grown, long and perfectly formed, all the ones frayed and worn by his earlier travels having been replaced. He took off and flew eastwards. He did not have to fly far before he came to a copse. In it there sat a group of seacrows including three young females. He skirted round to take a closer look and alighted in a nearby tree. He stretched, spreading out his new wings, and began to preen himself. The females noticed. All three came over to inspect him. This was new. Usually his luck with the females was sparse and short lived, but all three of these ladies began to answer his calls and they each turned, flicking their tails provocatively. He picked the prettiest, the one with the softest looking feathers and dark liquid eyes that followed his every move. She was too good for him but it would do no harm to attempt to impress her. He took off skywards and then dropped, swooping past her, close enough for her to feel the air stir as it spilled off the tip of his wing and, Harg be praised, she took off and followed him, leaving the group behind. They found a tall tree and Sakki started to lay sticks across a fork in the branches that offered the potential to hold a nest. The female went to fetch a stick. She placed it carefully across his half-formed framework and the match was made.

Sakki used to think that the slavish carrying of material to nests and food to chicks looked exceedingly tedious and tiring, but suddenly nothing gave him more pleasure than to find a good stick, bring it back and weave it carefully into the nest. Mrs Sakki seemed as willing as he to take part in the process. They mated several times. A clutch of smooth, pebbly eggs was laid and they shared the sitting, taking turns in sunshine, wind and rain, whether in darkness or in light, over many days. Four chicks hatched out. They were funny and adorable at the same time. Sakki joyfully swooped backwards and forwards to bring them food and willingly continued to sit on the nest while the world turned and the rain dripped into his eyes. For more than a moon he devoted his life to them, feeling as if this was precisely what he had been born to do, forgetting almost completely about his duties in caring for his Morthern charge.

***

At the time when Sakki was preparing to become a proud father, Kesh was still wrestling with his jealousy of Ahbrem's forthcoming wedding.

"Ahbrem seems to always be in control of his emotions," he complained to himself as he sat at his desk one evening. "Yet I suppose it is unfair to assume that Ahbrem's feelings are shallow compared to my own." He stared blankly at Hannala's Xouthan language notes on the desktop in front of him. "Ahbrem has a more reserved personality, it is true, but I should not assume that he is not capable of the same depth of emotion that I feel myself."

Kesh had slouched over his desk, head in his hands, digging his fingertips into the day-old bristles that covered his skull. Unfortunately, massaging his scalp was not sufficient to drive out the evil of the jealousy that was still plaguing him. He wearily lifted his head from his hands and his eyes lighted on the inked drawing of Mattouk Calim that hung on the wall above his desk. A particularly artistically gifted monk had made it several rounds before Calim's death and had given it to Kesh after the funeral.

"Dear great-uncle Calim!" Kesh breathed. "This mattoukhood is far more difficult than you made it seem. Did you ever struggle with your desires as I have to struggle with mine? If you did, I think you were far better at concealing it. Perhaps you were just a better monk. You seemed to effortlessly maintain balancement throughout the day, always calm and always kindly, whereas I lose balancement somewhere between the meditation flames and my bed each night."

Kesh sighed. He pushed his chair away from the desk and stood up.

"I feel that I desperately need to get away from this place for a while and yet it has only been two moons since my visit to the Sacred Mountain. While Ahbrem is away helping Nathan I am tied to the monastery. I will remain so until his return and I have no way of knowing how long that will be."

There was a knock at his study door that made him start. The monastery was usually quiet by this time of night. Kesh stepped across the room to unlatch the door.

"Most revered mattouk," Grenholt stood in the darkened corridor. "I am sorry to disturb you but a messenger has arrived from somewhere called Ahn Dehar. He has travelled a long way across the sea, he says, and through the Dinash mountains. He insists that his message is urgent and cannot wait till morning."

"Thank you, Grenholt. Where is he?"

"He is in the kitchens, being given sustenance. Shall I send him up?"

"No, no. I will come down."

Kesh stepped into the dimly lit kitchen and saw a man seated at the table eating rapidly as if he had not taken food all day. Grenholt went across to him and whispered, gesturing towards Kesh. The man stood up abruptly, brushing crumbs from his beard and quickly swallowing his last mouthful. He bowed to Kesh.

"Kesh of Khoulan?" he skewed the name with a heavy foreign accent.

"Yes," Kesh nodded.

"I am Wanhild of Ahn Dehar. I am afraid I bring news of the death of our beloved chief, Ackhart of Ahn Dehar. His last words were to beg his son to fetch you. I understand that you offered to sing at our master's funeral and his dying wish was that you should be sent for in order to fulfil this promise. Will you come?"

"Um ... yes, of course. But it will surely take us several days to get there. Will they not have buried him by then?"

"Hernst, his son, has hired an ice house from the fishermen at Wadderhick. The chief awaits you there. The sooner we can get there, the better it will be, of course."

"Of course," Kesh took a deep breath. "Mittan, will you pack us up some bread and cheese for a journey? Grenholt, will you fetch a horse from the stable?"

"Certainly, Mattouk," answered Grenholt, but Mittan hesitated.

"Most revered Mattouk, I think this man must have rest before he travels more," he said.

"Yes, quite right." He turned to Wanhild. "You must rest a while, sir. I will pack to be ready to leave as soon as it is light." He turned back to Mittan. "But someone should leave tonight and fetch Ahbrem from the Sacred Mountain. I cannot leave Khoulan without a mattouk in charge."

"I will go, my Lord."

"Thank you, Mittan. I will write him a letter. Come to my study to collect it as soon as you are ready to go."

Kesh went up to his study and hurriedly wrote:

> To the Revered Mattouk Designate of Khoulan at the Community of the Sacred Mountain
>
> Dear Ahbrem, I am afraid I am obliged to interrupt your task of helping King Nathan with his translation. I have to travel urgently to Ahn Dehar in order to keep my promise of performing a lament for their chief, who is recently deceased, so you are needed to take over at Khoulan for a while. I will return as soon as ever I can.
>
> Yours sincerely
> Kesh of Khoulan, Mattouk.

Mittan knocked on his door just as he was sealing the letter. When he had gone Kesh went about his room packing items for the journey and then lay on his bed with the candle still burning, not expecting sleep.

He was woken by bright sunlight at the window and a loud knock on his door. Ahbrem greeted him with a grin.

"However did you get back here so quickly?" Kesh asked.

"Oh, with a fresh horse and an eagerness to take a break from the endless task of translation, the distance can be covered very quickly. It's mostly downhill, after all."

"But you must have started out in the middle of the night."

"Yes. I told Mittan to take a rest and follow me back this morning so that I wouldn't have to keep to his pace. So how long do you think you will be away?"

"I am not entirely sure, but it could be as little as ten days. It depends on how soon we can get passage, on how long the sea crossing takes and whether there are any unforeseen delays."

"I will see you back in another round-of-the-seasons, then," Ahbrem teased.

Kesh pulled his mouth down at the corners. "I will be very careful not to lose my horse this time. Anyway, it is springtime. I assume, as the Ahn Dehar messenger came via the Dinash Mountains, that the pass is clear and also that the sailings to Wadderhick are free of winter ice and can be expected to remain so for the season."

"Do not forget to take Sakki with you for protection."

"I think Sakki is away in the trees with his lady friend. I doubt he will notice my departure. I will have to learn how to look after myself."

"Make sure you do," Ahbrem laughed, but a little worried frown danced briefly across his brows before he said more seriously "Well, if you are ready, I will come down and see you off."

***

Wanhild set a brutal pace, pushing their horses to the limit, but Kesh felt obliged to follow without complaint. The pass through the Dinash Mountains was high and steep, and the weather grew colder as Kesh led his horse behind that of Wanhild. He pulled the cloak that Ship had given him tightly around himself and was never more glad of it. At the summit, he turned to look back over Morth. It was a glorious view, with Ahbresk a little to their right and close enough to trace the outline of the palace buildings. Kesh imagined that he could just make out the mound that was Khoulan and beyond it, surely, the twinkle of the sea. Then he turned to look ahead, out over Enaha, its roads and rivers all leading to another sea, grey and distant but more clearly visible than on the Morthern side. He took a breath of the bracing air and his troubles began to fade away, as if he could leave them behind him with the Morthern soil. He started to feel as if he was at the beginning of another great adventure, even if it might be all over in a few days time.

"Is that Odout?" he asked Wanhild, pointing to a brown smudge near the horizon.

"It might well be, but I can't be sure," the man answered. "If you are sufficiently refreshed, we should press on."

"Of course. Please lead the way."

Kesh's feelings of elation lasted until they got to Odout. He was standing outside the shipping office, having paid for their passage and for the stabling of his horse. He was waiting while Wanhild settled up for the hire of the horse that he had ridden to Khoulan. He looked along the harbour wall and saw a young woman with a small child toddling back and forth around her skirts. Although the woman had her back to Kesh she gave out an air of grace and dignity. For a moment, he imagined that he was seeing Maina, and that the child was Calim Bradmutt. The boy let go of her skirts and wandered towards the edge, where the wall dropped into the sea. The woman grabbed his little arm in alarm and pulled him back. She caught a glimpse of Kesh out of the corner of her eye, a stranger openly staring at her. She turned to face him, drawing herself upright, challenging his gaze. It was not Maina and Kesh dropped his eyes to the ground, embarrassed.

It was a painful reminder that Maina had, indeed, once stood on that very harbour wall, at a time when he had not felt about her as he did now, when he had wasted all the days that he had spent with her, not realising the value of the precious gift that had been given to him and only to be snatched away after so short a time. The anguish in his soul rekindled instantly. No onlooker would have then been surprised to learn that he was on his way to a funeral, for he carried a suitably sombre expression from that moment on.

***

Maina attended the festival of friendship but she did not want to enter the temple. Instead, she stood outside the gates in the public courtyard with her father. Women often elected to stay there with their men folk so she was not the only female present. Wyn's mother was there for some of the proceedings, standing next to Salwell. Maina nodded and smiled to them both in greeting. Salwell smiled back rather oddly and after that, whenever she looked in their direction, she found Salwell staring at her with a curious half-smile on his face. She wondered what could be on his mind. Did he find it strange that she was not inside the temple with his sister? Or was it something to do with the letter she had sent to Kesh? Did Salwell have a reply for her? Did it perhaps contain a personal message that had given Salwell some cause for amusement?

The celebrations began with a group of trainee priestesses filing out of the temple and arranging themselves along the top three steps. They began to sing a joyful anthem to the goddess of love and friendship. Maina knew the piece well and the maidens sang it so beautifully that she found her eyes stinging with tears. She did not feel tempted to join in their praise of the goddess, however. The anthem was intended to be moving, stirring the listener to more fervent devotions to the deity, but it was lost youth and lost peace of mind that Maina was inwardly weeping for. The happy days of her unquestioning worship of the gods of nature were now behind her. If Kesh's religion was more accurate in its perception of the Ship Prophet's origins, it might suggest that she should perhaps begin to worship the Morthern god, Harg. If she did not, she would be left with nothing. She would recognise no higher authority to guide her life and there would be no entity of supernatural power to protect her should she come to harm. It was a frightening prospect, and one that she had been pushing to the back of her mind for far too long.

Whilst listening to the familiar harmonies soaring and fading through the maidens' anthem, she decided that she should widen her studies from now on in order to consider religious themes. Perhaps she should study the religions of other cultures, that of the Enahet sun-worshippers, for instance. By gaining knowledge of a number of religions she would surely come closer to finding the essence of belief, that great elusive truth that might be a part of every religion which could then lead her to an ultimate understanding of all things. She made up her mind to set aside some of her time to seeking an answer to these greatest of all questions, but she did not know where she was going to start. She did not have access to books about the Enahet religion, nor indeed any religion other than the Xouthan worship of the gods of nature. The search for ultimate understanding would have to wait until she could travel abroad once again.

When the temple ceremony was complete, Maina stepped towards Salwell, hoping to ask him if there was any news from Morth but, at that very moment, Wyn came out through the temple gates to embrace her mother and brother. Maina did not want to interrupt. The emperor's retinue, which had taken a central position at the front of the courtyard, was now ready to depart and she would be expected to leave the temple with them. She would have to wait until later in the day to ask Wyn if Salwell had any news for her.

"No, I'm sorry," Wyn answered her inquiry that afternoon. "Ahbrem sent word that Kesh has gone to a place called Ahn Dehar for a funeral. It is overseas, I understand, so it might be some time before he gets back and reads your letter."

"Oh," said Maina, deeply disappointed. "But Salwell was... well ... grinning at me during the service. I thought perhaps ..."

"Yes, he said that he had caught your eye. He said you distinctly smiled at him."

"Indeed, I did. I nodded to Salwell and to your mother, but I did not get a chance to speak to them. My father left the temple quite promptly and I was obliged to leave with him."

"He has grown up to be quite a handsome man, don't you think?"

"Salwell? Yes, very handsome. When I think of how gawky he was at the time when you and I left for the Sacred Mountain, I am amazed at the change there is in him."

"Mmm," Wyn nodded, smiling.

"Your mother must be very proud."

"Oh, she is."

"She is a very lucky girl."

"Who? My mother?"

"The one Salwell is planning to marry. Has she accepted his

proposal?"

"Ah," said Wyn. " Um ... I don't think Salwell has spoken to her, yet."

"Tell him not to be so scared. He should seize the day, as Ship would say. Many are the chances lost through hesitation."

"Yes, I'll tell him that." Wyn was silent for a moment and then asked, "Maina, who is the current heir to the empire?"

"As soon as my father changes the law, it will be me."

"Yes, but your father has not yet changed the law, so it must, at present, be someone else. Someone who, should the heavens strike the emperor dead, the gods forbid it, would inherit the leadership of the empire."

"My father has no brothers but he does have a male cousin, the Duke of Anthra. He currently has charge of Anthra province. I think it would be him."

"And is he a good man?"

"He does not have the best of reputations. He is considered rather brutal in his judgements, I believe, but my father says he keeps the province functioning efficiently, ."

"And just when does your father intend to change the law?"

"As soon as he judges me schooled well enough to take the responsibility."

"How long is that likely to be?"

"I don't know," admitted Maina. "It seems to be a lengthy process."

"I have to confess I am a little uneasy about the future of our beautiful country. It would not matter for myself. I can go and live in Morth. But for all the other Xouthans who would suffer under poor leadership - for them I worry."

"Don't be anxious, Wyn. My father enjoys rude good health and I am studying hard. Xoutha is in good hands."

Chapter 5

As soon as the ship docked in Wadderhick, Wanhild sent a messenger on ahead to tell Hernst that Kesh had arrived and that it was time to prepare for the funeral. Then he took Kesh to the ice house where, with the help of some fishermen, they lifted a rectangular box of ice enclosing the withered corpse of chief Ackhart onto a horse drawn cart. Wanhild covered it with a cloth bearing the chieftain's insignia and they set off for Ahn Dehar. The cart was driven by a hired hand, and Wanhild rode ahead of it on his own horse, freshly retrieved from stables. Kesh was astride a hired mount and followed on behind. Soon water began to drip onto the road and an unpleasant smell started to fill the air. Kesh could not help feeling that the chief's mourners should not have waited for a Morthern monk to be fetched all the way from Khoulan.

At the base of the mountain, Hernst greeted him warmly, as an old friend, even though they had met but once before. He asked after Maina, and Kesh told him unhappily that he had not seen her for some time.

"I am sorry to hear that. She seemed a warm-hearted woman."

"Yes," Kesh agreed and sighed.

Hernst frowned a little, as if he was restraining his curiosity. Kesh would have loved to talk to Hernst about her but there were more urgent matters to discuss.

"Can you explain the proceedings to me? When exactly do you wish me to sing?"

Hernst told him that the ceremony would take place after dark, that a funeral pyre would be lit and that the best time for Kesh to sing the lament would be while the pyre was burning. He pulled the cover off his father's coffin and felt the sodden timbers. He called a young man over in his own language and gave him some instructions. Then he explained to Kesh that he was sending a message to the carpenter to send down a coffin for the chief, as this wet wood would be too heavy to carry up the mountain. It took all four men, Wanhild, Hernst, Kesh and the driver, to lift the box down from the cart so that the driver could start his journey back to Wadderhick.

As the three remaining men stood idly waiting for the arrival of the coffin, Kesh tried to think of something suitable to say.

"Please accept my sincerest condolences," he began.

"Thank you," said Hernst. "I could say that my father had a good and fruitful life, and so he did, but he suffered a deal of pain at the end of it and his time seemed all too short." He let out a heavy breath before continuing. "I suppose that it may seem so for all who die, to those that follow."

Kesh thought back to the shock he had felt on hearing of Mattouk Calim's death and how it had seemed to come much too soon. If his great-uncle had been the mattouk a little longer, Kesh might have learned from him how to maintain balancement in the face of constant jealousy and desire and so avoid the anguish that he daily struggled with.

"Lives are never long enough, that's true," he said. "For the loved ones left behind."

"But I must be strong. I have to concentrate on leading the people of Ahn Dehar. We must go forwards, take our place in the modern world. At least we can now sell our coal to the Four Kings. I suppose I could have started the process a while ago. My father would have been too weak to stop me. But I restrained my actions out of respect. Now, however, I am free to do as I think fit."

"Um ..." Kesh hesitated. "I think there is something you should know."

He told Hernst all he knew about the 'slow poison' that the four kings had sent to be placed in chief Ackhart's mattress.

"They poisoned my father?" All the colour had drained from Hernst's face.

"I think so, yes."

Hernst turned away from him, shaking his head, looking around him in bewilderment as if he could make no sense of what he had just been told.

Suddenly, he spun around and threw out,

"How do I know you are telling me the truth? Did my father suggest you told me this?"

"But ... you translated for us. You heard everything he said to me. And anyway, what motivation would I have for lying to you? What difference would it make to me, whether you sold your coal or not?"

Hernst shook his head again. "I am sorry. I have not been sleeping well. My temper is short. Forgive me."

"No need," said Kesh, and ventured to place his hand on Hernst's shoulder. As he did so he saw figures coming down the path towards them. "Here comes the new coffin, by the look of it."

It was not a pleasant job, lifting the dripping corpse from its bed of melting ice. The skin was grey and sunken into the hollows of the bone while the mouth was stitched shut with ugly blackened threads. The smell and perhaps the sight of it sent Hernst into the bushes from whence the sound of vomiting could be heard. He emerged soon after, ashen faced.

"Are you well enough to take a corner?" Kesh asked.

"Certainly," Hernst said. "I must bare my father's coffin to its final destination."

The procession walked slowly up the mountain, with men changing places to share the burden, but Hernst would not yield his corner and held on doggedly. They reached the defensive wall and passed through the gate up to the very summit, where a new rectangular construction stood over a pile of oil-drenched brushwood. The coffin was lifted onto the platform, and Hernst turned to the mattouk.

"Now I must get ready for the ceremony. There is traditional dress for such an occasion. Family members must all carry a torch. If you will excuse me ..."

"My wife has prepared some food," Wanhild stepped up to Kesh. "If you would care to come and eat with us before the ceremony."

"Thank you. That is very kind."

"She does not speak the language of the Four Kings," Wanhild told him as he led him away. "But she cooks a tasty meal."

The ceremony had great dignity and beauty. It seemed as though every member of the tribe of Ahn Dehar was present, down to the smallest infant. After earnest speeches given by several of the elders, Hernst took the narrow stage in front of the coffin's platform and faced his father's subjects. Kesh understood nothing except the solemn tone but was moved nevertheless. When he had finished, Hernst and several of his kinsmmen lowered their torches and set light to the brushwood. He nodded to Kesh, who stepped onto the stage and began the lament.

He started it well enough but, before the end, the roar of the flames behind him grew so loud that he doubted that his voice could be heard above it. When he had finished, he turned to face the burning fire and watched with the Ahn Dehar as the flames leapt up into the black night sky.

He could not help but recall the last occasion at which he had sung in front of a large group of people. At the winter festival in Enaha, they had applauded him enthusiastically and, at the time, he had felt embarrassment but now, when he looked back on it, he felt a glow of pleasure. At this present sombre event there was no applause and Kesh wondered if his foreign song had been appreciated at all, but Hernst thanked him with emotion afterwards and said that he was deeply grateful that Kesh had come such a long way to carry out his father's dying wish. It was for his father, cruelly wronged by the Four Kings, that Kesh had undertaken the long journey but it was for Hernst that he now felt pity, for his view of the world must have changed a little after receiving Kesh's information. His confidence in his future plans for the Ahn Dehar must surely have been a little shaken.

As the flames died down, people began to leave the area. Hernst was talking to other members of the clan and drifted away with them. Kesh was left standing in an increasingly empty space, contemplating the strangeness of using a funeral pyre to assist his flame meditation. Wanhild came to his rescue.

"Please forgive Hernst for forgetting his duties to his guest. He has other things on his mind. Would you like to come back and stay with us?"

If Wanhild had been a little formal with him on the journey, it was more than compensated for by his offers of food and accommodation. Kesh accepted his invitation and spent the night on the floor of Wanhild's family home on a deep pile of blankets generously lent by neighbours.

Hernst sought him out early the next morning, with profuse apologies for not making better provision for Kesh's comfort.

"Not at all," Kesh responded. "I was very well looked after."

"I will walk with you down the mountain a little way, if I may. I need to take a little air to clear my head. I drank a good deal of ale last night. My uncles and cousins persuaded me that it was the best way to drown my sorrow, and I did not have the heart to tell them that what I really needed was some time alone to think."

"The path down the mountain has a few good spots for contemplation, I expect. You get a different view of the world, I find, looking down from somewhere high. It can help to create a sense of a detached overview, helpful in clarifying ones thoughts."

"Precisely," Hernst agreed. "Let's take it slowly then."

They started down the path in silence each busy with his own thoughts. Kesh was thinking about how long he would have to wait for Ahbrem to complete his task of translation for King Nathan before the next time he could relieve Kesh of his duties at Khoulan.

Hernst was thinking rather different thoughts.

"I don't think I will be selling mining rights to the Four Kings after what you told me."

"No. I understand," said Kesh. "Mining would almost certainly damage the beauty of your land and the benefits might not be worth it."

"Ah, our tiny economy badly needs some income. Our ability to trade seems to dwindle year by year. I may still be selling mining rights but not to the Four Kings. What I would really like is to raise sufficient funds to pay for an army to declare war against them, to punish them for what they did."

A silence followed. Kesh understood Hernst's inclination towards revenge but could not imagine how so small a nation could take on the might of the powerful Four Kings. He did not like to say as much.

"You come from a wealthy country, don't you?" Hernst started to speak again. "Your king has powerful armies, does he not? And you have must have influence with him, I think. Did you not tell me that he is your uncle? You could persuade him to come and join with us. Together, I am sure we could dent the defences of the palace of the Four Kings. Together we could teach them a lesson that would not be easily forgotten."

Kesh shook his head. His first thought was that he could not possibly move against the Four Kings. They had a connection with the Prophet of the Burning Ship. Not one of kinship, exactly, but deeply held and timeless, nevertheless. To move against them would be to move against his greatest mentor and a beloved icon of his religion. It was unthinkable. Yet, the idea was implausible for other reasons.

"Our armies have to be ready to defend our kingdom from more local threats," was his first excuse. He considered what the king's reaction was likely to be to such a request and said, "Our peace with Xoutha is as delicate as a young shoot in spring, still fresh and fragile. Besides, we have no coastline on our eastern border facing in your direction. We would have to build ships in Enaha to bring our armies over here and the Enahet might not give permission. They are a peaceful society. They have no monarch to make treaties with. Their society is made up of loosely linked local governments. They do not have the same tradition of war that we have in Morth. They might not understand our motives and it would make me very sad if we damaged our friendship with them."

"No, no. You are right. It was wrong of me to ask for such a thing. You cannot go to war along with us. If we have battles, we must fight alone."

"Not necessarily," suggested Kesh. "The peoples of the north would perhaps be justified in resisting the march of progress from the south. You could form alliances with other states. The people of Wadderhick, perhaps, and the Tejwan. Maybe you should all join forces to resist the spread of the influence of the Four Kings. Perhaps you should fight together to keep your countries beautiful. Perhaps you would not even need to go to war. Merely to demonstrate a united opposition might make the Four Kings reconsider."

"I don't know," Hernst shrugged. "That seems a rather feeble response to the wrong that we have been done. I will think about what you have said though. You have great wisdom for one so young."

"Hernst, you are surely not much older than me. Do I seem so young?"

"The loss of my father ... I am now the oldest male in the family, as well as being chief of the clan. All that responsibility has made me realise that I am not the carefree youth that I imagined I was just a moon ago. It's time for me to shake off childish things and tangle with the greater challenges of life."

"Hmm," Kesh murmured. He felt a suspicion that Hernst's words should perhaps apply to him. "Then I wish you every good fortune. May Harg ... may your gods protect you and bring you success in all you do."

"I thank you most sincerely. It is time to say goodbye," said Hernst, coming to a halt and gripping Kesh's forearm firmly. They were not yet at the foot of the mountain but Kesh returned the farewell and turned to tread the rest of the path alone.

Kesh collected his hired horse from the barn at the bottom of the mountain. If he had thought about King Nathan's desires to have his documents translated as soon as possible or that Ahbrem might have been eager for Kesh's return so that he could hand back the reins of Khoulan, Kesh might have urged the horse to step more quickly. As it was, Kesh's pleasure at being free of the responsibilities of Khoulan, and his own appreciation of a little time alone for thinking, made him quite content to allow the horse to plod on steadily at a pace of its own choosing.

Hernst's determination to tangle with the real challenges of life should, he decided, inspire him to think about the future of Khoulan. What efforts could he make to improve the functioning of the monastery? It would have a wider influence on Morth if a greater number of monks passed through its education system. Perhaps Khoulan should offer schooling to boys other than those destined for the priesthood. A good grounding in religious philosophy would almost certainly improve the functioning of lawyers and administrators, perhaps planners and architects, too. He could spread great-uncle Calim's wisdom through the length and breadth of the country.

He needed some greater purpose to take his mind off his obsession with the Xouthan priestess. Though her smiling visage haunted all his days, he should try to concentrate on other things. Why was this so hard? Was his personality hopelessly unsuitable for the priesthood or was he just not meditating hard enough? He had to admit to himself that there had been times when his spirits had been at such a low ebb that he would deliberately allow himself to sink into a memory of his time with her, or into a dream of an impossible future, to find release. The memories would sometimes make him weep from lack of her, yet they seemed to have the power to subtly diminish his mental anguish. Perhaps this was an indulgence he should forego. He would never recover from his infatuation if he allowed his thoughts to wallow in such contemplations.

And so, as he passed the days, riding steadily to Wadderhick, crossing to Odout, riding through Enaha and up the Dinash mountains, he resolved to begin afresh and to concentrate on functioning better as a mattouk. It had been his dream, after all, to teach the Khoulan students and one day to become mattouk. He was more fortunate than most. Not only had his dream come true but it had happened relatively early in his life, without the delay that he had been anticipating. At the summit of the Dinash pass, whipped by a furious gale from the direction of Khoulan, Kesh urged his horse over the border into Morth. It was the morning of the tenth day since his departure. This would show Ahbrem that he could keep to a timetable. If he rode all day he could be back at Khoulan before night fell. But he had no real desire to prove Ahbrem wrong. He decided instead to make his way to Ahbresk and call in on his uncle.

The king had a visiting duke to dinner and, this time, the queen was in sufficiently good spirits to dine with the company. Kesh listened with interest to the news of Morthern affairs and realised it was not only his brief trip to Ahn Dehar that had caused him to lose touch with what was going on. Life at Khoulan was sometimes a little too secure and comfortable and its occupants tended to become detached from what was happening in the rest of the country. Kesh learned that, partly as a result of the previous good harvest, trade with Enaha and with Anthrakat was increasing, in addition to the cautious but growing exchange with Xouthan traders via the port of Fullabish. The treasury was enjoying improved circumstances and the army was being gradually enlarged.

Having exhausted the subject of trade with the duke, the king turned to Kesh.

"I hear you have a new little protégé at Khoulan? I am told you seem rather fond of him."

"Ah," said Kesh, realising that he must be talking about Calim Bradmutt. "Yes. He is being sponsored personally by the Prophet of the Burning Ship."

"Hmm. An honour, indeed. He must be very special. The Chosen

One. And you are happy with this choice?"

"Um ... yes."

"And how did he come to be so 'chosen'?"

Kesh coloured and shifted position slightly.

"Well, he was born on the Sacred Mountain."

"How so? I thought the mountain community was made up only of priestesses and trainees."

The company around the table became expectantly silent and Kesh sensed they were all waiting to hear an explanation. He remembered what Wyn had reported telling the midwife at the time Calim was born, and began.

"An ... um ... unmarried woman ... went to the priestesses ... on the mountain ... for help when ... um ... and left him in their care."

"I see," said his uncle and chuckled. "I do so enjoy watching you monks squirming in your struggle to explain matters of biology. You should marry, Kesh, and then these words would not be so difficult for you." He glanced, smiling, around the table at his other guests as he continued. "How your students ever manage to learn anything of the science of reproduction from their Khoulan masters, I will never know."

The duke laughed quietly.

Kesh smiled wanly but said nothing.

"So he is actually of Xouthan origin?" the king concluded.

"I suppose he is," Kesh answered slowly.

"And yet the Prophet of the Burning Ship sends him to be nursed and, presumably, educated in Morth."

"Yes," said Kesh but did not offer further explanation.

"I am pleased that the Prophet of the Burning Ship recognises the advantages of a Morthern upbringing, but I am not altogether comfortable with your protégé being of Xouthan blood."

"But he is the sweetest child imaginable," Kesh defended him.

"Quite so. But, however beguiling he is at the infant stage, his true nature may come out as he grows up. After all, I dare say that even the Xouthan emperor was sweet at that tender age – if you could have asked his mother's opinion, at any rate."

The rest of the company chuckled at this but Kesh tensed and drew himself upright in his seat.

"I shall make sure that his true nature develops into one bounded by integrity and good intent," he bridled. "It will be moulded by the very best in education that the monastery can offer."

"Yes, yes, of course. I know you will do your best with him," the king said. "But there is another aspect to consider. It is not good to show too much favouritism. This child may be chosen by the Prophet of the Burning Ship but if you, personally, show him too much regard, the other boys may come to hate him. Jealousy and resentment may be encouraged by your behaviour and then, if they should find out about his Xouthan origins, things could get very difficult. Do you understand what I am saying?"

"I think I do."

"Take it from a man who has been a father. Even between the closest of brothers there can be occasional resentment and hostility. Although ultimately there was such deep love that ... Tarleck gave his life ..." the king's voice trailed off.

The queen's face contorted as if struggling with emotion. Kesh was afraid she might get up and leave the table.

"I will take heed of your advice, you can be assured," he said quickly. "Thank you for sharing your wisdom in this matter."

The king changed the subject. "I suppose the new mattouk designate is in charge until you return."

"He is. I have every confidence in his ability to cope with the responsibility."

"Yes, I hear he is quite a capable young man."

"You seem to know everything about us at Khoulan."

"I like to follow the fortunes of my nephew as closely as I can."

"The peace with Xoutha is holding well, I understand," said Kesh. "Could you not withdraw the soldiers from the monastery now?"

The king smiled at Kesh having assumed that his information came from the soldiers stationed there.

"The peace with Xoutha only lasts until it is broken. We cannot forget that their attacks have taken us completely by surprise in the past. We should remain forever vigilant. Anyway, the threat to Khoulan comes from marauding islanders rather than from Xoutha. You need the soldiers there until the islanders can be trusted not to try their luck with another raid. It might be some time before I will feel able to put my trust in the so-called Prince of Benethan. You are too precious to me to risk letting you go the same way as your great-uncle. "

"Well, I thank you for your concern."

"The soldiers behave themselves, I hope? They keep their arms outside the Khoulan walls?"

"Yes, I have not heard any complaints about them."

"Ah," the king gave a satisfied grunt and turned the conversation to other matters.

As Kesh lay on his bed in the palace that night, listening to a late spring storm pelting the windowpane with rain, he went over the evening's conversation in his head and felt renewed dismay at the king's hatred for Xoutha. With two sons lost, it was only to be expected that he would feel ill will towards the nation responsible, but his attitude brought home to Kesh the importance of keeping the details about Calim Bradmutt's origins a secret. He dearly wished he hadn't given away so much information about him.

Kesh set off promptly the next morning following the road towards Khoulan, still musing about Calim Bradmutt's secret. He would have liked to be able to tell the king who Calim's father was. After all, it made the child the king's great-nephew and, but for the lack of a marriage ceremony, he should be second-in-line to the Morthern throne. Now was not the time, however. The time to announce Calim's true identity would not come until the king and the emperor of Xoutha were fully reconciled. Until then, truth avoidance must be the order of the day. He must be content with forever skirting around the subject and fending off all prying questions.

With Khoulan almost in sight, a seacrow flew down and landed near to the horse's feet, causing Kesh to pull up on the reins.

"Is that you, Sakki, come to protect me on my journey?" Kesh asked the bird. He dismounted and bent down to run his fingertips over the bird's sleek springtime feathers. "Well, you are too late. I think I've landed myself in hot water once again, letting out too much information about Calim Bradmutt. Anyway, I should not be loitering here, petting animals. I must get back to Khoulan."

Kesh straightened and the bird hopped off towards the trees. The monk went to remount his horse but the bird flew out again and landed close to his feet. Kesh stood still and watched as the Sakki hopped towards the trees once more. He looked back at Kesh and let out a single squawk. Kesh gave a puzzled frown and put his foot in the stirrup. This time Sakki flew so close to his head that Kesh was afraid he would collide with him if he tried to mount.

"Sakki, what is the matter with you?" Kesh asked, watching him start into a demented dance between the road and the trees. Finally, Kesh tied his horse to a branch and stepped into the copse. Sakki hopped off in front of him, turning every now and then as if to check that he was still following.

On the far side, where the trees had taken the brunt of the previous night's gale, there was a broken bough and a scattering of twigs and, next to them on the ground, four bedraggled baby seacrows just short of fledgling size.

"Oh, Sakki, you are a father too!" Kesh exclaimed. "Congratulations. Clever boy! But these babies are too small to be left on the ground and your beautiful nest has been destroyed. Shall I take them with me to Khoulan? Will you follow, if I do? What about Mrs Sakki? Is that her hiding in the trees?"

Kesh gathered the chicks up gently and tucked them into a fold of his cloak. He mounted with difficulty, afraid of squashing his delicate burden, and set off for Khoulan, with one seacrow circling close by and a second following a little way behind.

He passed by the saluting soldiers, who recognised him easily enough, and rode into the quadrangle. Mittan was on stable duty. Kesh asked him if he could find a shallow packing crate and put a handful of hay or soft straw into the bottom of it. He lifted up a fold of his cloak to show him the little birds by way of explanation. Mittan shook his head as he went off on his quest and Kesh imagined that he was wishing his mattouk would stop bringing back strays for the monastery to care for. In contrast, Ahbrem was thrilled that Kesh had rescued the babies and immediately called for two of the students to go and dig for worms to feed them.

"They look a bit bedraggled," he said to Kesh. "I think we should put them by the fire to dry them out."

So a fire was lit in Kesh's study and the window was opened so that Sakki could see what was happening to his chicks. He arrived on the sill quite promptly, seeming to know exactly where to find Kesh and his offspring, but the female would not come near. By the next day, Sakki was foraging himself and bringing food right inside the study for the chicks. Still the female stayed away. Kesh was worried that she might abandon Sakki and her family, so he arranged for a ladder to be set up and the packing case to be lodged outside, pushed into the roof thatch in a sheltered corner. He watched with satisfaction as the two adult seacrows began to take turns bringing food back to the little ones. Ahbrem came to join Kesh in the quadrangle and stood beside him watching the big black birds as they flew to and fro.

"Our very own family of seacrows," said Ahbrem. "I am certain they will bring good fortune to Khoulan. Oh, by the way, this came for you the day after you left. I must apologise for forgetting to give it to you yesterday."

He held out a parchment roll to the mattouk. Kesh broke the seal without looking at it and began to open the letter out. As soon as he recognised the hand, he quickly rolled it up again.

"Nothing urgent. I will read it later."

Ahbrem smiled to himself. He knew well that Kesh would not want to read this long awaited communication from Maina anywhere but in the privacy of his study.

"Well, I think our friends are settled now," he said. "If you can spare me from Khoulan, perhaps it is time I went back to the Sacred Mountain to continue my duties as translator."

"Yes," said Kesh. "I have had some time away. It is your turn now. Time was when we could set off on adventures together but now both our pleasures and our responsibilities have to be taken separately."

"Well, I am not sure that translating text for Nathan could be described as an adventure. I would be happy for you to take a turn at that too, if you like."

"Oh, no. My knowledge of Xouthan is almost non-existent. I intend to learn but I find the pronunciation difficult and the grammar seems so alien. I will study Hannala's notes some more while you are away. I hope to make some progress in that way but it will be a long time before I will have a skill sufficient for the translation of important texts."

"I am sure you will pick it up very quickly once you get back to your studies again," Ahbrem said. "Should I start to pack?"

"Yes, yes. Make haste. You should leave tomorrow morning, if you can."

As soon as Kesh settled back into the routine of Khoulan the plans that had begun to take shape in his head during his journey back from Ahn Dehar were forgotten. His idea of extending the offer of an education at Khoulan to students other than those whose career was to be in the service of Harg seemed to be impractical. Khoulan was too isolated a place for boys whose destiny lay outside the church.

Chapter 6

Maina was at her lessons once again. To her great relief her father had engaged three administrators to take over the task of instructing her in affairs of state. They were far more encouraging than her father had been. Only the financier was sparse in his praise. The lawyer and the political expert were both very complimentary. She thought perhaps they were simpering to her merely because she was the emperor's daughter but, even if this were the case, their frequent positive comments spurred her on to greater efforts. She began to have more confidence in her potential to administer the empire. She was still rather surprised by her father's next proposal, however.

"Your instructors seem, on the whole, to be pleased with your progress," he admitted grudgingly after half a moon of lessons. "But there is a world of difference between regurgitating theory and applying it in practice. To prove that you are actually capable of leadership there is no substitute for a real position of authority. I am therefore going to give you the opportunity of proving your worth by appointing you temporary governor of the Mardek province. You must be aware that Count Zandis of Mardek has been suffering from poor health lately. You can serve a round there for me, and give him some relief. Perhaps I will even allow you to serve for a second round, if you don't make a complete mess of the first."

Maina did not answer. She looked at the patterns in the marble of the floor while she considered her answer. If she refused, she might never be able to persuade her father to change the law so that she could take over from him. She would be continually under pressure to marry so that the responsibility could pass to her husband until there was a male heir. If she accepted, she would have to leave her beloved friend Wyn and the familiar surroundings of the palace to begin a struggle to gain and maintain authority in a strange province with no friendly faces to support her.

"You hesitate?" her father asked. "You do not wish to prove your worth to me in this way?"

"If I make a success of this, can I be assured that the law will be changed regarding the possibility of female succession?"

"You have my word."

Maina guessed that behind his prompt assurance lay his expectation that she would fail. It was a challenge she could not avoid.

"When would I have to leave?"

"You may have a quarter-moon to prepare. You can send what you like to decorate your accommodation. Two or three cartloads should be ample, but it will be your first independent home and I wouldn't want it to look sparse or shabby. Bradmutt's widow could go with you to help you choose suitable drapery and so on. She has always chosen well for me. She could probably spare a moon or two of her time, given her circumstances."

Yes, that would be a comfort, Maina thought, to have her nurse-mother accompany her at the start.

"Very well," said Maina. "Thank you, father."

Maina told Wyn of her father's plan when she next saw her. Wyn seemed horrified.

"How could your father send you away alone?"

"Not quite alone," said Maina. "He is going to send your mother along with me to help me decorate."

"Oh," Wyn was even more alarmed. "I don't know that my mother is strong enough to undertake such a move."

"She is only meant to stay with me for a moon or so."

"Even so, I'm not sure she is ready yet to travel anywhere. She still gets very tearful sometimes."

"I don't think my father thinks very much about how people feel. All he thinks of is that so-and-so isn't doing much at the moment so they are free to do his bidding."

"I suppose we must try to make the best of it, then," Wyn huffed. "Well, perhaps it will do my mother good to have a change of scenery. But I will miss you terribly. A whole round, possibly two!"

"And I will miss you, also."

"Oh, Maina, must you do this?"

"I think it is the only way that my father will be persuaded to change the succession law."

Wyn closed her eyes for a moment, summoning up the courage she needed to speak her mind.

"Maina, if you could only find a suitable husband, a man you could love, a man who would shoulder your responsibilities, it would remove the need for this trial of governorship," she said. "There is someone who would do all that for you, you know, if you would just give him half a chance."

"I don't want someone to shoulder my responsibilities. I must shoulder them myself."

"But you deserve to be loved, Maina. You deserve to have someone who will care for you and share your burdens. I know someone who would gladly do that and so much more."

"Yes, there is Kesh. I think he would have cared for me and helped me in my duties but my father would never accept a Mortherner into the Xouthan court. There is no chance that he would ever give the care of Xoutha over to him, no matter how good a man he is."

"I am not talking about Kesh."

"Then of whom can you be speaking? You know there can never be another."

"Why, I mean Salwell, of course," said Wyn. "Don't you realise how he feels about you?"

"Salwell?" Maina repeated. "I thought he was about to propose marriage to some local girl."

"But it's you! The local girl is you, Maina. It is to you he would propose, if he could get up the courage. Have you not noticed how he follows you with his eyes whenever you are in the room?" Wyn sounded exasperated. "You must concede that he has become a very fine young man and he is well educated, of noble blood, fluent in the sacred language. I'm sure your father would approve. Could you not love him? Perhaps not now but, given time, you would come to love him, I am certain."

"Wyn, I do love Salwell," Maina said.

"Ah," Wyn gave a little cry of delight but Maina went quickly on.

"I love him as a brother, as I love you. I was brought up in your household and I regard him as my brother. I could no more consider him as a suitor than ... than you could."

"Is it because of his age?" asked Wyn, disregarding the idea that her friend thought of Salwell as a brother. "Maina, he is only three rounds our junior. That will be as nothing in the rounds to come. You may think of him still as a child but he is maturing quickly. He will soon be someone you can look to for advice as well as comfort."

"No, it is not his age. At least, it is only a factor in as much as I clearly remember Salwell as a child. Wyn, I remember him falling into the fishpond in your garden. I can see him now, climbing out all caked in sludge from the bottom of the pool and dripping all the way into the house."

Wyn nodded and laughed quietly at the memory.

Maina went on. "I remember him throwing a stone at a mivva-sparrow and then crying because he regretted killing it. So many of my childhood memories are tied in with him. Your brother became my brother and he will always be that way."

Wyn hung her head and shook it slowly side to side.

"It will break his heart, you know. He had a crush on you before we became temple maidens and he has never overcome it."

"I can't believe that he still feels that way," Maina sighed. "I will ... speak to him. Tell him to be in the palace garden tomorrow at mid-day. You need not state my opinion of him but, on the other hand, don't say anything that will encourage false hope. Just tell him I would speak with him. Perhaps it is just as well that I am going to be working away from Zoradetra for a little while."

When Wyn told Salwell that Maina wished to see him privately, she could tell that he experienced a thrill of anticipation but she said nothing to destroy the childish grin that spread across his face. After all, once he and Maina were alone together, Salwell's obvious good qualities were sure to shine out and might cause Maina to change her mind.

***

Maina went to the walled garden behind the palace at mid-day and found Salwell already there.

"Greetings, brother," she began. "How goes it?"

"Very well," Salwell smiled. "And yourself?"

"The emperor is sending me to Mardek. Apart from that, all goes well."

"That is not good news," he took three steps towards Maina. "Perhaps I can help."

He was standing a little too close and he was looking down at her, which she did not remember him being able to do. The last time they had stood this close together they had still been children.

He had, indeed, grown into a fine young man but not a man that Maina wanted to be this close to. She stepped to the side and said,

"Shall we walk around the paths?"

Salwell offered her his arm and she took it. She did not want to seem churlish, after all.

"I will do anything you ask, you know," said Salwell, assuming Maina would understand what he meant. "Anything at all."

"Salwell, you know that I have pledged my heart to Kesh. Wyn must have explained that much, at least."

"But Kesh can be of no help to you stuck, as he is, in Morth. I am here, right beside you, Maina. I can help. I do not even ask that you care for me, just that you let me care for you."

"Salwell, that is a lovely thing to say. But I am not worthy of you. I will tell you a secret that will explain everything, as long as you promise never to breathe a word of it to any other."

"I promise. I will guard your secret with my life."

"Then listen carefully," Maina slowed and turned to face her nurse-brother. "I am no longer a maiden, Salwell. I bore Kesh's child and he took him back to Morth to hide him. So, you see, I cannot marry you. I am not fit."

Salwell's face broke into a joyful grin. "Maina, that is no secret in our household. Wyn told my mother all your problems and then my mother passed the secret on to me. I know all about your troubles. That is why I consider myself to be the very best person to support you now. For a moment then, I feared you had something worse to tell me but, if you don't, there is nothing more to worry about. If I know all your secrets and I love you still, does it not prove how strong my feelings are?"

"Oh, Salwell, You're very sweet and you deserve so much better. I am so sorry I cannot return your love in the same way. I adore you as a brother but I could never think of you as a potential husband."

"I know you do not love me now but please give me a chance to prove my love to you. I told you, I will do anything for you, anything at all."

"Then, if you really do feel as you say, I will be asking you to carry out that which might seem, just now, to be the hardest task of any. What you must do for me is to expel me from all the dreams you may have for the future. I want you to be happy, Salwell. Find a suitable girl and just be happy."

"There can never be another. You are my one desire. From the first time I noticed that you were becoming a woman, my only dream has been to love you as a man."

"Oh, Salwell. You are very handsome. There must be a dozen women in Zoradetra who would give themselves to you in an instant if a single kind word dropped from your lips," Maina said. "Wait and see. You may feel differently about me after a while. Give it time. If it's any consolation, I do know what it is to love where that love can never be returned. Our situations are not the same, I know, but, apparently, you find yourself suffering a love that has no purpose, as do I."

"Surely you could reconsider," Salwell burst out, suddenly catching hold of both her hands.

"No, Salwell. It is impossible," Maina pulled her hands away. "I am very honoured that you hold these feelings for me and I promise that you can always depend on my assistance and protection, if ever such things are needed. I do love you deeply, but as a brother only. I could never contemplate any other sort of relationship between us. In a few days I must travel to Mardek. This may be my only chance to wish you a personal goodbye. Embrace me as a brother, Salwell, then let us go our separate ways."

Maina stood on tip toes, put her arms round Salwell's shoulder and kissed his cheek. Salwell allowed himself to be held but did not return the kiss. He hung his head dejectedly and stood still as a statue as Maina walked out of the garden.

***

Maina left the palace with a heavy heart. There had been no reply to her letter from Kesh and now she was travelling even further away from him and from her son. Wherever her most beloved ones were in Morth, at Khoulan or beyond it, the south of Xoutha would be even more distant from them than the city of Zoradetra.

Wyn's mother sat opposite her in the royal carriage as it made its way in a procession of four vehicles heading for Mardek province. The older woman observed the misery on Maina's face and wondered why she chose to suffer so.

"You spoke to Salwell, I understand?"

"Yes," said Maina.

"But you could not accept his help? Surely, if this coming term of office in Mardek is so painful for you, marrying Salwell would be the obvious way of avoiding it."

"You make it sound so simple."

"Maina, you are young, I know, and you can't imagine growing old but look at your nurse-mother and you will see that the ravages of age come to us all. I am left without a husband and I am not ready yet to consider remarrying but, if I wanted to, it would not be easy. My flesh grows fatter while my hair grows thinner, my skin seems to stretch and sag and all the excess is gathering into creases."

"You are still a handsome woman," Maina interrupted. "If you don't look your best just now, it is because of your bereavement. You will soon regain your sparkle."

"I'm not so sure," she said. "I beg you, heed my warning. Don't wait until this wastage comes to you. Salwell appreciates your youthful beauty. You take it for granted now but, believe me, it will slip away in the blink of an eye. You will look in the mirror one day and an old woman will stare back at you. Then you will spend all your time wishing you could have your youth restored. Act now. Don't wait until it's gone."

"Nurse-mother, I tried to explain to Salwell, and to Wyn as well, that

I can only love Salwell as a brother. I could never take him as a husband, with all that such a relationship would entail."

"But Salwell would be patient. I'm sure he wouldn't force his attentions on you before you were prepared."

"I'm sorry, nurse-mother. I am sure you are right but I never could be 'prepared' to accept such attentions from my nurse-brother. He is a very fine young man but he is simply not attractive to me in that way. You can understand that, can't you?"

The older woman took a breath, as if to argue further, but then she sighed.

"Well, I am very sorry it cannot come to be. You would have made a truly wonderful royal couple. I am afraid I have long been harbouring quiet hopes that you would catch my Salwell's fancy, that he would become the emperor-regent and the father of the next in line. I had such plans for him. You must forgive me if I find it difficult to let go."

"Oh, nurse-mama," Maina embraced her. "I'm sorry if I've disappointed you."

"No matter, my dear. We must make the best of the gifts the gods choose to bestow. I will do my best to make your quarters in Mardek comfortable and pray that your governorship goes well. I am proud of you, too, Maina. I like to think I played some part in your upbringing and I will be very proud if my nurse-daughter becomes the empress of our country. You will be a pioneer, after all, a symbol of achievement for all Xouthan women to aspire to. I will help you all I can."

"Thank you, nurse-mama. Your support means so very much to me. I would not have liked to face this move to Mardek entirely on my own."

The governor's palace looked bare and unwelcoming, the Count Willdred having already moved all his belongings to his country residence a quarter of a day's ride away. The ladies spent the first night in a local inn, while the drivers of their vehicles camped in one of the empty rooms.

Maina's first duty the next day was to visit the count at his new residence to discuss arrangements for the ceremonial transfer of governorship. Wyn's mother stayed at the governor's palace to supervise the positioning of the furniture and hanging of the drapes.

At the count's country house, Maina was shown into a spacious room with large windows displaying an impressive panorama of the Mardek coastline. Her arrival was announced. The count was propped up on a daybed with a swollen foot resting on two pillows.

"Forgive me for not getting up."

"Of course," she said and held out her hand to him

He took it in his own and raised it to his lips.

"I don't suppose you remember me," he said with a twinkle. "When I last saw you, you were about the same height as my kirra-hound. You have grown into a beautiful woman since that time."

"Thank you, Count," Maina smiled at his flattery and bowed her head in acknowledgment. "I have come to ask about the arrangements for the transfer ceremony. It is to take place in seven days time, I understand."

"Yes, that's it. My administrator has drawn up a document detailing the whole procedure. I am leaving it all to him. He will no doubt be along with his plans in a little while. In the meantime, I hope you don't mind if I ask you one or two questions."

"Not at all."

"Far be it from me to criticise your father's judgement - indeed, he has never given me any cause until today - and I do not mean to question your abilities, but I have to confess to being a little bit surprised at his choice of temporary governor. Has governorship been an ambition of yours for long?"

"Indeed, it has not," Maina confessed. "I trained as a priestess and my ambition was to be high priestess like my mother."

"Ah," the governor frowned. "May I ask what changed your mind?"

"You may not," said Maina, and then relented. She did not want to make an enemy of the one man who had experience of the post she was about to tackle. "At least, you may, but I have to be assured first that the information will not pass beyond the four walls of this room."

"You may have my word on that."

Maina took a breath while she considered how she might best explain.

"I sailed to the Sacred Mountain, as all priestesses do, to complete my training. While I was there, I met many different people and I heard things, saw things, and learned things that caused me to doubt the beliefs I had held so firmly until that time. I began to question every aspect of my faith. I subsequently felt unable to carry out the functions of a priestess."

"I see. That must have been quite devastating for you."

"Yes, it was."

The count continued,

"Forgive me for asking a personal question but surely, as the emperor's daughter, would it not be normal for you to be considering marriage by now? I am sure the emperor is keen to see the birth of a suitable heir to the empire and you cannot tell me that there hasn't been an army of suitors lining up for a chance to take you to the temple."

"I am afraid none of the suitors has been entirely suitable. You may have heard about Thrull of Benethan and the revelation of his island family? He was the best of an array of young men that the emperor has invited to the palace over the last few rounds. I am afraid I don't share my father's taste in eligible men. I have asked him to change the law of succession so that I can take over the empire instead of marrying. He has agreed but demands that I prove first that I have the ability to govern. Hence, this temporary appointment."

"Your father has given you training in the leadership of men?"

"Not exactly. He has given me training in administration, finance and the law, but he hasn't really offered me advice on leadership as such."

"Then how does he expect you to succeed?"

"I think he rather expects me to fail. He probably expects me to return to the palace in a very few moons and beg to be married to the first single man who'll have me."

The ex-governor chuckled and shook his head.

"Well, now. That wouldn't do, would it? I have no wish to go against your father's plans but I think that would be a dreadful outcome. Your failure in Mardek province would undermine the emperor's authority in all the land. You are his daughter, after all."

The count gripped the sides of the daybed and tried to haul himself into a more upright position. Maina stepped forwards to help him but the count put up is hand to stop her. He went on:

"I don't think your father fully realises the value of Mardek province. To him it is probably a distant county, merely a buffer, a no-mans land between the Wildlands and the empire proper. But to me it is a beautiful place and one I am proud to call my home. So, I don't wish to see it slide into anarchy, even for a little while. Therefore you and I must strive to make your governorship a success. Tell me, lady, - you must have thought about this - how do you propose to maintain authority? How do you intend to make your subjects do as you command?"

"Um ... I suppose, by being fair. I suppose I had hoped that, if they liked me enough ..."

The governor interrupted. "No, no, you are not here to make friends. Fairness is important, yes, but don't expect those whom you command to like you. It is their respect that you should be seeking, not their friendship. That must be saved for those you love already."

"Oh," said Maina.

"The most important thing is to demonstrate your authority early in your tenure. It is so much harder later on. You will find that those under your command will be forever pushing you, testing you out, to see where they can take advantage. The young men are more than usually likely to be rebellious, I am afraid, because you are a woman. If you hesitate or put off the punishment for a particular misdemeanour, the culprit will see that he has got away with it and will try something worse the next time. Likewise, all other potential troublemakers will see you as soft and weak and will be expecting to get away with bad behaviour also. Restless subjects can be like children, do you see, forever pushing their luck, watching for the scolding from the parent, but carrying on as they like until it comes. So you must be the perfect mother, fair but firm, and use the earliest opportunity to exert control. So tell me now, my dear, from whence comes your authority? What gives you the power to command?"

"Um ... my father, I suppose."

"Ultimately, yes. If there was mutiny in the province, you could seek the support of the emperor and he would be obliged to send you soldiers. Even if he secretly wanted you to fail here, he would be bound, by law, to send you troops to help you regain control. But, besides your ability to call on your father's aid, what gives you your authority?"

Maina did not have an answer.

"You are about to take command of the military of the province and of all the servants of justice and the law. You must learn what all the various penalties and punishments are and how to instigate them. You have had lessons on the law. Now you have to find out how it works in practice."

"I am not sure that I'd want to use the law in that way. I don't wish to penalise and punish. Surely, most people are decent and respectful of one another, and we don't really need the law at all. So often it seems to work against the people. It becomes their enemy.

"The law is the servant of the people. It sets a pattern of acceptable behaviour which protects all citizens from evil doers, whether they are intent on doing evil for evil's sake, or whether they may make an unlawful action on a sudden impulse. Let me use, as an example, Anthrakati family law. You may be familiar with their law which prohibits any man from holding a conversation with another man's wife. Because every citizen of Anthrakat understands the rule, no man would speak to another man's wife unless he were prepared to risk punishment by the law and, because of that, I would argue that much misunderstanding is avoided. In contrast, in our own country, if a man sees another man in conversation with his own wife, he may be overcome with jealousy and may attempt to strike the individual who is causing him the offence. He knows, however, that in Xouthan law it is an offence to assault another person physically and, therefore, he would be protected by his knowledge of the law from committing the offence. He would have to reconsider his course of action, giving himself time to find out if there was indeed any justification in his jealousy of the other man."

"But the law is too restrictive. It takes away ones freedom to live life just as one chooses."

"Yes, it restricts our choices but it also protects us from the choices of others who might 'choose' to do us harm. Every law abiding citizen makes an unspoken pact with the state to live by its laws in return for protection from the dangers of the chaos that would inevitably reign in any lawless state. A system of clearly defined rules and clearly prescribed punishments are the prerequisites of any harmonious society."

"But during our training for the office of priestess, we were told that praise and encouragement produces more diligent efforts in the student than penalties and punishments."

"Yes, praise is powerful but there will be times, believe me, when you come across a subject who offers no evidence of taking any actions that would engender praise. Be prepared to act accordingly. You have a heart-warming smile but you must use it sparingly and only when it is truly earned. You must be watching at all times for moves that go against your wishes, and you must pounce on such moves with the utmost alacrity, like a detti-cat upon a mouse. Knowing exactly what powers you have and how to use them will give you the confidence to command. It is only if you believe in yourself that others will obey you."

The harsh advice continued over dinner even in the presence of the count's administrator and Maina left the governor's country residence in dismal spirits. She was grateful for the older man's support but when she had asked why he was helping her he had told her that it was his chance to do penance and that giving her assistance would atone for all the bad deeds he had committed whilst in office. This had made her feel distinctly uncomfortable. The Sacred Texts made it clear that penance could be paid to atone only for acts which were not recognised as bad until after the event and then only if the perpetrator felt genuine remorse. It could not be used as a promise to do something good in the future in order to make up for evil acts knowingly and consciously committed. If the ex-governor's help was being offered to her as part of his plans for cancelling out his previous misdemeanours in the judgement of the gods she should refuse it, and yet it would doubtless benefit the people of the province if she took advantage of his advice. How she was going to rule successfully and yet remain within the bounds of what her conscience judged as righteous, she did not know. She now had no expectation that she was going to enjoy any part of her governorship.

Chapter 7

Kesh's evenings at Khoulan were quieter than ever with Ahbrem away at the Sacred Mountain. He looked forward to Calim's visits as to a rare ray of sunlight piercing the prolonged periods of gloom that had to be patiently endured with the scant assistance of fervent meditation. When there was no visit due he brooded over Maina and his memories of their time together. He now had two letters to ponder over in such moments but the one that had been handed to him on his return from Ahn Dehar was just as formal and enigmatic as the first.

> *To Kesh of Koulan*
> *Most Revered Mattouk*
>
> *I am writing to keep you appraised of the situation here in Xoutha. The emperor enjoys good health but is investing much time in the training of his daughter in affairs of state with a view to changing the Law of Succession. To this end, the Xouthan lady, having undergone four rounds of religious education, is now devoting herself to the study of politics, social administration, finance and accounting. She is putting every effort into this endeavour and regrets the fact that there is currently no opportunity for her to travel abroad or to enjoy any kind of recreation. She would, therefore, much appreciate a reply to this epistle to be sent via the route by which it has reached your location.*
>
> *I hope that this letter finds you and all your kin in perfect health. Please pass on the very best of good wishes to those of our joint acquaintance. I look forward to receiving your reply forthwith.*
>
> *Yours sincerely*
> *Maina, Trainee at the Palace of Zoradetra.*

Kesh noted that she gave her address at the palace rather than at the temple and no longer referred to herself as a priestess. What that meant, exactly, he could not be sure. However, she was still unable to travel, so was unlikely to be visiting the Sacred Mountain in the near future and now, surely, far less likely, if she was no longer serving as a priestess. How was he ever going to arrange to speak with her again? In the long term, he pinned his hopes on learning the Xouthan language and travelling to Zoradetra. In the short term, if he could not see her, he could at least communicate with her by replying to her letter. He prepared a letter to be ready for when Ahbrem returned so that it could be dispatched along with his next to Wyn.

> To Maina of Zoradetra
> Most Honoured Trainee at the Palace
>
> *Your communication was very much appreciated and has brought sunlight into the corridors of Khoulan. I am sorry to hear that you are too busy to visit the Sacred Mountain. I visited the community myself recently and have begun lessons in the Xouthan language. I have been honoured to receive the help of a lady of the highest office in that establishment, who has supplied copious notes for my perusal. However, I find the pronunciation difficult and I fear it will be some while before I am sufficiently proficient to be able to travel south of the border. Nevertheless, I will persevere and hope to pay my respects at the palace at some point in the future, albeit a little while away. I look forward to it with an eager heart.*
>
> *Please pass on best regards to those trainee priestesses who were studying on the mountain in the round of my first pilgrimage and please accept my very best wishes for your own well being. May the coming times bring you lasting peace and a long and happy life.*
>
> *I am yours sincerely
> Kesh of Khoulan, Mattouk.*

Kesh had put the letter on the mantel in his study while it awaited Ahbrem's return. A few days later, Kesh received the letter from Ahbrem telling him that the translation project was going to take much longer than anticipated. Ahbrem asked Kesh to send for him if there was the need, as he would probably be glad of an excuse for a break from his endeavours, but Kesh could hardly send for him just to take a letter to Fullabish. Kesh decided he must send someone else and called for Mittan to find him a monk who could be spared from monastic duties for a day or so.

The monk chosen did not know the sea captain that Ahbrem had been using to carry his letters. He found someone willing to take the letter to Zoradetra but it was not a man who could then find Salwell to pass the letter on personally. Instead, the letter found its way to the palace buried in a bundle of sundry other missives that were then delivered into the hands of the emperor.

Any letter arriving from Morth was of interest to the emperor but, as it was clearly addressed to Maina, the emperor sent for Dorran. He was a specially trained military man who had carried out certain tasks for the emperor on previous occasions when there had been the need to gather intelligence from Morth.

"You can open this without damaging the seal?" the emperor asked him when the soldier arrived in the stateroom.

"I think I should be able to, with a little care, my liege."

"Bring it to me as soon as you can unroll it. There is no need to read the contents."

The soldier bowed and took three paces backwards before turning to leave the room.

He brought the letter back after a short while, balanced on a platter. The seal was intact but the parchment freed from it except at the very top edge.

"Hmm ... you have done well," the emperor told him and unrolled it to read.

"Communication?" he growled to himself. "Sunlight to the corridors?" the emperor quoted the sacred language words disdainfully and asked Dorran; "Do Mortherners always write such poetic garbage, or is it a secret code which we must break?"

"I believe that Mortherners are, indeed, prone to using unnecessarily airy phrases, my liege. I am not aware of any code of which this could be a part."

"Pay his respects at the palace?" the emperor read. "Not if I have anything to do with it! Dorran, go to the Sacred Mountain for me. Make sure this 'lady of the highest office', I assume he means the principal, gives no more lessons to this Morthern mattouk. Make it plain that the Xouthan language is for Xouthans only."

"I will, my liege," said Dorran. "Do you wish me to have the letter forwarded to the new governor of the Mardek province?"

"I do not think that will be necessary," said the emperor, handing the scroll back to him. "It does not appear to be urgent or important. Reseal it, would you, and have the housekeeper take it to the governor's old room. No doubt, my daughter will receive it soon enough."

Dorran nodded.

"Very well, my liege."
Dorran bowed low and backed away.

***

Maina had followed the governor's advice. She had listed all the offences she could imagine taking place amongst her staff and learned the appropriate punishments off by heart. It was, indeed, the younger men who were the least respectful. On the first day after the official transfer of governorship, one of them had interrupted her when she was giving out a command, questioning her judgement.

She reacted swiftly.

"When you are a senior official of long standing service," she began frostily "You may well be asked for your opinion, but in your present position you will not express your opinion unless it is specifically requested and it will certainly not be given any consideration whatsoever should it occur again in the form of an interruption of the governor's commands. I fine you one day's pay and I await your apology."

The young man duly apologised, but other minor offences occurred, making the first moon of her governorship a constant struggle. The older administrators fell into two groups. Individuals of the first kind were inclined to behave like fond uncles who were aware of her inexperience but ready and willing to offer assistance, while individuals of the other kind seemed to acquiesce to her wishes while in her presence but, once away from her, blatantly disregarded her instructions and proceeded to do just as they pleased. These people were the hardest to deal with. Maina lacked the confidence to confront senior officials who had so much more experience than herself.

When the first moon of her office was complete, Maina was invited to dine at the old governor's residence to discuss her progress. It was her problems with the senior officials that she first brought up with him.

"Who in particular has disobeyed your wishes?" he asked.

"Finance Administrator Pitchet has caused me the biggest problem. I asked him to reorganise provincial taxes half a moon ago in order to reduce the burden on those with smaller incomes. So far he has done nothing. Twice I have asked him to draw up a detailed plan for redistributing the tax burden but each time I ask he mutters some excuse and no plan appears. Am I to punish him with a fine? Threaten to release him from his post? I know he has such long rounds of experience that he could easily give me all the advice I need, and yet he wilfully ignores my requests."

"Ah," the ex-governor sighed. "Pitchet is a good man, but very traditional in outlook. I can imagine that he finds it difficult to take orders from a woman, especially one so youthful. I remember he made some comment about the emperor having taken leave of his senses when he first heard of your forthcoming appointment." The ex-governor cleared his throat. "Two things you should know about him: first, that he was once chided by a priestess for taking a willow switch to his daughter when she disobeyed him. He has not been near a temple since, and he will not know that you have relinquished your priestess status. Second, that it was he, as you may have already guessed, who drew up the present regime for tax collection and he probably feels that it is already as good as it needs to be."

"Oh, of course," Maina breathed. "Why didn't I think of that? Not only have I made him resent my authority, I have insulted his work into the bargain. But what can I do? Will I have to relieve him of duty before I can make the changes?"

"Perhaps not," said the ex-governor. "You could offer to relieve him of his duties, perhaps by offering him retirement on half-salary. But give him a choice. Make your youth work for you. Suggest that if he does not have the energy to produce the new plan, that you would be happy to give him a generous pension and appoint a younger man, although you would be sad to lose a man of such great experience and wisdom, that you were rather looking forwards to working with a man of such obvious talent et cetera, et cetera. I am willing to bet ten dipnats that, in order to prove that he still retains his youthful vigour, he will produce an alternative taxation plan before the next new moon."

"I don't know," Maina hesitated. "I would rather he worked for me willingly than have to rely on manipulating him with threats."

"Ah, I see. So this is the first time that you have used such methods to get your own way? You must have been an exceptionally angelic child."

Maina stared at her feet, remembering guiltily how she had tricked her father into signing a peace treaty, how she had suggested to Imgrin that he could repay her for her financing his wife's treatment by delaying his announcement of Thrull's fatherhood.

"Or perhaps you are wishing that you had not already done such things?"

"I am afraid I have indeed been guilty of using similar ploys in the past," she shuffled the documents in her lap aimlessly. "I am amazed at how I manage to block such things out of my consciousness. I tell myself that

I am a good person. I convince myself that I aim only to do what is right, that I am virtually without sin, faultless, and yet, so near to the surface, is the realisation that I have already been a wicked person, manipulative, dishonest, ruthless. I have done awful things. I do not deserve to be in a position of power. Perhaps I should go back to my father, beg his forgiveness, agree to do his bidding from now on. Or better still, I should devote myself to a life of study and self-denial in an isolated religious community where I can do no more harm."

"Maina, Maina, enough! Don't spend your life agonising about the past or about your own failings. You are here for a purpose. You are here to take care of the province of Mardek, to keep its administrators functioning and its people prosperous. Think of the good things you can do tomorrow and the next day, not the bad things that are gone and dead. Holding a position of power will always force you to compromise your desire for what is right and good. A good governor is one who can keep an acceptable balance between necessary evils and unrealistic ambitions of righteousness."

"But I don't want to be evil. Can't I just be good?"

"Not in my experience. If there are two spheres of activity in which it is impossible to act in a way that will avoid one's consignment to the Dark World after death, they are business and politics, and a governor must inevitably have dealings with both. Now, I remember, when we first met, you told me that you had experienced something that made you question your faith. I, too, have had cause to question the teachings of Xouthan priestesses and yet I still believe that we should all aim to do good rather than harm. But, I also believe that the first thing a successful leader must be willing to sacrifice for his people is his aspiration towards a place of honour in the Palace of the Gods. I will be due to pay a good deal of penance, I can tell you, before I can hope to atone for my misdemeanours. The secret is to keep your evil deeds small and your good deeds large." He leaned forwards and patted the hand that held the documents. "Anyway, you will not really be manipulating Pitchet. You will be challenging him to show his worth. He doesn't have to accept the challenge. It will be his choice, whether to meet it or to accept retirement. It is a fair choice. No governor can work with administrators who won't take orders."

Maina returned to her quarters feeling that she wanted to abandon all ambitions to run the province, much less to inherit the rule of the empire. Nevertheless, the quiet words she had with Administrator Pitchet the next day seemed to have the desired effect. A detailed plan for a new taxation regime appeared on her desk before the new moon arrived.

***

Hannala was teaching a class of natural philosophy to five of the Sacred Mountain trainees when she was interrupted by one of the maidens who should have been on kitchen duty.

"There is a soldier at the Xouthan gate, Madam. He is demanding to be let in. He says he needs to speak to you."

"Doesn't he know that men are not allowed on the mountain? Don't let him in. I will come straight down. Excuse me, girls, you must find some personal study work to do for a little while."

Hannala left her class and went with the maiden through passages above the kitchens in the old building that led out onto a walkway overlooking the gate in the wall.

She called down to the man below her.

"Who is there?"

He looked up and scowled.

"I am Dorran of Zoradetra. I have a message from the Emperor himself for the principal. I demand admittance."

"I will be honoured to receive a message from the emperor but you are a man. You cannot be admitted unless you have taken Holy Vows and no man of Xoutha is allowed to take Holy Vows."

"Nevertheless, I must obey the emperor's command to deliver the message. I must speak with the principal."

"You are speaking with the principal. Deliver your message."

"Humph. This is no way to receive a messenger from the emperor!"

"Are you going to give me the message or will you leave without fulfilling your objective?"

Dorran huffed a second time.

"Most unsatisfactory! Very well. Hannala, Principal of the Sacred Mountain, you are hereby informed that, by ruling of the emperor, the Xouthan language is decreed to be for the use of Xouthans only, and you are forbidden to teach it to anyone of nationality other than Xouthan, failure to obey this decree being on pain of imprisonment for a minimum period of five rounds. Do you hear and understand the emperor's decree?"

"I hear it."

"Then I require that you promise by way of oath to uphold the demands of this decree."

"I am not swearing an oath to a messenger at the gate. I have heard and understood the decree. That must be sufficient for you. You have delivered your message and now you must go. I have a class in natural philosophy to get back to. I must wish you good day."

With that Hannala turned on her heel and left the walkway. The maiden looked down at the soldier. He growled grumpily and started back down the path into Xoutha.

Hannala had no idea how the emperor could have known that she had been teaching Xouthan to anyone of a different nationality. It rather frightened her that such things could be found out. Who was sending such information to Zoradetra? Had one of the trainees been bribed, or worse, blackmailed to pass on information? She considered telling Kesh that she could no longer teach him but her pride told her that she should be free to do what she thought was right. Goodness and the gods came before the decrees of an emperor. She decided that would pray to Tarn and hope for his guidance to become apparent during her devotions.

**

After three moons without a reply to his letter, Kesh was in despair, fearing that he would never hear again from the Xouthan lady. Even if the letter had taken a whole moon to get to Zoradetra and the reply a whole moon to get back to him, that still left a moon during which Maina had not seen fit to put pen to parchment. Kesh did receive a letter from Ahbrem, however, in which his friend said that he was finding the translation task a little tedious and that he would be pleased to take over at Khoulan for a little while to give himself a break from his labours. He was planning to return before the new moon.

Kesh took out his notes on the Xouthan language and studied hard in anticipation of a trip to the Sacred Mountain. Then a second letter arrived, explaining that Ahbrem would be delayed by at least a day as he had been instructed to deliver the first copy of the initial section of Nathan's sacred document, now translated into the Morthern language, as a gift from Nathan to the Morthern king. Kesh was unperturbed. After four moons without Ahbrem, one more day made little difference.

Chapter 8

Ahbrem rode down the path on the Mortbern side of the Sacred Mountain on a fresh morning in late spring. The brilliance of the sunlight and the warmth of the breeze intoxicated his spirits with its heady promise of freedom. For the first time after many weeks of dutiful translation at Nathan's side, he now dared to look forward to the coming summer. At the end of it, when the suggested two rounds had passed since the death of her father, there would be his wedding to Wyn.

He rode straight for the palace at Ahbresk, ignoring the turning that lead to Khoulan. He was not sure how he would explain the gift. He could only tell the king that the book he had in his saddlebag was of such great importance to Nathan that he had spent six moons producing a translation of just this single section, amounting to perhaps a quarter of the whole document. Nathan was hoping that the king would be so inspired by it that he would want to find out more, but Ahbrem very much doubted that this would happen. Personnally, he had found the study of the human sacred text only mildly interesting, despite having chosen to devote his life to religious matters. The alien document was wordy and ambiguous and described events that had little in common with the history or experiences of Mortherners. Nevertheless, he was duty bound to deliver the gift, and deliver it he would.

Ahbrem arrived at the palace and introduced himself at the gate as the Mattouk Designate of Khoulan. He was formally announced in the main hall of the palace. He approached the king's dais with bowed head, Nathan's gift clutched before him in both hands.

"Welcome, Mattouk Designate," the king said. He could tell that the young monk was nervous. "So what brings you here to see us?"

"I bring a gift from King Nathan of the Land of the Four Kings." Ahrem held out the book.

"Well, I thank you," said the king and signalled for a footman to take the book from Ahbrem and hand it to him. "And what is the purpose of this gift?"

"Um ... It is a symbol of friendship from King Nathan. It is a translation of part of a sacred text that is of supreme importance to him."

"I see,"

The king took the book from the hands of the footman and opened it to see the title page, beautifully scripted by one of the trainee priestesses.

She had been set this as her task from the Ship Prophet, and had copied it stroke for stroke from Ahbrem's original translation into the Morthern language, without any understanding of its meaning.

"Do the Four Kings worship Harg as we do?" asked the king.

"They worship but a single god, unlike the Xouthans, but they do not call him Harg, The book I bring is about a being, believed to be the son of that god, who became a mortal and began a new religion. King Nathan has already devoted six moons to the translation so that Mortherners may read it. He is deeply convinced of its worth and hopes that you will be able to find time to study it."

"You can assure him that I will study it with interest," the king told him. "Please offer him my sincere thanks. I will endeavour to find a suitably meaningful gift for you to carry back in return. You will dine with us, I hope, and spend the night before travelling again."

"Thank you, sire. I would be honoured to be your guest."

At dinner, a quiet meal in private with the monarch and his queen, the king seemed to have a favourite topic of conversation and kept returning to it.

"So this protégé of Kesh's is an engaging child?"

"Indeed. The happy relationship between them encourages me to be less fearful of fatherhood."

The king raised one eyebrow and Ahbrem hurriedly went on, suddenly aware that he had made a blunder, trying to deflect any further conversation about Kesh's relationship with the infant.

"I am betrothed," he explained. "I expect to become the first Khoulan monk to marry. The ceremony is to take place this summer ... Indeed, I would be most honoured if you could attend, your majesty ... your majesties."

"Oh!" The king smiled at the sudden stumbled invitation. "Well, it would, indeed, be an historic occasion," He glanced questioningly at the queen. "If we have no other engagements at the appointed time, I'm sure we would be delighted to accept. Yes, we will both attend, providing that no urgent matter demands my presence in some other place. Have you set a date?"

'What am I doing?' Ahbrem asked himself before saying aloud, "No, not yet but I am hoping it will be late summer, in the eighth or ninth moon of the round."

"A beautiful time for a wedding and most auspicious. Summer wedding, springtime baby, don't the old wives say?"

Ahbrem coloured and looked down at his plate, showing an

embarrassment that was delicious to the king. The monarch's questions sprang back to his favourite topic.

"So Kesh has a special relationship with the Sacred Mountain child?"

Ahbrem answered slowly, "Ye-es."

"Yet the mother is a Xouthan woman?"

"Yes."

"Who is the father? Do we know?"

Ahbrem said nothing.

"Ahbrem, do we know the father?"

"I cannot answer you, my king."

"You refuse your monarch a reply?" he waited a moment before continuing, "I know your training forbids that you should ever lie. Answer the question. Is the identity of the father known, yes or no?"

"Um ... It is."

"Is he a Xouthan man?"

Again Ahbrem hesitated.

"Ahbrem, is he a Xouthan man?"

"No."

"Mmm. So not a Xouthan. Who could it have been? An Anthrakati?"

Ahbrem's lack of expression led the king to dismiss that possibility.

"Enahet, perhaps."

Again Ahbrem's face remained expressionless.

"Surely not a Morthern man?"

Here Ahbrem's brows flickered slightly and his features tensed as if his fingernails were slowly being extracted.

"But we were at war! It was surely not a Morthern man!" the king exclaimed. "So who was this man who so betrayed his country?"

"Please, your majesty, I am sworn to secrecy. Please do not put pressure on me to break my oath."

This only served to intrigue the king yet further.

"You are sworn to secrecy by one who would cause you to withhold information even from your monarch. To whom could you have made such an oath?"

Ahbrem now stared straight ahead, determined not to give his friend away.

"My nephew Kesh went on a long journey," now the king spoke quietly, as if to himself. "When he came back, he was a much changed man, much grown in stature, if not in girth, far more self-confident, sure of what he wanted and determined to achieve it. He told me that he wanted Khoulan monks to be allowed to marry. I jokingly asked him if he had someone in mind and he did not respond, which, of course, I assumed indicated a negative reply. But perhaps he did have someone. Perhaps he did. He certainly sprang to the child's defence when I suggested, at our last meeting, that his Xouthan temperament might prove to be a problem. Ahbrem, tell me, is Kesh the father of this child?"

Ahbrem's tortured silence was all the confirmation that the king required.

There came a low rumble from his monarch's throat that struck terror into Ahbrem's heart. It rose in pitch and volume until it burst out as a roar.

"While his cousins were being drained of their life blood on Xouthan swords! How could he?"

Ahbrem was sure, in that moment, that he was about to pay for Kesh's misdemeanour with his own young life.

"Guards!"

Two guards instantly entered in through the main doors of the dining hall. They came to attention on the opposite side of the table to the king.

The king pointed his finger at the monk "Escort our guest back to Khoulan. Once there, find me Kesh, the Khoulan mattouk, and bring him to me. By this time tomorrow night he must stand before me!"

The two guards walked the length of the table and stood behind Ahbrem. He looked down at his plate still holding the remains of his unfinished meal. So he was not to be executed after all, but he was being evicted in disgrace. He stood up slowly. One of the guards touched Ahbrem's elbow gently, almost respectfully, as though embarrassed to have received a request to arrest the mattouk designate. Ahbrem bowed his head and allowed himself to be guided out of the dining hall.

***

Woken suddenly from deep sleep, Kesh was confused by the loud banging on his chamber door in the middle of the night. He could not grasp the significance of Ahbrem's arrival at his quarters with four burly soldiers but his friend was clearly in distress.

"I did not tell him, Kesh. Please believe me, I said nothing. It was through my silence that he guessed it. Please forgive me. Oh, my brother, my dear friend. I did not betray you. Please."

Ahbrem's words were not making sense. Kesh's first thought was that the monastery was once more under attack, that perhaps fire had broken out again. Then he remembered that Ahbrem was not yet at Khoulan and thought for a moment that he must still be dreaming. But the chill of the room and the rasping sounds of Ahbrem's rapid breathing seemed all too real.

It was not until one of the soldiers said, 'I am afraid, my Lord, you must come with us,' that Kesh realised that the men with Ahbrem were not part of the contingent based at Khoulan to protect them but that they bore the insignia of the King's own palace guards.

"You are speaking of the king?" Kesh asked Ahbrem, still perplexed.

"Nathan sent me to the palace, as I told you in my letter, to hand over the first copy of the translation, part of the translation, to the king, as a gift," Ahbrem spoke too rapidly, garbling his explanation. "He invited me to stay and dine. Then he started asking questions. I could not lie. He guessed, and I could not deny it. I am so very sorry."

"Guessed? What has he guessed?"

Ahbrem could not bring himself to explain in the presence of the soldiers. He hung his head in silence. The meaning of the brusque intrusion began to dawn on Kesh and his face lost all its animation. He stood stock still and stared at Ahbrem. His friend was close to weeping, standing there before him. Kesh reached out and put a hand softly on his shoulder.

"Look after Khoulan for me," was all he said.

He was obliged to dress in the presence of the soldiers, with Ahbrem standing by, shame faced. He reached his cloak down from its peg and nodded to the guards to let them know that he was ready.

"Kesh ..." Ahbrem was afraid he was going to leave without farewell. "Peace and long life, my brother."

"Peace and long life, my dearest friend."

Each clasped the others elbows in a parting embrace. Then Kesh was lead out into the night. Sakki slipped silently from the thatch and followed a little way behind the party. With his babes now fledged, he was solitary and vigilant, watching over his Morthern charge once more. He flapped lazily and coasted into gentle swoops across the path where the horses had just passed.

By the time they rode into Ahbresk it was mid-morning. Kesh was taken to the palace but not by the usual entrance. Instead, he was taken through a side door and put into a dungeon room. This did not augur well. The king must have been very angry about whatever Ahbrem had told him. Kesh wondered whether he might be merely awaiting execution, or whether he might first be subjected to a trial. At around mid-day, the dungeon railings were unlocked. The gaoler bowed his head briefly, as if acknowledging the status of the mattouk. He indicated that Kesh should follow the two fresh guards who had come to fetch him. He was taken up to the main hall and held between the guards until he stood before the king.

Kesh bowed low and did not dare to look his uncle in the eye. He kept his gaze on the stone flagging of the floor. The king dismissed his men and they were alone in the great space of the hall. There was a heavy silence in which even the sound of his own heartbeat seemed to reverberate around the chamber. Then the king drew a deep breath and spoke in a low voice.

"Is it true, Kesh of Khoulan? That you are the father of the Xouthan brat?"

"Apparently," Kesh said quietly. He immediately regretted that he had considered expressing his doubts on his relationship with Calim Bradmutt.

"Speak up, mattouk. Do not mumble when you answer to your monarch."

"Yes," said Kesh. "Yes, I am his father."

"But we were at war. We were at war with Xoutha and you were lying with this Xouthan harlot? You, a man sworn to celibacy, a man of Harg, the mattouk designate, no less, the nephew of the very king of Morth! While your cousins were dying on the battle field you were taking your pleasure with a Xouthan whore!"

Once the king had mentioned his dead cousins, there was no thought of making up excuses. It would have seemed churlish to point out that he had not known that their countries were at war. Nor would it have helped his case to explain that he hadn't been aware of what he was doing at the time. Not much good to argue that he was too drunk to remember anything that had happened on that fateful night. He was tempted, though, to defend Maina's honour but he did not know how. Should he explain about the potion? He decided not.

"I will resign my post, of course," said Kesh, hoping he might avoid execution at least.

"Get out!" roared the king. "Get out of my sight. I don't want your filthy flesh in my hall a moment longer. You are defiled, you are contaminated, you are ... disgusting. Guards! Get him out of here."

The guards came back in and escorted the mattouk to the dungeon once again. Kesh was desolated and in misery. A deep self-loathing crept over him for so letting down his uncle and his profession and yet he could hardly believe that an action he couldn't even remember could have such far-reaching consequences.

The cell had an iron bedstead. Although his sleep had been disrupted the previous night, he could not rest. He sat, head in hands, going over again and again the weakness that had brought him to this point. He feared for his future but, worse than that, he began to fear for Calim Bradmutt. What would happen to the child once he was gone? Would the monastery still oversee his welfare, would Ship continue to pay the costs of his nurse-family? Or would the king vent his rage on the infant and dispose of him? If the king was prepared to have Kesh, his nephew, executed, then being partly of the king's flesh and blood would obviously be of no benefit to the child.

He looked around him at the damp stone walls that imprisoned him. There was a small high window on one side. Kesh caught hold of the bars and pulled himself up so that his face was level with it.

"Maina, Maina, where are you, Maina? You need to know that I have failed you," he shouted out. "My promise to you is crumbling. I have let you down. I have failed our child. My loose tongue has put his life in danger!"

A seacrow flew up from the paved courtyard outside the window and fluttered at the glass, as if trying to get in.

"Sakki? Are you still my follower even in my darkest hour? I am so sorry. I have let you down, also. I cannot open up this window and I have no breadcrumbs for you."

Kesh held on to the window bars until his arms ached unbearably, watching the seacrow fly around the tiny yard. Eventually the prisoner let go and his feet found the flagstones of the floor. He sat down gloomily on the narrow bed to wait out the time remaining to him.

As sunset put the cell in shadow there was another rattle of keys against the bars. Again, the gaoler bowed and Kesh was instructed to follow the guards. He feared the worst but they led him this time up a familiar stairway into the guest wing and he was shown into his usual room. He walked into the chamber, where a candle was already burning and a fire lit in the grate. Had he been forgiven?

A tap came on the door and he went to open it. A tray of food lay on the floor outside and a serving girl was walking away down the corridor. Two guards stood at the end where the corridor joined the main passageway and they nodded to the girl as she passed by. He judged by this that he was not to be invited down to dinner. He was still detained but now imprisoned in comfort, so surely not under threat of death.

He slept fitfully so that in the morning, when he was woken, he was bleary eyed and not at his best. He was summoned into the king's presence soon after breakfast.

The king was once again alone in the main hall. He sent the guards away and scowled at Kesh.

"What am I to do with you?" he shook his head slowly. "For two nights now I have had no rest. At first I was too angry. I just wanted to leave you to rot in the dungeon. But I soon realised that you might be missed and I might be required to supply an explanation. It is no small thing to imprison a revered mattouk, after all. So it is not possible for me to lock you up and forget about you."

The king stared sourly at his nephew for a while before he asked,

"So who else knows the truth about this matter?"

"Ahbrem only," said Kesh. He was on the Sacred Mountain with me but no one else. The other monks had been sent back to Khoulan because of the war."

"What about the nurse-family?"

"They have not been told anything of the infant's parentage, only that he is sponsored by the monastery."

"The child? Does he know? Does he call you father?"

"I deeply regret that he does not. I could not risk allowing myself that pleasure. He does not yet know."

"What about the Xouthans? How many of them know of him?"

"The principal at the Sacred Mountain, the child's mother, of course, and the mother's nurse-sister. I do not think any others will have been told."

"There was a midwife, surely."

"She was not told of the true identity of the mother, much less the father."

"The true identity?"

Kesh was silent.

"Was there a special need to keep the mother's identity a secret?" asked the king.

Still he could make no reply.

"Kesh?"

His monarch demanded a response.

"Um ... She was one of the trainee priestesses."

"Ah! One of those beguiling Xouthan priestesses," said the king. "Not such a good example for a priestess to set her congregation, though, giving birth to a bastard child. So, what is her name?"

"Maina," answered the mattouk.

"Maina?" the King repeated. "A pretty name, and one I have heard before, I fancy. What is her family name?"

Kesh let out a sort of groan for a reply.

"What was that? I didn't quite catch what you said. Speak up, young Kesh."

Kesh felt the king was playing with him now. He bowed his head low and said quietly, "She is the emperor's daughter."

"Oh, by Harg!" the king wailed. He lifted both hands and slid them wearily down his face. There followed a few moments of silence during which the king seemed to be considering the implications of this information. Once he had thought things over, however, he seemed to find some humour in Kesh's predicament. He almost chuckled as he exclaimed, "Oh, Kesh, my boy, you certainly don't do anything by halves! I assume, as you're still breathing, and there's no army at the gate, that the emperor knows absolutely nothing of this?"

"I think not."

"What about the Ship Prophet? You spoke before of the infant being sponsored by him. Now you say he is being sponsored by the monastery. Which is true?"

"The Ship Prophet kindly provides the finance. Obviously, it would not have been ethical for me to have the monastery provide the finance for my son and, as a monk, I have no personal wealth to draw on. The monastery administers the sponsorship."

"I see."

The king fell silent. With his short-lived good humour gone again, he sat staring gloomily into space.

"Of course, I will resign my mattoukhood," Kesh repeated. "I am not worthy. Ahbrem can take over."

"You cannot resign." The king slowly shook his head, staring blankly ahead of him. "How would we explain your resignation? We could not. Not without throwing all the family into shame. It is imperative that no one ever hears of this. I still need an heir. I still need you to follow after me. You must *say* nothing and you must *do* nothing, except that you must make an oath to me, Kesh. You must swear to me here and now, by Harg, that you will never disclose the truth of the situation. My reputation and all my hopes for the future, as well as your position and present career, all depend on your continued secrecy. Say it, Kesh. Say that you swear, by your love of Harg, to maintain this secret."

Kesh said solemnly, "I swear, by my love of Harg, that I will maintain this secret."

"You must never tell another soul, not even the child himself."

"Oh!"

Kesh was not expecting to keep the secret from his son forever.

"Promise me?"

Reluctantly he promised.

"In view of the circumstances," the king continued. "I think I will double the guard on the monastery. I will also order a consignment of tiles for the roof. That thatch is far too vulnerable to fire and I don't want my nephew going the same way as my uncle. I only regret I didn't think of doing it before, many years ago."

"It is not long since the roof was re-thatched after the fire. It does not need replacing yet," said Kesh, thinking that the seacrow wouldn't like the tiles."

"My decision is not negotiable," said the king. "I will order it to be done quickly so that it can be finished before the wedding. Ahbrem is to be married at Khoulan, I take it?"

"Yes," answered Kesh, trying to hide his surprise that the king knew about the wedding.

"I take it that you will conduct the ceremony? Has he asked you to?"

"He has, yes."

"I am rather looking forward to it. I think I like the idea of monks marrying. As you once suggested, a married monk will have a deeper understanding of the difficulties encountered by the ordinary man."

Kesh did not reply. He somehow guessed that such approval did not extend to monks who wished to marry Xouthan women. The jealousy he had felt until now was replaced with concern for Ahbrem's plans. He surmised that the king was not yet aware of the nationality of his future wife. If the king intended to attend, he might soon find out, and that might make things difficult for Ahbrem.

Chapter 9

Kesh was released and allowed to find his own way back to Khoulan. He spoke to Ahbrem as soon as he could get him alone in private.

"The king told me he is looking forward to your wedding. I take it that he doesn't know that Wyn is Xouthan?"

Ahbrem shook his head.

"Are you going to tell him? What will happen when the king offers her his congratulations and hears her replying with a Xouthan accent?"

"I do not know. I cannot imagine that he will be very happy. I wish now that I had not mentioned the wedding, but I was trying to distract his attention away from the topic of your relationship with Calim Bradmutt. Before I knew what I was saying, I found myself inviting both the king and queen to the wedding. I have been trying to think of ways of avoiding revealing Wyn's true origins ever since. The king is obviously still full of hatred for the Xouthans."

"Impossible for him to feel otherwise when he has lost both his sons to their warriors."

"If I was not a monk, I could lie and pretend that she was Enahet, or better, Anthrakati. I don't suppose the king has met many Anthrakatis. He might not know the difference."

"The only thing you can do is to instruct Wyn to say as little as possible when the king speaks to her. Perhaps you could train her to speak a few phrases of the Sacred Language without an accent."

"You mean, with a Morthern accent. The Xouthan maids on the Mountain thought my Morthern accent quite amusing, I remember. Did Maina never tease you about yours?"

"Tease me?" Kesh thought about it. "She teased me about our religion but never about my accent, as far as I remember."

"Aha," said Ahbrem. "She must have been absolutely besotted with you if she never made her criticisms personal."

"Really?" asked Kesh. "Well, I think she must have forgotten about me now. She hasn't replied to my last letter."

"When did you send it?"

"A few moons ago, soon after you left to help Nathan with the translation."

"So how did you get it to her?"

"I sent the primer Altan to Fullabish."

"Did he give it to Captain Gintrog to give to Salwell of Zoradetra?"

"I do not know. He gave it to one of the Xouthan captains."

"Ah. She may not have received it, then. I will ask Wyn if she knows what happened to it."

"Thank you."

Kesh was comforted by the thought that his letter may not have reached Maina, rather than that she had read it but not taken the trouble to reply. With Ahbrem back at Khoulan, Kesh was now free to visit the Sacred Mountain for further instruction in the Xouthan language. He decided that he would concentrate on the phrases he was most likely to need as a traveller, and venture into Xoutha, perhaps even as far as Zoradetra. If he could see Maina face to face once more, he could discover whether her feelings for him lived on. If her heart was still his, as she had once told him it was, then he might still find the strength to endure the long wait that lay ahead of them before they could be together. He might dare to dream of a time when they could declare their relationship publicly.

Kesh packed for a long trip, but did not say anything to Ahbrem about his plans to cross the border. He spent half a moon in the Sacred Mountain community practicing his pronunciation with Hannala, memorising the rules that indicated when a certain sound should come from deep inside the throat, or when whole syllables at the end of certain words did not require being pronounced at all. When he could wait no longer to achieve a better standard, he packed his bags and took his leave of King Nathan and the Prophet of the Burning Ship. Hannala walked with him down the steps to the Xouthan gate. Kesh drew back the single bolt and stepped through. He sucked in a large breath of Xouthan air.

To Hannala, he looked quite different now he was dressed in Xouthan travelling garb, with his hair just beginning to grow back, hidden under his felt hat. She had not mentioned anything about Dorran's visit or his threat to her. She hoped Kesh was now good enough to pass for a friendly foreign visitor without immediately giving away his Morthern nationality. She made him practice one last time.

"Say again, 'I am seeking lodgings for the night.'"

Kesh translated into Xouthan. Hannala replied, and Kesh translated back into the Sacred Language:

"We charge two dipnats, payable in advance."

Hannala laughed lightly.

"Very good, but you must take care, Kesh. I am still not happy that you are risking making such a journey on your own."

"Do not worry. All will be well."

"I have grown very fond of you lately, Kesh. I would so hate to be responsible for sending you into hostile territory underprepared."

"I am well prepared, Hannala. You have given me excellent instruction. And I have grown fond of you, too. If Maina does not want me anymore, I will come back here and marry you."

He put his arms around the Sacred Mountain principal and hugged her. Hannala hesitated, holding herself stiffly for a moment. She must have been a little taken aback by his sudden display of affection. But then she relented and put her arms around him in return.

"I wish you wouldn't joke about such things," she said. "I mean, love and marriage. You should not talk of them so lightly. You may be new to these concepts, but we Xouthans take them very seriously."

"Oh, I take my relationship with Maina very seriously. Next to my love of Harg and, I suppose, my love for my son, it is the utmost sentiment in my heart."

"But, sometimes, you do not seem to consider other people's feelings."

"Oh," Kesh said, ashamed now that he had been so free with his embraces. "I am so sorry. I did not mean to offend you."

"No, no. You didn't offend me, but you should perhaps consider other peoples' emotions more carefully. You have grown into a fine young man. You must not underestimate the effect your words and, even more, your deeds could be having. Young women's hearts are easily captured. You should show a little compassion now and again."

"Compassion? Yes, alright. I will try."

"May the gods of Xoutha watch closely over you - in league with the God of Morth, of course."

"Thank you. May Harg protect you until we meet again."

Kesh trod lightly down the path into Xoutha. He had a feeling that Hannala had just paid him an enormous compliment, but he had not yet fully worked out what she had meant by it.

Hannala was not the only one worried about Kesh's excursion south of the border. The last time Kesh had been this side of the mountains there had been a strong aroma of blood and torn flesh. There had been an open space strewn with many corpses and, although seacrows were usually highly attracted to the smell of a fresh corpse, Sakki had no wish for his crumbdropper to become one. He circled nervously behind him, watching anxiously over his head for signs of trouble, determined to stay close.

Kesh walked all day, passing through the settlement that served the historical fort at Ghaba Head and on along the road to Zoradetra. By the time the sun had set he was within the outskirts of the city. He found lodgings, a room with its own fireplace, and he carried out his evening's meditation before going down to eat with the other guests.

The next morning he asked for directions to the palace and the innkeeper pointed to an elaborately decorated building which stood out majestically above the older part of the city. It looked out over the ancient harbour and, beyond it, to the sea. At the palace gates he did not dare to ask for Maina. Instead, he asked for Salwell.

A young man who had the same colouring as Wyn soon appeared at the gate and Kesh introduced himself. Salwell was polite and welcomed him, but did not invite him into the palace. He told him that it might not be wise. Kesh was happy enough to postpone his encroachment onto the emperor's personal territory. Instead, Salwell took Kesh to their family home, offered him tea, and sent a servant to the temple to fetch Wyn.

"It will be delightful to see your sister again, of course," Kesh told him. "But I was really hoping to see your nurse-sister, Maina, while I was here. Do you think that it could be arranged?"

"I am afraid my nurse-sister is away in Mardek province at the present time."

This was the first time that Salwell had cause to feel glad that Maina happened to be so far away. He explained about the posting.

Kesh felt his expectations crushed but did not give up hope completely.

"How far is Mardek?" he enquired.

"It is to the south, on the border with the Wildlands, Salwell told him."About as far away as you can get without leaving Xoutha."

Kesh's heart sank. He did not have the time to ride, let alone walk, across the whole country. He was expected back at Khoulan within the moon.

"Oh, that is a pity," Kesh said, trying to hide the depth of his disappointment as best he could. After a moment he asked, "Do you know if Maina got my last letter? I sent one of our primers to give it to a Xouthan sea captain at Fullabish, but I do not know whether the letter reached you as I had intended it to."

"I do not remember seeing any letter from Khoulan addressed to Maina. There is usually one to collect for Wyn every moon or so."

"Ah, those would be from my friend, Ahbrem. He seems to have mastered the Xouthan systems of communication a little better than I."

Salwell lifted his chin as if to nod but said nothing.

"Perhaps ... Would it be possible to get a letter to Maina in Mardek province?"

"Er..." Salwell hesitated.

Wyn arrived. She bowed formally to Kesh. Salwell excused himself to return to his duties at the palace.

Sakki recognised Wyn and knew that Kesh was now amongst friends, despite the absence of his mate. Perhaps it was not the season for crumbdropper matings. There was no sign of food as yet and he began to feel a little bored. He took to the air and turned towards the sun, intending to go down to the coast to seek scraps of crab or fish but, as he looked southwards, a line of blue hills seemed to beckon to him from across the sparkling bay. It was a beautiful day and long flights were best begun on empty stomachs. He beat his powerful wings and was soon sailing out across the water.

Wyn studied Kesh and her face broke into a smile.

"You look different in your travelling clothes," she told him. "They remind me of the clothes you were wearing the night you arrived back at the Sacred Mountain. I was so relieved to hear news of Maina that night. I was so grateful to you for bringing her back to Xoutha safely. So, how are you?"

They exchanged pleasantries and then Kesh broached the subject of communications once again. If he could not see Maina in the flesh, at least he could send a letter from within the same country so that it might have a better chance of reaching her.

"We could have a letter taken to Mardek for you, certainly," Wyn told him." But you haven't travelled all this way just to send a letter."

"No," said Kesh. "I was hoping to visit Maina. I did not know about the governorship."

"I am sorry that you have had a wasted journey."

"Oh, no, it has not been wasted. It is wonderful to see you once again. And there is something else I should discuss with you, in any case."

"What could that be, Kesh?"

"I do not know quite how to begin," Kesh said. "Did Ahbrem mention anything about the king in his last letter to you?"

"Yes. He told me that he had invited the king and queen to the wedding but that they did not yet know that I am Xouthan."

"And they must never know, Wyn," Kesh said. "The king lost both his sons in battle during the last war so he would never approve of Ahbrem marrying a Xouthan, much less be willing to attend the ceremony."

Kesh could have illustrated his statement by describing the king's reaction to discovering Calim Bradmutt's parentage but he didn't want to frighten her.

"I see," said Wyn.

"So we are going to have to find a way of hiding your identity."

"How could we?"

"I am afraid that you will have to wear Morthern wedding garb."

"I don't mind that."

"And you will have to avoid speaking to either the king or the queen if at all possible. It might be a good idea if you could learn to mimic the Morthern accent when you speak the Sacred Language, just in case you have to speak to one of them, and it would help if you could learn a few Morthern phrases in case anyone addresses you in the local language. The other thing is ... Well, hiding one Xouthan will be difficult enough. I am afraid I cannot see how we can accommodate any members of your family at the ceremony. I am so sorry. It may not quite be the celebration that you would have hoped for."

"That's alright, Kesh. Ahbrem has suggested that we hold a Xouthan ceremony for my family here in Zoradetra before I come to Khoulan."

"Um ... that is a good idea but ... will you not have the same problem? I mean, will you not have to hide the fact that your husband-to-be is Morthern?"

"You are probably right. My mother knows, of course. She thinks I am making a mistake marrying a man who does not share my beliefs. A recipe for disaster, she called it, but I have told her what a good man Ahbrem is, how he is more earnest in his beliefs than many Xouthans, how he always seems to know, and to do, what is right. I think she understands. I'm sure she would prefer me to be marrying a Xouthan, but she is no longer saying so."

"What about the other guests?"

"We have decided not to invite the emperor," Wyn smiled.

"Very wise."

"I will just invite a few close family and friends."

Instead of asking for details, Kesh's thoughts sprang back to the object of his obsession.

"Will Maina be coming?"

"I hope so. I would have asked her to conduct the ceremony for us but she is refusing to even set foot in the temple these days."

"Oh? Why is that?"

"She says she is having doubts about her religious convictions. She blames you. She says she spent too long in your company."

"Oh ... That is ... um ... unfortunate. I did not intend to have that effect, nor would I have believed it possible."

"Don't worry. I don't think it was all your fault but it was something that happened during the round we were away from here. Something powerful that shook her faith. I'm not sure what exactly."

"Is she alright?"

"Yes, I think so."

"How is she getting on with this governorship?"

"She seems to be coping well. Mind you, she has the old governor in her pocket. He is bending over backwards to help her make it a success, it seems."

"Good," Kesh said, but in his heart he felt a pang of envy. Another man was helping Maina, there with her, providing support when he could not. "So, how long will her term of governorship last?

"Initially, the appointment is temporary and is due to terminate after one round but the emperor has said that he will extend the position to a second round if she does well."

"Oh," said Kesh.

It seemed to him that the more the old governor helped her, the longer she would be away.

"But she might come to your wedding? Wyn, may I request an invitation to your Xouthan ceremony? It seems it may the only chance I can hope for of seeing Maina once again."

"Of course, Kesh. We would be honoured to have you there."

"Thank you so much," Kesh said, now brimming with renewed hope. "So, about this letter to Maina. If I write it tonight, I could bring it to you tomorrow. Or should I give it to Salwell?"

"Bring it here to me. I will see that it is forwarded to Mardek. Salwell has enough to do at the palace."

"Very well. Thank you again," said Kesh. "Now, if you will excuse me, I will return to the inn. I must set my mind to getting some thoughts down on parchment."

That evening, Kesh sat next to his fire writing by the light of a shaded lamp. The monastery at Khoulan did not have anything so elaborate. To burn scarce lamp oil and then use a shade to reduce the amount of light it gave out seemed extravagant in the extreme. Nevertheless, it lit the parchment well. Kesh wrote:

> To Maina of Zoradetra
> Honourable Governor of the Province of Mardek
>
> Dear Maina, I have recently received an invitation from your nurse-sister, Wyn of Zoradetra, to attend the Xouthan celebration of her marriage to my friend and colleague, Ahbrem of Khoulan, and I wondered whether I might look forward to the renewing of our own acquaintance at that event.
>
> Forgive me for failing to contact you before this time. I was away from Khoulan when your last letter arrived there. It brought me great joy, however, to read its contents on my return. The reply, which I wrote a few moons ago, failed to reach Zoradetra as it should have done. It seems to have gone astray somewhere. I hope this missive succeeds where the previous one failed and I look forward eagerly to a reply. Wishing you peace and long life.
>
> Sincerely yours
> Kesh of Khoulan, Mattouk.

Kesh read through what he had written, rolled it up and warmed a piece of red sealing wax on a spoon above the lamp. He pressed his seal gently into the wax and put it ready to take to Wyn the next morning. Then he collected the crumbs from his supper and threw them out of the window onto the roof of the inn where a seacrow had come to sleep for the second night running. He assumed it had always lived there, but it had not been there when he had first returned to the inn earlier that evening. It had spent the day elsewhere, exploring the coast-line, perhaps, or enjoying a foray up into the mountains. What joy it must be to have the freedom to go anywhere you liked at any time. It was a fine cock-bird, glossy black and in its prime. It looked like Sakki, but then, all seacrows looked the same to him. Only Ahbrem could reliably tell one seacrow from another.

***

When Maina felt the pressures of governorship pressing too heavily on her shoulders she often took a walk into the gardens of the governor's residence, seeking solace in its quiet beauty, hoping for inspiration, looking to find new ways of dealing with her problems. A stream ran through the gardens and the decorative bridge that gave access to the area on the far side of it was becoming one of her favourite spots for contemplation. Out of habit, once she had reached this bridge, she thrust her hand into her pocket and felt the reassuring presence of the envelope with its secret coil of stolen hair. She realised that she hadn't been thinking of Kesh quite so much since she had been in Mardek. She had been so busy with meetings and with trying to work out how best to deal with her administrators that there was little time for reflection on personal matters. In the old days at Zoradetra she had forever been stealing moments to savour her own company so that she could conjure up his spirit, imagining him close to her, so close that she could feel the warmth of his flesh, breathe the scent of him hanging in the air, feel the touch of his fingers on her hand. In her mind she had held lengthy conversations with him at such times. Of course, she had consulted his spirit as to whether she should leave Zoradetra to take up this position in Mardek. So had it advised her to go? Indeed, it had not. In her daydream, Kesh had begged her to turn down the posting, had told her she should, instead, run away from her father, leave Zoradetra, escape into Morth and marry him; that he would find her a little house near Khoulan where she could hide and take care of Calim Bradmutt. Better still, the vision had said, we'll run away together and go and live as a family of three, in Enaha.

A shepherd's cottage, was it not, that he had wanted to take her to when he had first learnt of Calim Bradmutt's coming? Oh, she had dreamed such sweet discourse between them! Thinking back, however, only served to remind her that Kesh had not replied to her last letter. He had become so distant from her. Had he forgotten her? Perhaps she should throw away the coil of hair, concentrate on her new life. Perhaps the habit of touching it so often in her pocket was just that, a habit, and one she should try to break. She took the envelope out and held it between her fingers above the gushing water. If she dropped it there, it would soon be carried away into the sea and gone forever. She would be released from her memories of their time together, released from the constant yearning to be with him once again. Her fingers twitched and the envelope twisted between them, suspended above the water. A seacrow was flying in the garden, wheeling round, passing up and down between the trees, following the line of the stream. Was it looking for insects? She thought perhaps Sakki had come to visit her again like he had at Zoradetra but then told herself not to be so foolish. This bird was bigger than Sakki and Sakki could not have wandered all the way to Mardek from the Sacred Mountain.

The afternoon light refected off its glossy feathers as she watched. Suddenly the bird dropped and landed next to her on the parapet. Maina stepped back in surprise, nearly dropping the envelope. She clutched it in panic, realising in that moment how devastated she would have felt if she had lost that reminder of her love. She quickly put the envelope back into the safety of her pocket.

It was not over, then. She was not yet ready to give up hope of a relationship with Kesh. The seacrow let out a squawk and took off again. They were getting so tame, these crows, happy to land within an arm's length of a person. She did not remember them being so bold in her younger days.

Chapter 10

There was a guest in the east wing of the Palace of the Four Kings. Hernst of Ahn Dehar had arrived and requested an audience with the humans to discuss arrangements for the mining of coal from under his lands. He was invited to dine and the kings asked him what he would want in return for mining rights. He had not been very specific about his terms, however, and after the meal was over, King Kevin had suggested that Hernst might like to retire to the east wing to recover from his journey.

"He doesn't seem to be quite all there," Doug complained to the others. "He seems distracted somehow."

"Perhaps he is in shock after his father's death." Kevin suggested.

"He's suddenly responsible for his whole tribe," Ted offered. "That might take some getting used to."

"I suppose so," said Doug. "All the same, I didn't think he was being completely honest with us. He wouldn't commit to any of the terms we suggested. To me it almost felt like he was playing games with us."

"Perhaps he needs some support," said Ted. "Perhaps we should suggest he employs a lawyer to look over the agreement before he signs it."

"That's a good idea," agreed Doug. "We should put that to him in the morning. He might want to bring in someone neutral though. A lawyer from Wadderhick, perhaps. He might not trust anyone from around here."

"That wouldn't matter. We're not that desperate. If he wants to postpone an agreement until he finds a lawyer it will give you more time to put together a team of suitable engineers."

"That's true, I suppose."

"I don't know about you two, but I'm pretty tired," Kevin said. "I think I might turn in early, too."

"Okay," said Ted. "See you in the morning."

The remaining kings finished the wine in their glasses before bidding each other a goodnight. The palace soon fell into a quiet darknes, but not all its occupants were asleep. By the light of a stump of candle that he had brought from home, Hernst was sharpening a hunting knife, his father's old knife. It had the chieftain's symbols engraved on the side of the handle. Hernst tested the blade edge on his thumb. Seemingly satisfied with the feel of it, he gave the blade one last polish and slid it into a sheath on his belt.

Quietly he unlatched the door to his chamber and stepped out into the corridor. The candle flickered with the movement of the air, and his shadow danced briefly on the wall, a dark silhouette in a pool of light amidst a sea of darkness. Hernst solemnly drew himself to his full height and stepped silently towards the main body of the palace. He had chosen King Doug, because he understood Doug to have been responsible for preparing the poison. He would have liked to get rid of all three but he doubted that he could reach them all before being discovered. Besides, Nathan wasn't at the palace. He was out of reach, somewhere overseas, so Hernst couldn't hope to rid the world of all of these creatures at one time, as he would have liked to do.

He knew which room to make for. He could hear Doug snoring even from the corridor. The door wasn't locked. It opened easily, without a sound. Hernst stepped across to the bed. For a moment he held the candle out and looked down at the hairless being breathing noisily, deep in some carefree dream. Doug breathed and dreamed, while his father breathed no more and would never dream again. He raised his knife. It glinted briefly in the dark. He brought it down with all his might, slicing through the sheets, thrusting it into the flesh beneath.

The king woke and gave a strangled cry, twisting violently round. Hernst lost his grip on the blade. His victim started to scream hysterically. Hernst could not understand why he wasn't dead. Had he bungled his stab or were these people protected by an unworldly magic? Before he could decide on an answer, two palace guards appeared in the room and Hernst was seized.

The other kings stumbled in sleepily one after the other, followed by a gaggle of curious servants and confused administrators. Ted was first to realise the gravity of the situation. He sent one of the servants to fetch bandages and ointment for Doug's wound, while Kevin hurried another off into the city to find a doctor.

Hernst expected the kings to order him to be executed on the spot, but instead Ted told the guards to take him away to a cell and lock him up.

Doug's wound gave him a good deal of pain, but nothing vital seemed to have been pierced. The doctor arrived and stitched the edges of the gash together with boiled thread. He covered it over with an evil smelling poultice that encouraged Ted and Kevin to bid Doug goodnight as soon as they had arranged for extra guards to stand outside his door.

Within a few days Doug was up and about again, wanting to know where they were going to get their coal from, now that their planned supplier had made it impossible to trade with his people. The other kings could not come up with a solution regarding their future supply of fuel, but they did all agree that they should reinforce the palace defences, doubling the number of guards posted at each position both night and day.

"We need to react properly to this crime," said Doug. "It isn't enough simply to lock him away. We need to demonstrate that murder attempts on humans are not to be tolerated. I'm afraid that, if we don't deal with this harshly, we'll be giving out a signal that murderers can get away it."

"How do you mean?" asked Ted. "What else do you think we should do?"

"I'm thinking like for like. How about a public execution? That should get the message across."

"That's not like for like. He only attempted murder. He didn't actually kill you."

"He could have. Another couple of inches further down and I reckon it would have gone straight into my heart. Don't you care?"

"I care. Of course I do. But a public execution would be going a bit too far."

"I don't see why." Doug turned to his other colleague. "Kevin, what do you think?"

"I don't know. A public execution does seem a bit extreme."

"But to keep it private defeats the object," argued Doug. "We're not going to deter future attempts unless we demonstrate our reaction publicly."

"Why don't we see what Nathan says?" suggested Kevin.

"Nathan's not here and it would take him a month to get here."

"We could at least send a message," said Kevin. "We could explain what's happened and ask him for his opinion."

"So what do you say to that, Ted?" Doug asked the other king. "You'd agree to an execution if it was a majority decision, I take it?

"I think I could predict that Nathan would be in favour of an execution," Ted answered. "I know how his mind works. But, yes, we should at least ask for his input. We've always decided these big things between us in the past. It will at least give us some time to cool off while we wait for his response."

"I'm not sure I'm going to cool off. I've been traumatised, you know. Perhaps you'd understand how I feel if you were the one to have been stabbed in your bed in the middle of the night. I haven't slept properly since it happened."

"I'm sorry," said Ted. "I didn't mean to sound unsympathetic, but an execution would be a big thing. We haven't killed any Penethellans since we first made peace with them - except for this guy's father, of course."

"You think he found out about that?" Kevin asked. "But who could have told him? The only person who knew anything about it was the guy sent to place the power unit in the chief's mattress and I thought he wasn't told what it was, anyway. Do you think he betrayed us?"

"Perhaps we should ask him," said Doug. "Where is he now?"

"Perhaps we should just ask Hernst why he tried to murder you," suggested Ted.

"Like you could trust a word he said," grumbled Doug. "Okay, get some sort of investigation going. Appoint a detective, send a message to Nathan. I don't care what we do as long as we do something. What we mustn't do is sit around just talking and getting nowhere."

***

The Sacred Mountain was alive with talk about the attempted murder when Kesh arrived there on his way back from Zoradetra. Nathan assured him that Doug was alive and recovering but he told Kesh that he felt inclined to advise his colleagues to have Hernst executed as a warning to anyone else that might get similar ideas. Kesh was most alarmed at this suggestion but said nothing out loud. He could understand exactly why Hernst might have been stirred to attempt to strike back at the Four Kings. After all, he clearly remembered telling Hernst that his father had probably been poisoned on the orders of the Four Kings, and he also remembered denying him the chance to request military help from Morth, so rendering it impossible for him to take revenge by declaring war, as he had originally intended.

'Another blunder with monumental consequences!' Kesh told himself, once he was alone in the guest room on the mountain. Why could he not have kept his mouth shut? If he had not mentioned the poison to Hernst, the Four Kings could have had their coal and the Ahn Dehar could have had increased prosperity and there need not have been any war or attempted murder. He must save Hernst somehow. It was his duty. And what about the Ahn Dehar community? Who was in charge, with Hernst locked up at the palace? What could he do to put right the awful situation he had created? First, he decided, he must convince Nathan to change his mind and advise against an execution. Kesh realised that he should confess his blunder to Nathan straight away and explain that it was his own words that had, in all probability, caused Hernst to turn. But Hernst was likely to remain imprisoned even if he escaped execution, so the Ahn Dehar would still be without a leader. Kesh decided that he must visit them and offer help in recompense for his mistake.

He sought out Nathan the next day.

"Have you sent a message back to the other three kings yet?"

"I have written a message, yes."

"And has the messenger taken it?"

"He is due to set off this morning. I saw him saddling a horse in the stable as I passed."

"Did you advise execution, as you said you were inclined to?"

"I did, yes."

"I think that execution might be a mistake."

"Oh, you do? Really!"

"King Nathan, I think the murder attempt was my fault."

"How could that be? Why would you want Doug murdered?"

"I do not want Doug murdered. Most certainly, I do not, but when I attended Hernst's father's funeral I think I gave away some information that I probably should have kept to myself. I am afraid I told Hernst what I had learnt on my last visit here, namely that his father had been slowly poisoned on the orders of the Four Kings."

"You told him what?"

"Did I misunderstand? I thought that that was what I had heard. Of course, I now realise that I should not have passed the information on without some sort of ..."

"No, you certainly should not have passed that information on. Can't you tell when you are being told something in confidence? You idiot! Thanks to you, one of my friends nearly lost his life!"

"Yes, I realise that now. I am so sorry. I hope I can pay recompense somehow. But first, may I implore you to retract your advice on the execution? It is my fault that Hernst was driven to the murder attempt. It is I who should be executed, if anyone."

"You're not wrong there."

"So will you change your advice? Please do not have Hernst executed. He was just upset. He had just lost his father."

"Your involvement doesn't change the fact that he attempted to commit murder. He is a dangerous man."

"So he should be kept safe. He should be confined, perhaps, until he has been counselled. But please give him a chance. At least, let me speak to Hernst again before you decide to end his life."

"The messenger has probably left by now."

"I could go after him."

"Send you? You have done enough already."

Kesh searched desperately for another line of persuasion to reinforce his argument.

"If the other kings execute Hernst, they will have to explain to his people that he attempted murder," Kesh said. "Otherwise more murder attempts could follow, in revenge for Hernst's death. On the other hand, if the truth gets out, all of the Ahn Dehar will find out about the poisoning and other members of the tribe might follow behind Hernst, attempting to avenge Ackhart's death. The only way to put an end to this business, as I see it, would be to apologise to the man, offer him some recompense and return him to his tribe."

"Well, thank you so much for your advice. Forgive me if I do not immediately follow it. You're the person that's created this problem for us, remember. You're hardly in a position to go giving out good advice. And if you want recompense to be paid, it should be you that pays it."

"I agree, absolutely," said Kesh. "Unfortunately, as a Khoulan monk, I have no private wealth."

"How convenient."

"But I am willing to travel to the Land of the Four Kings, or to Ahn Dehar, to wherever you deem fit. I will offer service to the kings and to the Ahn Dehar, if there is anything I can do."

Nathan let out an exasperated huff and turned away while he thought for a moment.

"You are a stupid and irresponsible young man. I can't see how you come to hold such high office in what is meant to be a religious institution. Head of a monastery, indeed! However, you may be right that a holding a public execution could cause more problems than it solves. I still think an execution is the right thing to do, though. We can't just ignore the fact that this man intended to murder one of us. Let's go and see if that messenger has gone yet. Perhaps I will send you back with him to see if you can intercede on our behalf with his people and calm things down a bit, but I will also send a warning that you are not to be left alone with this man, Hernst, and that everything you say to him must be closely monitored."

The messenger had left, but one of the most fleet-footed of the maidens was sent down the mountain path after him and a little while later he came back in with her through the Xouthan gate of the mountain community. By that time, Nathan had written a second letter to suggest that Kesh might be useful in patching things up with the Ahn Dehar but warning his friends not to let Kesh near Hernst without supervision. Kesh had, meanwhile, prepared himself for another journey, sending a messenger to Khoulan to say that he would be away for a little longer than planned, adding another few moons to his expected duration of absence. When Nathan realised that Kesh's trip would delay his translator's return, he changed his mind about wanting Kesh to go but Kesh begged to be allowed to go to speak on Hernst's behalf. Nathan took him to Ship's study to see what his old captain thought about the situation. He first made Kesh confess what he had told Hernst about his father's death.

"I agree with Nathan that you should think a little more carefully before you speak," Ship told Kesh. "And I think a man who has attempted murder should be confined, for safety's sake, if not for punishment. I agree with Nathan that he has committed a serious crime – far too serious simply to pardon it and take no further action. Nevertheless, I think that the original fault lies with those who conspired to speed up chief Ackhart's death. The Ahn Dehar are creatures of intelligence, after all, the same as all the peoples on this planet. They should be treated with respect. They should not be played with like animals in a circus. I'm sure you agree with me, Nathan. You are now devoting yourself to their spiritual salvation, so you must see them as I do, as worthy equivalents to human beings."

"I say they deserve respect but I also think that an attempted murder should be punished appropriately."

"We could say that this man, Hernst, has already suffered a degree of punishment. After all, he has suddenly discovered that the people he was about to do business with murdered his father. I dare say all his hopes and plans for the future crumbled rather abruptly at that point."

"It was not handled in the best way, I will grant you, but murder is very strong word for what was done to chief Ackhart. It was better than fighting them for their coal, which probably would have caused many deaths on both sides."

"A little more patience might have avoided both scenarios."

"You weren't there. You don't know anything," Nathan said irritably. He turned on his heel and walked out of Ship's study.

"Oh, dear! I seem to have caused yet more conflict," said Kesh.

"Don't blame yourself for his rudeness. Nathan and I see things a little differently, that's all. He'll be nice as pie again tomorrow. In the meantime, I hear you're all packed up and ready for yet another journey. You never stay in one place for long, do you, Mattouk Kesh?"

"I have to go and see if I can put right what I have done wrong."

"You shouldn't be shouldering all the burden of blame, as I tried to make Nathan see," Ship told him. "Take care of yourself, and come back safe. I wish you a speedy journey."

"Thank you. I hope it is indeed speedy. I must be back in time to appoint a deputy mattouk designate before Ahbrem's wedding. I am hoping to attend both the ceremonies, so we will both be away from Khoulan for a few days at the time of the Xouthan celebration."

"Ah, yes. It is always good to have some joyful event to look forward to. I have been invited to Khoulan for the Morthern ceremony, and I hope to get there, if my aching joints will let me."

"Oh, that is good," said Kesh, although it did cross his mind that it was going to be even more stressful than he had expected, conducting his first wedding ceremony with the Prophet of the Burning Ship himself in attendance.

"Goodbye, then," said Ship.

"Peace and long life," said Kesh, and he pulled the door of the cosy little study closed behind him.

Hannala was with a small group of monks and maidens who had come to the Xouthan gate to say goodbye.

"It's a long journey, Kesh," she said.

"It is one I have taken before, albeit with a slight diversion across the winter ice."

"I feel uneasy about you going to a strange land to speak to a murderer."

"Hernst is not a murderer, even if he once intended to be. I think he is a good man at heart. He has simply been overwhelmed by his father's death, by the circumstances of it. I think he will soon recover and will look back on his actions as being the result of a temporary insanity."

"I hope you are right. Take care of yourself, dear Mattouk Kesh."

"I will," Kesh embraced her and then his colleagues "Good bye. Peace and long life. Goodbye."

Chapter 11

Kesh led his horse down the Xouthan path behind the messenger. Sakki was puzzled by this. He could not understand why his charge had returned to the Sacred Mountain but was now going back down the dangerous side of it instead of going home. Nevertheless, he followed as before, always looking behind and ahead for potential threats to his crumbdropper.

Kesh found himself constantly thinking about the two letters which the messenger was carrying, one condoning the execution of his friend, the other criticising his own character. He was prepared for the temptation that presented itself each night as the messenger slept: the impulse to simply steal the letters and save his friend and his own reputation in one action, but he did not want to load his conscience with any more bad deeds and he could not work out how he would explain the disappearance of the letters to either the messenger or to the three kings. Nevertheless, if Harg had seen fit to wash them away in a sudden flood or to send a mighty wind to blow them into the camp fire, he would have been very grateful.

While he and the messenger made their way towards the Palace of the Four Kings, Kesh spent much effort on trying to calculate whether he could hope to win a reprieve for Hernst, visit the Ahn Dehar and get back to Xoutha in time for the Xouthan celebration of Ahbrem's wedding. His one chance of seeing, and perhaps speaking, to Maina in two whole rounds seemed to be slipping through his fingers. Was that going to be his punishment for getting Hernst into trouble? He imagined the worst possible scenario, that he would get back to Xoutha the day after the ceremony, with Maina already half-way back to Mardek and his return to Khoulan seriously overdue. Were they destined never to meet again?

Taking this route with the messenger made his anguish all the more acute. A painful reminder to Kesh of the journey he had made with Maina, it was exactly the reverse of the route they had taken home when they had come across the battlefield near Larkat. Beyond Larkat, therefore, there was a long trudge across the arid plains, dismounting frequently to water their horses. Cam-horses had been bred on these plains. They were able to store small reserves of water in swellings on their haunches, yet even they could not cross the whole of the desert without stopping to drink.

Then, when they reached the port of Anthrakat, the messenger paid for their passage with money provided by Nathan. Obviously the human king was now reluctant to trust Kesh with anything. That snub was just another part of his punishment, to be relegated to a status lower than that of messenger. Kesh bore it without resentment to the servant, who seemed to carry out his duties to the Four Kings faithfully and, for the most part, cheerfully.

***

As the Anthrakati ship approached the coast of the Land of the Four Kings, Kesh could see a distant line of peaks that he guessed must be where the territory of the Ahn Dehar lay. He wondered if the Ahn Dehar even knew yet that their leader had been imprisoned by the Four Kings. Was Wanhild still watching daily for his return? He wished there was time to go and see them but his most urgent mission was to get to the Palace and speak to the Four Kings, preferably before they read the letters that the messenger was carrying. He tried to rehearse in his head what he should say to them. He must speak with care. The life of his friend depended on his finding exactly the right words.

They disembarked at the Port of the Four King's after a crossing of only ten days. Harg had kept their journey speedy, with a good following wind and no hinderance from either storms or becalment. The messenger knocked on the gate of the palace. During the moment it took for the wooden slat to be drawn aside, Kesh recalled how he and Maina had waited hours before being admitted, but the messenger was recognised straight away and the gate was opened. The palace seemed busier than he remembered, with soldiers crossing this way and that, and guards standing all around the walkways that topped the substantial walls. The messenger spoke to an administrator and asked him to inform the kings of his arrival and then he took Kesh not to the staterooms, but to the kitchens, where they were both given food and hot tea. It was another reminder of Kesh's lowly position. It was strange how, at the Sacred Mountain, he considered it an honour to be allowed into the kitchens with the trainee priestesses, yet here he felt it was another sign of his recent demotion to a status equal to the servants. No matter. It was better than waiting until the evening to dine with the kings and the food was just as good.

He felt a sudden pang of extreme anxiety as he followed the messenger up a spiralling stone staircase from the kitchens to the stateroom after their meal. He wished he had not eaten quite so much. He was announced ahead of the messenger but this didn't help matters much as Kesh saw that Nathan's letters had got there before him. Doug was holding one in his hand, while the other sat on the table in front of the kings, loosely curled, the seal obviously broken.

"Welcome, Kesh of Khoulan," said Ted. "So what have you got to say for yourself?"

"Please, I beg you, let Hernst go" Kesh said. "It was my fault that he did what he did. I told him what I knew about the poison. I should not have spoken. I gave no thought to the possible consequences. Please accept my humblest apologies."

"Poison?" repeated Ted.

"I think he might be referring to the power unit," Doug offered.

There were a few moments when no one spoke. Doug broke the silence.

"Well, I suppose that explains how Hernst found out. So we now have two of us proposing execution, with one against. It's up to you now, Kevin. Have you made your mind up yet?"

"I'm still not sure," said Kevin.

"We should count you as an abstention. That would give a majority for an execution. You happy with that, Ted?"

"No, not really."

"Please," Kesh blurted out. He stopped himself, waiting for permission to speak.

"Well?" prompted Doug irascibly.

"Hernst is a good man. He was driven to his crime by my foolish outpouring. It should be me who takes the punishment, not him."

"You didn't really commit a crime, Kesh," said Ted. "I don't think punishing you would achieve anything."

"But Hernst is the leader of his people," Kesh said. "Who will they look to without him there?"

"Can't they elect someone else?" Ted asked.

"I do not know if their laws would allow such a possibility," Kesh answered. "Chieftainship has to be inherited, I believe, just as kingship is in our country."

"We could appoint someone," suggested Doug. "That way we could just put our own man in and there'd be no question of any problem with the mining."

"I thought we weren't going to extend our rule out any further," Ted complained. "Didn't we say we'd trade rather than conquer from now on?"

"Yes, we did say that, I know," admitted Doug. "But that was before one of us had been nearly murdered. Things have changed since then."

"What about you?" Ted turned back to Kesh. "Nathan seems to think we should make use of your friendship with them. He seems to think we should send you as a kind of go-between. Would they accept you as a leader, do you think?"

"Me?"

A vision flashed before his eyes of himself leading the Ahn Dehar from a room in the fortress, in the same way that he ran the monastery from his study at Khoulan. Yes, that was what he deserved. He should devote his life to paying recompense for his foolish actions. He should spend the rest of his life trapped in a foreign country, all hope of seeing Maina gone for ever. But after another moment of thought he realised that there was a reason why this might not prove to be the best solution for the Four Kings.

"Acting as their leader might be difficult," he told them. "Even if they were willing to accept me, I don't speak a word of their language. I know of only two people who could translate for me, namely Hernst and his messenger, Wanhild."

"Mmm," Ted agreed. "Not an ideal situation."

There was another silence. Kesh broke it reluctantly.

"If I was to serve in this way, with Wanhild's help, would Hernst go free?"

"We can't just let him go free," said Kevin. "He tried to commit murder. He must be kept locked up. Doug would never rest easy if he was allowed his freedom. I would, however, consider voting against the execution if I knew that there was a viable alternative plan."

"If Kevin votes with me, you no longer have a majority vote," Ted was quick to tell Doug.

"Ha! Are you really voting against it now then, Kev?"

"I can't say I was ever really comfortable with the idea."

"Well, can we at least have a public trial?" Doug demanded. "I'm not allowing this attack to be completely brushed under the carpet, unchallenged. It can't just be forgotten."

"Yes, yes, I'm sure we can arrange some kind of trial," Ted told him. "And we'll make sure that he is sentenced to a lengthy imprisonment." He looked from one to the other and asked, "Everybody happy then?"

Kevin nodded slowly. Doug shrugged his shoulders and turned away but said no more.

'So this is it?' Kesh asked himself. 'My freedom relinquished in exchange for Hernst's life. Hernst's freedom taken as punishment for his crime.'

On the second day Kesh was allowed to see Hernst. He was taken down to a dungeon not unlike the one his uncle had held him in a few moons before at Ahbresk. Seeing his friend brought out in shackles and chains was a shock to him. They sat in the gaoler's room on opposite sides of a small wooden table. Hernst's eyes had lit up in recognition when he first saw Kesh but he did not speak.

"I am so sorry," Kesh said but got no response. He went on, "This is my fault. I told you about the poisoning and then I denied you the chance of military assistance. I left you with no options, as if I expected you to simply shrug and get on with your life. I did not give sufficient consideration to your feelings on the matter."

Eventually Hernst spoke, slowly and deliberately. "This is not your fault. It was not you who murdered my father."

"I am afraid the Kings are not willing to allow you to go back to your people."

"No. I did not ever think they would." Hernst let out a sigh, more of disgust than sorrow. "My mistake was in not planning more carefully. I should have waited and attacked when the kings were out of doors, where there would have been some chance of escaping. I have let my people down."

"The kings have suggested that I go to Ahn Dehar." Kesh told him. "Does anyone there know that you are in prison? Will they still be expecting you back?"

"I have no idea. Word may have got back to them, or it may not. I couldn't say."

"You have had no visitors from Ahn Dehar then?"

Hernst shook his head.

Kesh coughed nervously, knowing that he must tell Hernst of the deal that had been done.

"The kings have suggested that I act as leader there for a while."

He watched for Hernst's reaction, but saw only an expressionless face staring at the wall.

"Hernst, who is next in line? Who is due to rule after you?"

"I have a son," Hernst said quietly.

"Really? Oh, Hernst, you never said."

Hernst looked sadly at the table top.

"Could he ...?" Kesh began. "How old?"

"Six rounds."

"Ah. So who takes charge while you are away?"

"I left my mother in charge. My brother will be old enough in another round or so."

"A brother. May I ask how old he is now?"

"Fifteen rounds. I told him to look after our mother when I left but I fear taking responsibility for the whole tribe is a little beyond him yet. It was beyond me, after all. I have not looked after their interests very well."

"Could I help?"

"In what way?"

"I do not know. You must tell me."

Hernst shook his head gloomily. For a few minutes he was silent but then a thought seemed to strike him and he said in a low voice: "You could perhaps do something. Someone has to make sure that the coal is never sold to these people." He furtively cast his eyes sideways towards one of the guards. "Perhaps you could find someone else to mine it or find some other way for the Ahn Dehar to trade. The people are better off without me but they still need an income. If you wanted to do something for me, and for them, that would be the thing."

"Alright, I will try. Harg knows I am no business man but I will look into it. So Hernst, can I go to your people with your blessing? You understand, do you, that the kings want to put me in a position of responsibility? They want me to take charge, but I cannot do it if it offends you, and the Ahn Dehar will not accept me unless you give me your permission."

"It does not offend me but I do question why they want you, in particular, to be in charge of my people. They must think very highly of you. No doubt, they expect that you will make it easy for them to take the coal. You are a friend to the Four Kings, I suppose? And I have just asked you to do the opposite. How will you reconcile your obligations?"

"My obligation to the Four Kings stems from my position as a religious leader. In our religion the fifth human is a very important figure. He is our Prophet of the Burning Ship and revered most highly. I owe allegiance to the other humans because of him."

"Then you will naturally choose to help them over the Ahn Dehar."

Kesh glanced across at the gaoler and whispered his reply. "A greater debt is owed to you, my friend, because I am responsible for your imprisonment. Believe me when I tell you that I will do your bidding first. Satisfying their demands will come a sorry second."

"Then I would ask that you be guided by my mother. She is wise and good-hearted. Please tell her how ashamed I am, and tell my wife what a great love I have for her, and for our children. Take my good wishes to them all and say I hope the day will come soon when I can be with them once again."

At this point, Kesh judged that his yearning for Maina was as nothing compared with this man's anguish at his imprisonment and separation from all his kin. First Hernst had mentioned a son, now it was children, and Kesh had not even realised that he had a wife.

"Hernst," Kesh began hesitantly. "Does your wife know why you came to see the Four Kings? Did she know that you planned to ... what you planned to do?"

"No, no, of course not," he answered. "When I left for the palace I wasn't even sure myself that I'd actually have the courage to carry it out. I decided it was best that she didn't know."

"But should I tell her?"

"You can tell her I tried - and then you must tell her that I failed."

"You do not regret trying?"

"Certainly not! After what they did? How can you ask?"

Kesh frowned uncomfortably but did not say more. He remembered that, when he had first heard of his uncle Calim's death, he probably would have been quite happy to join a raiding party in an attack on the Xouthan Palace. He had spent a good deal of mental effort at the time wrestling with his instinct to seek revenge and, if Maina had not reminded him of his uncle Calim's great longing for peace and reconciliation, he would have been eager to continue the war with Xoutha. He surely could not condemn Hernst's desire for revenge now, and yet he could not explain why Hernst's attack seemed like a terrible crime for which he should now be showing remorse, while a Morthern raid on the Xouthan palace would have seemed like a legitimate act of war.

***

When the kings discussed Nathan's letter again, Kevin declared that he couldn't understand the warnings about Kesh's character. He said that, after spending several weeks and travelling many miles in Kesh's company, he would happily trust him with his very life but Doug told him that Nathan would not have sent the warning letter without good reason and that they should take heed of it. Ted had merely shrugged his shoulders when asked for an opinion. Doug, however, insisted that they should send someone with Kesh. An administrator named Applad, who had worked for the kings for many years, was therefore appointed to accompany him to Ahn Dehar and to report back on everything that took place.

A few hours after the pair had left, Ted came into the stateroom carrying a wicker cage with a large seacrow in it.

"I found a fisherman with this bird. He'd captured it by throwing one of his nets over it. Apparently, it had been stealing the fish from his drying rack. He was about to despatch it, but I thought it looked a bit like Kesh's pet."

"It does," said Kevin. "Lucky you were there to rescue it."

"Well, what should I do with it?"

"I suppose we'd better keep it until we can find someone to take it to him."

"Keep it where?"

"I don't know. I guess we'd better make a cage."

"Then we'd have to feed it."

"Well, we know he likes dried fish," Kevin laughed. "Perhaps you'd better go and buy some."

After three days riding, the travellers turned off the road to go up the mountain track to Ahn Dehar. Kesh looked into the surrounding fields and saw no workers. He stopped with Applad at the barn and dismounted to look inside. All was quiet.

"Usually there are people working here. I do not know where everyone is," Kesh said. "There are hay nets and water troughs in these stalls. I think we should leave our horses here. The path up the mountain is very steep. I remember that leading a horse up it was difficult and leading one down was quite beyond me. Hopefully, the Ahn Dehar will not mind too much."

They tied their horses to the rings set into the walls of the barn and walked up the ever steepening track to the fortress of Ahn Dehar. Applad was not a young man and he carried a slight excess of weight. He had to stop several times to catch his breath. Kesh remembered the Ahn Dehar runners who had trod so swiftly up the path on his first visit. He was closer in physique to Applad than to them.

When they reached the fort, the great timber door sat across the entrance. Kesh shouted, but he had no words that would encourage the Ahn Dehar to let him in. He resorted to shouting Wanhild's name and after a good while of calling it out, Wanhild finally appeared, looking down on them from the top of the enormous mound of stones that formed the wall on the south side of the door.

Wanhild recognised Kesh but seemed suspicious of Applad.

"He has travelled with me from the Land of the Four Kings." Kesh explained. "Wanhild, I have news for Hernst's family. Would you be willing to act as my translator?"

"I'll warrant it is not good news, then," said Wanhild gloomily. "Is he dead?"

"No, not dead. Let me in and I will tell you all."

The heavy timbers of the door were slowly lifted with the accompanying grinding of cogs and creaking of rope.

"I apologise for being a little slow to welcome you," Wanhild said as he waved them through the portal. "Hernst's protracted absence has made his mother very cautious. Few people are being allowed off the mountain at the present time, and the door remains down both day and night."

"I understand," said Kesh. "Can you take me to Hernst's mother, please?"

Wanhild lead them to a part-timbered house situated at the heart of the community. It looked familiar. Kesh slowly realised that he and Maina had been given supper there the night of their first visit. It must have been Hernst's mother and his wife who had served them.

Wanhild spoke to the women and then the older woman, introducing herself as Iyerra, waved her hand in the direction of some chairs, indicating that they should sit by the fire. Kesh accepted the tea that was offered to him and then Wanhild said:

"Now you must tell us all you know about Hernst. Where is he? How is he? When is he coming back? Why is he not here with you?"

"It is a sad tale, I am afraid, and Hernst may not be back for quite a while."

Kesh solemnly told the whole story as he understood it, a concoction of what he had heard from the Four Kings and from Hernst himself. Kesh trusted Wanhild to translate as faithfully as he could, although he stumbled now and again, seeming to be seeking the appropriate word. Applad listened to Kesh's words attentively and Kesh did not fail to describe his own part in Hernst's downfall but when he came to explain exactly what the Four Kings wanted him to do, he found it difficult to tell Iyerra.

"The Four Kings have asked me to act as go-between. No, that is not quite true. They want me to act as leader – your leader, leader of the Ahn Dehar. I did not want to lead your people on their behalf. I did not want to be a puppet under their control but it was part of a deal. I agreed to serve them in return for them sparing Hernst's life. Two of the kings wanted to have him executed, you see. They have sent Applad to accompany me, so that he can report back to them. However, I have a duty to Hernst also, as his friend, and he has asked me to be guided by you. Of course, I can do nothing without Wanhild to act as my translator."

After listening solemnly to Wanhild's translation, Iyerra sat in silent thought for a while. It was growing dark and the flames of the fire cast dancing shadows onto the hangings that clothed the walls.

"Are they treating Hernst well?" she asked in a small voice immediately translated by Wanhild.

"I think so, yes," Kesh told her. "He does not seem to have any cuts or bruises. He does not even seem to have lost weight."

"That is good," she nodded. "But they have him. What can we do? He is their hostage and we must do as they say."

"I do not think that is quite how they would put it," Kesh said, glancing questioningly at Applad.

Applad turned down the corner of his mouth, shrugged and shook his head.

"But it is how I would put it," Iyerra said.

Kesh considered her words. "Well, then, there are options," he told her.

"What options?"

Kesh did not answer. Again the question came to him via Wanhild.

"What options do we have?"

Reluctantly Kesh said:

"They have Hernst. You have ... "

As Wanhild translated the unfinished sentence all the eyes in the room turned to Applad. A sudden spasm of alarm gripped the man's features and he stood up abruptly, but Hernst's young brother had already moved to bar the door.

***

When the net had first come down over Sakki, he had been annoyed, but not overly concerned. He had cried out at first in surprise but had otherwise felt quite calm, assuming that it had been done by mistake. It was not until the fisherman raised a club above his head that he realised this particular crumbdropper was a threat to him, that in fact the man intended to end his life. Sakki was so relieved when one of the humans had come to his aid but then he had been unceremoniously bundled into a wicker basket and carried to the palace, as if he could not fly. He had tried explaining that he was perfectly able to get there by his own efforts but it did no good. Worse was to come, when Sakki realised that the monk was no longer with the Four Kings. It was imperative that he be released to follow him. He cried out again and again and struggled against the confines of the basket but one of his primary feathers broke and after that he forced himself to be quiet and still. It was not that he needed to impress the ladies, not until next spring at any rate, but it was crucial to maintain the power of flight. He could never hope to follow and protect his crumbdropper if he couldn't fly straight.

After two days the human incarcerator had put the basket inside a larger cage in an otherwise empty room and opened the lid. Sakki had climbed out and stretched his wings cautiously. He tried to convey the importance of being allowed to go and protect his charge, but he was not set free. Instead, he was given food and water and kept confined. Twice each day the gaoler came with fish and fruit – all very acceptable to a seacrow – but he always re-fastened the cage afterwards. Sakki started to watch him carefully each time he opened the fastening and soon he had worked out how to operate it, but he had to spend some time stretching and softening the wicker around the catch before he could manage to reach it. It was many days before he finally got a good enough grip on it with his beak to pull it across and release the cage door.

He hopped out cautiously. He guessed that a hunt might begin as soon as his escape was discovered. It would do Sakki no good to be found in full view in the middle of the room, so he hid behind the door. Then, as soon as it was opened, he strutted around it and out before the human had even noticed that he was no longer in the cage. The room proved to be part of an out-house, and so Sakki found that he was now free to seek his crumbdropper. He spread his wings and took off, but flying was not so easy with uneven feathers and, after so many days in a cage, he was a little stiff. He wobbled and barely made it over the palace wall before he had to stop for rest. Luckily, he still had good health after being so well fed, and he merely needed to regain fitness and learn how to compensate for the unbalanced wing. By flying just a little way at a time and taking frequent rests he began to track his charge northwards. He dreaded to think what terrible things had been going on in his absence.

Chapter 12

Maina was reading through the previous moon's reports returned by the colonel in charge of the defence of Mardek province. It was mainly about how much food had been consumed, how many new weapons had been allocated, how many men had been recruited and so on but there was a section entitled 'Active Service', in which a skirmish with Wildanders was described, with a summary stating the losses as ten foot soldiers and zero officers, with estimated enemy casualties at around thirty.

Maina checked the dates. It was during the last moon. She laid the documents down and stared out of her study window. During her last moon's governorship, ten of her people had died, alongside around thirty Wildlanders, and this was the first she had heard about it! So many deaths, so many bereaved families, so many broken hearted mothers, distraught wives, perhaps even fatherless children, were now suffering the effects of these devastating losses and yet it warranted barely a few lines at the end of the one of the most tedious reports she had ever had the good fortune to plough her way through.

She sent for the colonel. The sun was low in the sky by the time he arrived at the governor's residence, so she offered him dinner. During the second course, with general pleasantries exhausted, Maina voiced the questions she had been waiting to ask him.

"These 'skirmishes' with Wildlanders," she began. "How often do they occur?"

"Every couple of moons or so. They are more frequent in the summer when the weather is dry and there is less for them to hunt."

"Do they always attack the border wall, as described last moon?"

"Usually, yes. Occassionally, they get more ambitious and try landing boats."

"And what, do you think, is their motivation?" Maina asked. "I don't suppose they are trying to take over the province?"

"Nothing as serious as that, Ma'am. Don't you worry. There is no chance that they could ever come close to threatening the integrity of the province."

"So why do they do it, do you think? Are they bored?"

The colonel laughed. "No, I don't think that's it Ma'am, although it wouldn't surprise me to learn that taking part in, and surviving, one of these attacks engenders a degree of admiration from the females. It may be that they form part of a coming-of-age-ritual, or some such thing."

"Or?"

"Or?" The colonel pulled a face as he tried to think. "Well, ma'am, they could just be hungry. As I said, these attacks usually occur during the dry season."

"Perhaps we should try to find out," Maina said. "I don't want these skirmishes to continue indefinitely. It's a waste of resources. Do you have anyone who speaks the Wildlander's language?"

"No, ma'am."

"I don't suppose there are many Wildlanders who speak Xouthan?"

"I wouldn't think so, Ma'am."

"So what should we do? We need to increase our knowledge of these people. We need to understand what motivates them, I think, so that we can take some action."

The colonel's forehead knitted into a frown.

"Do you want me to send men into the Wildlands, Ma'am?"

"I think we must, yes. A small team of men. But I don't want soldiers. I want 'researchers' – young men who would be willing to live with the Wildlanders for a while, to learn their language and to learn about their customs."

"How do we know that their throats won't be slit before they can even learn to say 'Hello'?"

"Mmm, I take your point," said Maina as she helped herself from a dish of green salad. "So how else could we learn about them?"

The colonel shrugged.

"Do the Wildlanders ever manage to breach the wall?"

"No, ma'am," the colonel sounded shocked. "There has never been a breach of the wall. Well, not under my command, anyway."

"Do they ever succeed in climbing over it?"

"No, Ma'am. It is always vigorously defended by our archers and then swordsmen go through one of the gates and finish them off on the Wildlanders side."

"How about allowing it to happen next time? Allow one or two Wildlanders over and arrest the intruders. We could take them prisoner and then we could learn from them in safety. Some of our men could be instructed to start learning their language, could they not?"

"You think prisoners will cooperate in that way?"

"Perhaps not, but we could try offering rewards for cooperation – better quality food or some such. It may be a bit devious but it's got to be better than suffering this constant loss of life - on their side as well as ours."

"Very well, Ma'am."

"From now on I would like you to issue orders that no swordsmen should go through to the Wildlander side. An occasional show of force from the top of the wall can be made if we are heavily threatened but, as a prelude to our efforts to increase our understanding of these people, please ask your archers to avoid killing them if at all possible. They should aim their volleys just above their heads, perhaps. Alarming but not lethal. Is that acceptable to you, colonel?"

"I am willing to make this change as long as I have your leave to return to tried and tested tactics if they attack in overwhelming numbers. You must do what you have to do, of course, but do not put our men at risk and use lethal force on the Wildlanders only as a last resort, I beg you."

"Very well, ma'am

"Thank you," said Maina. "Now tell me colonel, you are a married man, are you not? Do you have children?"

After finishing the meal with conversation limited to lighter topics, Maina showed the colonel to the door herself. She watched him as he walked away into the darkened streets. She saw him shake his head and was sure he muttered 'Women!' once he thought that he was beyond her hearing. That attitude, she had found, was typical of Xouthan men in positions of power but it didn't necessarily mean that he wouldn't do as she had asked.

***

Applad watched fearfully as Kesh strode up and down in front of the fire, one hand on his forehead, as if it would help him to concentrate.

"Applad, please sit down," Kesh said eventually. "There is something I must explain to you."

Applad cast suspicious glances around the room. There were many pairs of eyes on him. He froze like a statue.

"Applad, sit down," Kesh commanded.

Applad sat.

"Two rounds ago," the monk began as if starting a fireside tale. "I was sent across the sea from my country to seek out the Four Kings. There is a fifth human, you see, who lives on the borders of our country and he has become an important figure in our religion. He is our Prophet of the Burning Ship. He is very wise, generous, those who meet him almost always come to love him and all of us admire him greatly. He had heard of the Four

Kings and he sent two of us to find out if they were human like him and, therefore, might be some of his former colleagues. King Kevin travelled back with us. I am proud to call King Kevin a friend and, given time, I am sure I would come to know all of the Four Kings as friends. However, my colleague and I had travelled overland to the Palace of the Four Kings from Wadderhick and, on the way, we were offered hospitality by the Ahn Dehar. We were given supper and offered space at the fireside in this very house. I did not know then that it was the chief's wife, together with the wife of the future chief, who had served us our meal. Afterwards, we spent a long evening talking with Ackhart. He was their leader but he was dying and obviously in great discomfort. We talked through his son, Hernst. My heart went out to him and to all the Ahn Dehar. So, you see, my friendship with the Ahn Dehar is actually a few days older than my friendship with the Four Kings. You can, perhaps, imagine my predicament, then, when one set of friends asks me to do something which goes against the wishes of the other set." Here Kesh paused and drew in a deep breath.

"Now, on the one hand, I have Four Kings who want me to rule this tribe on their behalf so that they can come and mine its coal without hindrance and, on the other, a tribal chief to whom I have promised that I will seek some other kind of trade to bring income to the Ahn Dehar so that they will never be obliged to sell their coal to the Four Kings in the first place." Kesh paused and looked at the administrator, hoping to see some sign of recognition of his quandary, some understanding of his predicament. The hostage stared back blankly. Kesh went on.

"What I need from you, Applad, is time. I need you to allow me time to find some kind of solution to this problem. I need you to stay here with the Ahn Dehar while I find some way of enabling them to maintain their independence. However, I will not try to persuade you to renege on your duties to the kings, and for that reason you will be made a prisoner here. It will be made clear to the Four Kings that you are kept here totally against your will. You will be treated as well as the most honoured guest, but a message will be sent to the kings explaining that you are forcibly detained. I will take the blame for this situation wholly on my shoulders."

Kesh started to pace up and down again, now with both hands on his head as if to tear out the short lengths of hair that grew there. He began to speak more to himself than to Applad.

"Harg knows how I will ever explain myself to the Four Kings but then I only agreed to do their bidding in order to save Hernst's life." He addressed Applad once more. "You see, it was only when Iyerra said that she thought of Hernst as a hostage that I saw that you might also be made to play the part of hostage. At least, you can be sure that you will be well treated because Hernst's safety is my primary concern, and I realise that any harm done to you is likely to be reflected in the Four King's treatment of Hernst. What family do you have, Applad? They should be told, in confidence, that you are not in any real danger."

The administrator stared at Kesh in silence.

"Applad? Should they not be told?"

"You think I would give information to you about my family?" he spat out.

"Very well," Kesh shrugged and nodded to the two men waiting to take him away.

With Wanhild's help, Iyerra wrote to the Four Kings informing them that Applad was being held to ensure Hernst's safety. Wanhild was to deliver the letter to the palace, but Kesh advised him that it might be better to leave it at the gate than to deliver it to the kings personally. He did not want to risk losing his only translator as a hostage to them. Wanhild was also given a letter written by Kesh, begging the Four Kings to support Applad's family while the breadwinner was being held by the Ahn Dehar. He knew that this would bring some ambiguity into his own role in the operation but he hoped that the confusion might help him to smooth things over with them later, when he had to confess his failure to persuade the Ahn Dehar to sell their coal.

In the meantime, Kesh had to search for a way to improve trade for the Ahn Dehar. He could do very little at the fortress with his translator away, so he packed his belongings for a trip to Zoradetra for Ahbrem's wedding. After all, he told himself, he was as likely to get inspiration for trading prospects there as much as anywhere. He would just about have time to call in at Khoulan first, to appoint a deputy mattouk designate. He thought Grenholt would be the best man for the job. He was a senior monk and had already visited the Sacred Mountain and climbed the waterfall, so he was fully qualified.

Kesh left the next morning, heading for Wadderhick to seek passage to Odout, his heart light now that he had a temporary reprieve from his responsibilities to the Ahn Dehar and to the Four Kings. It was made lighter still by his calculations that, barring unforeseen circumstances, he would have plenty of time to call in at Khoulan to appoint Grenholt and then accompany Ahbrem across the border into Xoutha for his first wedding ceremony where, Harg willing, Kesh would see Maina once again. He urged his horse to go faster and took out a chunk of Dehar bread to eat as he rode. A seacrow was wheeling around him, and he knew it would be picking up any fragments he let fall. Kesh suddenly realised he hadn't seen any seacrows for a long time. The first time he had visited the Ahn Dehar, the seacrow had stayed behind in the trees and they only grew halfway up the mountain side, but this time Kesh couldn't remember seeing a seacrow since leaving the palace of the Four Kings. He had been so taken up with his worries that he hadn't really given a thought to his usual friend and follower, Sakki. What had happened to him? This crow was similar to Sakki but looked so dishevelled, with broken feathers, as if he had been mistreated by someone. Could it be him?

Kesh reined his horse to a stop and dismounted. He threw down a chunk of bread and the bird came to eat.

"Sakki?"

Kesh bent to touch the broken feather. Sakki took a step but then allowed himself to be petted.

"Oh, Sakki. What have they done to you? How could I forget you and not be there to keep you out of trouble?"

The bread was nearly gone.

"Or was it you who should have been there to keep me out of trouble?" Kesh asked, uneasy now. "What have I done? I hope Applad copes with being the guest of the Ahn Dehar. They will treat him decently, won't they, Sakki? Perhaps I should turn around. Is that what you've come to tell me? But if I turn back now I'll miss the wedding and I'll miss Maina. Should I do that, Sakki?"

The bird took off when the bread was gone and seemed to fly off down the road, the way Kesh had been heading. That was all the encouragement he needed. He remounted and urged the horse on.

***

At the Palace of the Four Kings the monarchs were waiting expectantly for news from Ahn Dehar. Ted felt guilty for having failed to keep Kesh's pet safe for him, Doug was short-tempered and listless. Kevin was worrying about Doug. Even if they'd been free to start the mining operation immediately, Kevin doubted that Doug would have been capable of getting it organised. He seemed to have lost his enthusiasm for life. Until then, Doug had been the one who had motivated the rest of them. He had been the prime mover in all the progress they had made since their arrival but lately he had taken to wandering around the palace like a lost soul and, if he said anything at all, it was only to moan or criticise.

"How are you sleeping these days?" Kevin asked him at dinner one evening.

"Don't ask," was the reply.

"Perhaps you need a holiday," his friend suggested.

"Yeah, that'd be nice," Doug said bitterly. "A couple of weeks in Hawaii, or a fortnight in the Caribbean. Perhaps it was a weekend in Paris, or a little Mediterranean break, you had in mind?"

"Okay, we can't have holidays like we used to but what about travelling around a bit? You could go and see Ship. He'd be really pleased to get a visit. I daresay he's seen enough of Nathan to last a lifetime by now."

"Hey, Nathan's alright. Leave him alone."

"So you would get to see Nathan as well."

"You really want to get rid of me, don't you?"

"You might sleep better once you're away from here," Kevin suggested." It can't be a good thing, being constantly reminded, with Hernst right downstairs and everything."

"Well," Doug hesitated. "Perhaps you're right. Perhaps I should make the effort and book passage over there, but you'd better draw me a map. I'll need to know where to go once I get over the sea. And how would you feel about it, Ted? Wasn't it meant to be you going there once Nathan got back?"

"He still can, once Nathan gets back," Kevin said. "Come on, there's nothing happening around here these days. It doesn't need more than two of us to look after things."

"I suppose," Doug shrugged. "Come with me to the docks? You know where to go, who to ask."

"Of course."

By the time the letters from Ahn Dehar arrived, Doug was on his way to Anthrakat. Ted and Kevin read them through several times.

"I don't understand," Ted complained. "Kesh is pleading on Applad's behalf. Does that mean he's a prisoner, too?"

"I wouldn't think so. He's big friends with our murderer in the dungeon down there," Kevin said, pointing to the floor as if it would help Ted know who he meant. "I don't think the Ahn Dehar would try to take him prisoner."

"So what's he playing at? Do we get a deal on the coal or don't we?"

"Well, it doesn't look like it. Not yet, at any rate. Good job Doug isn't here at the moment. This wouldn't cheer him up at all."

***

Maina wrote to her father a moon before Wyn's wedding to inform him that she was intending to come back to Zoradetra for the ceremony. She would rather have made the trip in secret and simply stayed at her old home with her nurse family but she would inevitably have been seen at the wedding by some gossip with an eager tongue. Her father might have felt hurt if he had learned about her visit from someone else. She considered restricting the information in the letter by simply referring to "a" wedding, but she knew her father's first question would be to ask whose wedding she was attending. She knew also that her father would want to know why he hadn't been invited, so she described the forthcoming event as just a quiet family ceremony on a modest budget, explaining that Wyn didn't want to have a big celebration so soon after her father's death.

Maina had not foreseen what would actually cause her father the most consternation.

He wrote a long letter in reply in which he complained:

'Bradmutt was my right hand man. I like to think that I was also his most important friend. Why has Wyn not asked me to stand in for her father at this wedding? Does she think I am not worthy? Should she not be proud to have the support of the emperor at such a time? What have I done to upset her? Her wedding should be second only to yours as a royal event. The celebrations should take place at the palace with all the nobles of the empire in attendance!'

He asked Maina to tell Wyn that she should avail herself of the palace and all its facilities for her wedding. Maina wrote promptly to Wyn, explaining why she had been obliged to tell her father, apologising for the predicament it had put them both in and asking what she thought they should do about it. The plan had been, after all, to have a quiet celebration for the benefit of Wyn's mother whilst avoiding the need for the Morthern groom to have to meet anyone except immediate family. Now Maina's father was threatening to change all that. If the emperor and other noblemen were present, the nationality of the groom would almost certainly be discovered.

Wyn wrote back to Maina to say that she had now invited her father but that she had explained to him that the family definitely did not want to be involved in a major event at the palace so soon after her father's death. They would, however, be very honoured if the emperor would care to join the celebrations due to take place in their humble home.

> *'This way, there will be only one non-family member to hide Ahbrem from. We can try, between us, to keep your father engaged in conversation with the family most of the time and so keep him away from Ahbrem and from Kesh.'*

Kesh! With the concerns over Maina's father's involvement in the wedding, she had nearly forgotten that there would be two Mortheners at the celebration. She reached into her pocket and took out the precious letter that Wyn had forwarded to her a moon before. It was formal and impersonal, for the most part, but it somehow suggested a hint of an emotional undertone which did not dare to be expressed in words on the open page. Most thrilling to Maina was the news that Kesh had replied to her previous letter. He had not lost interest, nor forsaken her, nor been too busy to reply. He had written and the letter had simply been lost on the way. She did not pause to fret over where the letter might have ended up. She was too thrilled to learn of its existence to worry over its present whereabouts.

Chapter 13

Once on Anthrakati soil, King Douglas paid a local messenger to go ahead of him with a note to warn Ship and Nahan of his arrival. He could only give the messenger directions according to Kevin's instructions, based on the sketch map he had drawn for him, but the messenger assured Doug that he would find the Sacred Mountain easily enough.

The human followed behind him at a steady pace. He had not expected that this holiday would magically dispel his depression but he had slept better on the ship, at least when the sea was calm, than he had been sleeping at the palace. Kevin had probably been right to suggest some time away. The empty arid Anthrakati landscape was not exactly cheering but at least there was sunshine every day. He had plenty of time to think while his horse plodded on towards the distant mountains. He made a concerted effort to concentrate his thoughts on the curiosities that he came across: lizard-like sand dwellers that darted down burrows as soon as they saw or heard him; stubby succulent plants that were the only spots of green in the vast expanse of yellow-grey earth; copses of thin trees, leafless in the height of summer and yet not dead - their greenish bark enveloped supple living branches. All these things helped to keep his mind off the night of the murder and the other nightmares that had come back to haunt him. The memories of the deaths of the two female crew now crowded in on him as if the one new trauma had invited back a whole party of previous horrors, breaking through to consciousness just when he least needed to bring them to mind.

On the day of Doug's expected arrival on the Sacred Mountain, maidens kept watch on the walkway above the Xouthan gate and, when they saw a figure approaching, they sent for Ship, Nathan and Hannala. There was a full welcoming committee assembled by the time he reached the top of the path. Nathan's embrace could not have been more enthusiastic if Doug had just returned from the dead, but what gave Doug a bigger surprise was seeing how his captain had changed over the years.

"Wow!" Doug exclaimed. "Just look at you, Captain Shipham. No wonder they think so highly of you. You really look the part. Wise old ... wise man. Grey beard, long grey hair, flowing robes."

"Less of the old, thanking you," Ship complained as he shook hands with the engineer he had not seen for so very long. "And just call me Ship, for Heaven's sake."

Doug found the trainee priestesses absolutely charming. They seemed to float around the passageways on a cushion of air, their long white skirts hiding the movement of their feet. They were eager to provide for his every need. He was shown to a guest room and then guided through a labyrinth of corridors to take tea on the balcony with Ship and Nathan.

It didn't seem as though it was only women in the community, though. On the way to the balcony, following behind the trainee priestess he saw a Penethellan monk with a shaven head coming the other way. His face looked awfully familiar.

"Hey, aren't you supposed to be with the Ahn Dehar?" he called out, but the monk had hurried past and was lost in the dim passageways. Perhaps Kesh had a twin.

It all started so well. His spirits genuinely felt lighter. The company was good, the food simple but hearty, the bed comfortable, the view from the balcony of the great hall spectacular - probably the part he liked the most. Seeing Ship again was almost cathartic and yet there was never an opportunity to talk privately with him. Nathan was always there as well. Doug had always liked Nathan and was glad to see him. If anything, of all his surviving crew mates, Nathan's outlook was most similar to his own. He sympathised with, and thought he understood, his mission to convert the Penethellans, although he regarded Nathan's expectations of a Second Coming on Penethella as probably a little over optimistic. Nevertheless, it was several days before Doug got what he had begun to long for, a chance to talk man-to-man with his old captain. He thought Ship was the one person he could be honest with, not needing to hide the awful thing he had found out, the source of his original nightmares, the ones that had recently come back to plague him every night.

It happened one afternoon when all three humans had taken tea on the balcony, as usual, but Nathan had finished his drink and left early for private bible study. Ship had poured them both a second cup and now sat looking seawards. The balustrade hid the horizon when you were sitting down, but Doug could see the water between the uprights, and the sky above it and he still got the feeling of space and distance that it produced. It created an enjoyable sensation of ... freedom. Yes, that's what it was, Doug decided, with the sea breeze in his nostrils and a reddening sun sinking in the west.

"Do you ever think back to the old days?" he asked Ship.

"Sometimes," Ship answered. "Mostly I try not to. I think it's better to concentrate on the present. I don't like to remind myself of a life I can never go back to. Some of my more recent memories are not good to dwell on, either. I'm not proud of losing the ship and killing two of my colleagues. Of course, I didn't actually know about Candace until Kevin told me, just a couple of rounds ago."

"What do you mean? Who did you kill?" Doug asked, shocked.

"Angela and Candace, of course. I just wasn't careful enough. I didn't think enough about the details. I was in too much of a hurry, I suppose. Every last piece of equipment should have been checked and double checked before we used it and I failed to get that done."

"You didn't kill them," said Doug. "I can be pretty certain you didn't kill Candace, at any rate."

"I thought her seat harness failed. I should have had them checked."

"No," Doug said.

"Wasn't it the harness? That's what Kevin told me."

"We all thought that, at first, and I let the others go on believing it, but I checked the harness afterwards. It was functioning perfectly. The clasp was working; the straps weren't ripped, nor even frayed; the anchor points were undamaged. I'm pretty sure, actually, that Candace killed herself. The way I see it, she must have waited until she could see we were about to come to a sudden stop and just pressed the release. I guess she just couldn't cope with the thought of being stranded on an alien planet with the four of us. Pretty understandable, I suppose. She made it pretty clear she didn't fancy any of us and, I guess, there's no denying, there would have been pressure. Maybe not at first, perhaps. We might have all behaved like perfect gentlemen for a few months, but then, as I'm sure she imagined, we probably would have all given it a go, trying to persuade her. The only human female on the planet, stranded with four young men, all with healthy appetites. Before long, I bet we'd have been ready to murder one another to get a go. If the others didn't fancy her, I know I did and I don't suppose for a minute I was really the only one. Poor Candace."

Ship frowned and coughed uncomfortably.

"Well, I don't suppose it matters now," he said to himself. "Keeping the old secrets – they're pretty irrelevant." He turned to face Doug. "Candace was in a very fragile state," he told him. "She and Angela were - had been - an item. She'd just lost someone very special to her."

"An item? You mean ...?"

"Yes. It was all part of Brannon's plan. He was too old to make the trip himself, but there were 23 frozen embryos on the ship, all deemed viable, all David Brannon's progeny. There were also some frozen unfertilised eggs and semen as back up. Angela and Candace were going to act as surrogates. It was what they volunteered for, what they, apparently, wanted, but I was the only other person who knew. Brannon thought that recruiting two women who were already in a stable, long-term relationship, and who wanted children, was the best way of ensuring that his embryos got used. I guess he was worried that heterosexual females might prefer to mate with one of you boys, once they were here, instead of carrying his babies."

"Great! So we were just the transport mechanism to get Planet Brannon underway."

"Oh, you were a bit more than that. You boys had been carefully chosen. Afterall, you were likely to be the fathers of the next generation. His own children couldn't be expected to mate with one another, obviously."

"My God!"

"You should feel honoured. The richest man on the Earth picked you as potential husbands for his daughters."

"That's ridiculous. What about the age gap?"

"Oh, I don't think David Brannan had a problem with a younger woman seeking the security of an older man. His third wife was thirty-five years his junior, after all." Ship watched contortions of disgust twist Doug's mouth. "He was likely to have been pretty choosy, if my ex-wife's parents were anything to go by. No one is ever really good enough for the daughter of a wealthy man."

"It's ... sick. Whoever did he think he was?"

"Perhaps he was just a man desperate for his children to survive. He was convinced that human culture on Earth was collapsing. The way he saw it, even if a few people were left to start again, with all the pollution there'd been and all the resources used up, there wasn't much hope of another civilisation rising out of the ashes. He was suffering a kind of depression, you might say, but he had this crazy idea, and he was the one person who could afford to try it."

"But we were told we were going to be pioneers, the ultimate adventurers, the first humans to travel to an extra-solar planet, possibly the first to make contact with an alien intelligence."

"Actually, I don't think you were promised anything like that. Brannon was looking specifically for a habitable planet without intelligent life, in order to maximise his offspring's chances."

"We weren't told that."

"No, you weren't. Would you have volunteered if you had been?"

Doug was silent.

"So, you see, Candace's hostility had never been anything personal. She didn't kill herself just because she didn't happen to be attracted to any of you. It was more than that. She was never attracted to any man. And the one woman on the crew, the one person she would have loved on the whole planet, had just been horribly asphyxiated right in front of her eyes. I'm not surprised she didn't want to go on living."

"I guess it must have been pretty awful," Doug slowly drew in a breath. "You haven't told any of the others about this?"

"This is the first I have spoken about it in all this time."

"Should I tell them?"

"That's up to you. I don't think it matters anymore whether they know or not."

When Doug went to bed that night he was still thinking about what Ship had said. It seemed as though part of his anguish might be over. All these years he had kept the knowledge of Candace's suicide to himself, judging it to be too insulting, too depressing to share with the others. The other three were having a hard enough time just coping with being stranded for life on an alien planet. The awfulness of a Candace's actions might just have pushed them over the edge. But now he knew the likely cause of her extreme behaviour, he didn't have to keep it to himself any longer. He had told Ship about it, and now he could tell his colleagues. He lay quietly in the dark in the peaceful little room in the Sacred Mountain Community and fell into a deep and dreamless sleep. He did not wake with the image of Candace's blood smeared all over the forward screen of the lander, nor with the excruciating pain of Hernst's knife lodged in his shoulder. In the morning he felt strangely serene and refreshed, as though he had been given a chance to begin his life again.

It hadn't really changed anything, though. They were still all stuck light years away from home with no women and no possibility of children, at the end of the line for humankind. For all he knew, civilisation on Earth had gone into total meltdown and they could be the very last humans in the universe. Over the next few days more questions came to him.

"So where did you land the ship?" he asked his captain as the three humans sat drinking tea the next day.

"I didn't land it. It crashed," Ship told him. "Into the sea. Luckily I was able to swim to the shore."

"Where was that?"

"In the bay out there."

"And the ship disintegrated, I suppose?"

"Some parts were still intact. The part of the forward section, where the bridge was, where I was, that is, was still airtight. The cargo bay on the port side was all ripped to pieces, but some of the other sections were okay. I dived down a few times to reclaim what I could. I got some wiring to rig up some lights and so on, but the power units I got out are on their last legs now."

"Wow! It's still down there?" asked Doug. "I'd love to see it. How long ago was your last dive?"

"Oh, many rounds ago. I was still young and relatively fit then. But I think the ship's power system was running out of steam. It took ages to pump out the air lock the last time I dived. I didn't think it would manage it again so decided that would have to be my last trip."

"How deep is it? The pressure down there will be more than those airlocks were ever designed to cope with. If you think about it, they were only ever designed to cope with a difference of zero to one atmosphere. Pressures under water go way above that, so the pumps will struggle. You were lucky the ship's hull didn't crumple as soon as it sank. Did you repressurise the atrium each time you went through?"

"Doesn't that happen automatically?"

"No," Doug told him. "You have to top it up from the compression tanks. You know, the valves in the panel just opposite the airlock door?"

Ship shrugged and shook his head.

"The power system was probably fine," Doug told him. "You were just putting the pumps under too much strain."

"Oh," said Ship.

"We should probably go take a look. Fancy a dive, Nathan?"

Nathan pulled a face. "Sounds a bit dangerous to me."

"Too good a chance to miss. We could do a bit of training first. See how long we can hold our breath and so on. Then we could try a few practice dives. We'd just look at the hull the first time and not go in. What's the visibility like down there?"

"Pretty poor," Ship told him. It's cloudy green near the surface, as I remember, and pretty near pitch black by the time you get to the bottom."

"Still worth a go, though," said Doug. "Conditions can change according to the weather, I imagine, and with different seasons. It might be better now."

The chance of visiting the wreck of the mother ship gave Doug something to look forward to. Now he had a definite goal to aim for, an adventure of re-discovery. Who knew what he might be able to reclaim? His life began to have purpose once again.

"Those power units you took off the ship," he turned back to Ship. "I could maybe charge them up again, if I took them back with me. We've rigged up generators back at our place, you know."

Chapter 14

Kesh had hoped to stay out of Doug's sight. Ashamed though he might be to admit it, on this occasion he and Ahbrem were using the Sacred Mountain community more as a convenient place to spend the night than as a place of pilgrimage. Meeting Doug in the passageway was an embarrassing accident, and he regretted being so rude, just walking past him as he had but, with his mattouk's robe and shaved head, he had hoped that Doug wouldn't recognise him. When Doug had called out to him it was already too late to put things right. It might have taken quite a while to explain the situation and time was a commodity of which he had little to spare at that juncture. He and Ahbrem had to get changed into travelling clothes suitable for their trip into Xoutha straight away. They were already running late. They needed to be at the inn in Zoradetra before nightfall ready for the wedding ceremony the next day. Ahbrem had to be dressed in his Xouthan bridegroom's costume and delivered to the gates of the temple at Zoradetra by mid-day.

For the first time in many moons, as they walked down the path on the Xouthan side of the Sacred Mountain, Kesh's jealousy of Ahbrem started to subside. Ahbrem was growing more anxious with every passing moment. It was his first time over the border, except for the time he had gone down this same path to see Kesh and Maina off three rounds before. He had never met Wyn's family. Kesh described Salwell to him but Kesh had not met Wyn's mother. Then there was the ceremony. Ahbrem was wondering whether he would remember the Xouthan marriage service, whether he would pronounce his responses correctly. Hannala had gone over it with him a hundred times but he was still worried. And, perhaps most terrifying of all, he was to be presented to the emperor. How would he manage to speak to him without letting it slip that he was, of all things most hateful to the man, a Morthener. Kesh tried to reasssure him. He told Ahbrem that his knowledge of Xouthan was far superior to his own and yet *he* had survived a trip to Zoradetra.

"You are not a good comfort to me, Kesh," he said. "You tell me that my knowledge of Xouthan is superior to yours but all that says to me, in my present state, is that you are more of a liability than a help. Not only should I worry about my own performance, but I should also worry about yours. What if your poor Xouthan gives us both away?"

"Do not worry. I have no desire to speak to the emperor. I will stay well out of the way when you are presented to him."

"Quite right. Desert me in my hour of greatest need!"

"You will not need me, Ahbrem," Kesh smiled at his contradiction. "You will be fine."

"Ugh!" Ahbrem exclaimed in desperation. "I am beginning to wonder if marrying is such a good idea. The life of a celibate may be joyless, but at least it is simple."

"It will be worth it, I am sure. You love Wyn, do you not? You want to be together? You want to take her home to Khoulan and show her the married quarters, I know you do, with the fresh whitewash you have applied and the potted plants you have been growing. It will all seem worth it then, I am convinced."

"But what if she does not like it there? She is used to wandering around palaces and temples. Khoulan is going to seem very small and dingey in comparison."

"The Sacred Mountain community is modest and not unlike Khoulan, yet she likes it, does she not?"

"That is true. But Kesh, what if she does not like me? We have not seen one another for such a long time. Two rounds ago she seemed to like me as much as I liked her but what if her tastes have changed? Then, I did not fear closeness but, now, I am terrified."

"Ahbrem, stop worrying. Everything will be fine. Two of my favourite people in all the world. I just know that you will still like one another, that you are perfect for one another."

***

The usually sensible and level-headed Wyn was no more at ease than Ahbrem. She held out her gown to show Maina, newly arrived from Mardek.

"It's beautiful," Maina gasped. It was Anthrakat silk, the colour of fresh ox milk, shiny and smooth and wreathed with lengths of creamy Xouthan lace. "And this the headdress? You will look absolutely stunning."

"Do you think Ahbrem will like it?"

"I'm sure he will love it."

"Mother went to Anthrakat herself to choose it. We have had to have one or two alterations done, to make it fit properly, so it has cost more than we were planning to spend."

"How are finances now in the household?"

"Not too bad. Salwell is now giving mother something for his board and lodging, so that helps. He is well paid for his administrative work at the palace. And mother still helps now and again with decorations and furnishings for the palace, so she has some income of her own. I have been living at the temple school, of course, so I haven't been paying her anything. I have managed to save a little, though. I thought it might be as well to have some money behind me. Morthern monks don't get paid and I doubt that there is much call for priestess teachers in Morth. However, Ahbrem says he still has much translation work to do on the Sacred Mountain, so I am hoping that I can go there with him and help out with the trainees."

"Oh, that sounds ideal," Maina said. "And I will tell nurse-mama to come to me if she ever needs a little extra. I am finding that a governor's pay is far in excess of my needs, even after the costs of running the residence are deducted."

"You will keep an eye on her for me, won't you?"

"Of course."

"I will visit her whenever I can," said Wyn.

"I know she will look forwards to your visits. You have resigned your post at the temple school, I suppose?"

"Sadly, yes. One of this round's Sacred Mountain girls has agreed to take my place. They will be graduating half a moon from now."

"Another round gone. I pray the next one flies by as quickly so that I can come back to Zoradetra."

"You're not enjoying your work?"

"It seems to be more struggle than reward."

"I have heard rumours that you are a harsh master," Wyn teased.

"Oh dear. The old governor would say that it would be a good thing to acquire a reputation for strictness, but I would rather have one for kindness and wisdom."

"I am sure that will come with experience."

"Perhaps. But enough about me. Has all the food been prepared for tomorrow? Can I help with anything?"

"Mama assures me that everything is absolutely ready. I am not allowed into the dining room. She has decorated it specially and she doesn't want me to see it until tomorrow. All the food is waiting for the guests in the larder and she has half a dozen trainee priestesses who, she claims, have volunteered to act as servers. She won't let me do anything."

"Of course. I should have known that she would have it all organised down to the smallest detail. I look forward to seeing the results. Nothing for you to worry about, then."

"I'm still terrified of having to present Ahbrem to your father. He's never going to pass for a Xouthan."

"I thought you said that Hannala has been instructing him."

"Yes, but ... "

"I'm sure she will have him fully prepared. He won't have to speak Xouthan, afterall. He just has to be able to lose his Morthern accent when he speaks the Sacred Language."

"I think that's going to be harder than it sounds."

"He'll be fine. Stop worrying. Anyway, if the worst happens, we will just have to tell the emperor that he's not from round here. That will explain why he doesn't have a local accent."

"Oh, I hope people like him. I wish my mother had met him already. I will be so unhappy if she decides she doesn't approve of him."

"Everyone likes Ahbrem. He's kind, sensible, reliable, and very handsome. A mother's dream."

Wyn smiled for the first time. "I'm so glad you're here. You always say what I need to hear."

"Only when it's true. Anyway," she began stepping towards the door. "I suppose it's time I went to the palace to say hello to my father. I expect I shall get his assessment of my governorship so far. And then I need to unpack my own outfit for tomorrow."

"So what's it like?"

"You'll have to wait and see. It's nothing special, really. I had a seamstress in Mardek make it up for me, and she insisted that I have to have the Mardek emblem embroidered on the bodice and on the cape. I will look like I'm on an official visit, I'm afraid."

"I'm sure you will look splendid."

"I just hope I can do justice to your special day. I'll see you in the morning, sister. Sleep well tonight."

"I doubt I'll sleep a wink, but I'll try to rest. Goodnight."

"Goodnight."

Once in her room Maina hung up her new dress, carefully smoothing out the wrinkles it had picked up from being packed in a trunk. She looked around her old room. Everything was as she remembered it, except that there was a scroll on the table by the window. She picked it up. The seal sprang open easily, as though the wax had not melted onto the parchment properly. It was the Khoulan seal. Maina unrolled the letter and saw Kesh's handwriting. Her heart skipped a beat. Was it a letter to say he wouldn't be coming to the wedding, after all? She scanned the first few lines. It didn't seem to be about the wedding. She checked the date and saw that it was from many moons ago. She slowly realised that it must be the missing letter he had mentioned. So she could still hope that he was going to be at the wedding with Ahbrem tomorrow. The man she had not set eyes on for two whole rounds would be there, in the same room as her, breathing the same air. She might get to speak to him, face to face, and look him in the eye, once again. She looked at the familiar, beloved handwriting and put the parchment he had touched to her lips. Then she read the text.

Kesh had written that her letter had 'brought sunlight to the corridors of Khoulan'! He seemed to have appreciated her communication, then. 'Pay his respects at the palace'? Maina rather hoped he hadn't tried to do that, especially not while she was away in Mardek. She knew her father would not have reacted well to such a visit, but the fact that Kesh said that he was 'looking forward to it with an eager heart' set her own heart singing. Was Kesh as eager to see her tomorrow as she was to see him? She started imagining what it was going to be like. If she got a chance to talk to him what would she say? How could she condense all her feelings into a few short sentences so that she could convey them to him in what little time they might steal alone together? If they were merely going to pass by one another in a crowded room, how could she communicate anything? She would have to be so careful not to invite gossip. How could she convey all the love and longing that she felt when their conversation would have to remain formal and restrained, when they would have to pretend to be no more than mere acquaintances? There was a knock on the door and her thoughts were interrupted by the maid who had come to help her dress for dinner.

Maina and her father dined alone together.

"Apparently young Salwell is to take Bradmutt's place at the wedding," her father commented grumpily. "I think he is too young. I would have been happy to do the job. Indeed, I would have been honoured."

"Salwell is head of the household, now," Maina told him. "It is his place to carry out Bradmutt's family duties."

After eating in silence for a while her father came out with, "The old governor seems very taken with you."

"Really?"

"I think he is just being polite. Does he not dare to offer honest criticism? Does he think, because you are my daughter, that nothing must be said against you?"

"I'm sure I couldn't say."

"They're all the same, those Mardek officials. They have no spine. They are all like fawning kirra-dogs, thinking to please me with their praise of you."

"Probably," agreed Maina, smiling at the compliment that was being conveyed by such a circuitous route. "With their sterling efforts, catastrophe has, indeed, been avoided in the province, so far."

"So it would seem," her father conceded. "So you are looking to gain appointment for a further round?"

"I would be honoured to serve, if you think I have done well enough so far."

"If you can continue to charm them as you have been doing, I suppose I am happy enough to let things run on a little."

But after chewing for a while he said, "Why don't follow your nurse-sister's example and find a man to marry? Surely Mardek province has noblemen as handsome as anywhere?"

"Indeed, it does," said Maina. "But I cannot govern and court suitors at the same time. The old governor told me that I am not there to make friends. I have to maintain a certain aloofness, he says. Perhaps it is different for a man. I imagine that, for an emperor, it would be possible to be a ruler and a suitor at the same time."

"I hope you are not presuming to comment on your mother's relationship with me, young lady."

"I am speaking in generalities, of course."

"Humph!"

Her father was silent again for a while and then said,

"So what's he like?"

"Who?" In a brief moment of panic, as her private thoughts were interrupted, she thought her father might have found out about Kesh.

"Wyn's fiancé - I take it you have met him?"

"Oh, yes. Well, he's reliable, good natured, intelligent and very good looking. All the maidens noticed him – I mean," she corrected herself quickly "All Wyn's friends, at the temple."

"So she has introduced him to them already. How come I haven't met him yet?"

"Oh, he's quite shy. He's rather nervous about meeting an emperor, I understand."

"Ah. Well, I suppose I shall meet him soon enough," he said. "Oh, by the way, did you notice that a letter had arrived here for you?"

Maina froze. A tingle of dread started behind her ears and spread down her spine. Her father had seen Kesh's letter!

"Ah, yes." She started cautiously. "It was dated many moons ago. You did not think to send it on to me?"

"Hmm, no. It didn't look important."

How much had he seen? Had he read it? Did he know who it was from?

"How could you tell?" she dared to ask.

"Well, it was from Morth. I didn't think it could be anything to do with your work in Mardek."

"No."

"So was it important?"

He hadn't read it, then. Was it important? It was merely a letter written by a man who was nearly as important to her as life itself.

"No," she said. "It wasn't important, but may I request that any other communications that arrive here for me are re-directed straight away?"

"I'll make a note to instruct the reception administrator. Let's see. That's young Salwell, isn't it?"

"I believe it is," she agreed. "Thank you."

When she had spent what she judged to be sufficient time with her father, she went back to her room and turned the key in the lock. She opened up the letter and studied it again. It seemed as though her father hadn't read it and yet the seal had been weak. If he had read it, what would he have gleaned from it? The 'sunlight to the corridors' sentence – was it obvious that it had been written by a lover? How about looking forward to paying his respects with an eager heart? Did that give their relationship away? How suspicious was her father? They had circled round one another at dinner like two Cweel island stags eyeing one another up before a fight. Was her father going to challenge her the next day on the meaning of this missive? She fervently hoped he would not do so in public, at least, not at the wedding.

Chapter 15

At the harbourside inn in Zoradetra, Kesh and Ahbrem were up early, washing and shaving ready for the forthcoming event.

"It does not feel right, not getting my head shaved," complained Ahbrem. "It itches."

"You will be able to shave it again in a day or two."

"But I will be wearing that Xouthan headdress all day. What difference will it make? You could shave it for me, Kesh," Ahbrem said, holding out his razor to him.

"I could, but I am not going to. We do not want to do anything unnecessary that might make us late."

"We have plenty of time."

"Even so," Kesh took Ahbrem's razor from him and wrapped it in a small towel. "You need to pack this ready to take to Wyn's house. Did you not tell me that you are spending your wedding night there?"

"Yes, but I have already packed everything else I could possibly need."

"Then it is time to get you into that Xouthan wedding costume."

"No, I must have breakfast first."

"A little while ago you claimed you could not eat."

"I must try to. I do not want to collapse through lack of sustenance in the middle of the ceremony."

Kesh sighed. He had never seen Ahbrem in such a state. "Right, we will go down for breakfast then."

Mid-day arrived. The weather was not sunny but it was dry and comfortably warm. Family members were already waiting in the courtyard between the two sets of temple gates. Salwell was organising them, arranging their positions according to how closely they were related to the bride, asking them to stand a little further forwards or a little more to the side. When Kesh and Ahbrem arrived, he showed them to a position right at the front and told them to stand facing the inner gates at the bottom of the temple steps.

They soon turned around, however, when noisy trumpeting announced the arrival of the emperor. The emperor's party filled in the space just behind them, so that the emperor was only an arm's length away from Ahbrem. Kesh caught his breath as he recognised the young woman who came to take her place next to the emperor. She was standing very straight. She seemed taller than he remembered and was staring fixedly straight ahead. Kesh tried to concentrate on studying the carvings on the temple doors but, as they waited, he found his head turning and his eyes straying sideways every so often to look at her. On one occasion she must have been looking at the back of his head for their eyes met as he turned. A surge of excitement set his heart racing. She did not smile and yet her look was full of meaning. He hardly noticed as Wyn's mother, later to be the hostess but presently the chief guest, took up her place just behind the empty space next to Ahbrem where Wyn was due to stand.

A hush fell on the assembled company once the guests were all present. After a few moments the doors of the temple opened slowly and out stepped two young women in the mauve robes of trainee priestesses. They each carried a staff, between which was suspended a swag of milk-white silk adorned with flowers, lace streamers and satin ribbons. They held it aloft to frame the doors and under it ranks of women in pale coloured gowns, some holding musical instruments, passed out onto the steps, arranging themselves on either side of the temple doorway. A pause ensued, the silence of suspense broken only by a distant cough from somewhere in the crowd. The sun came out briefly and flooded the quiet space with light, lifting all the colours and warming the backs of the guests. Finally Wyn, dressed in a flowing gown of white silk, stepped through the door of the temple and the trainee priestesses burst into song, accompanied by the playing of their instruments. It all sounded rather strange to Kesh. Their voices seemed scratchy and high and yet they projected a certain beauty.

Wyn stood under the canopy as two other women unfastened the inner gates and swung them open, to release the priestess from the temple confines. With the bearers holding the canopy above her head, Wyn came slowly down the steps but was taken to one side once she stepped through the gates. She bowed her head to the emperor and then to Ahbrem and turned to stand at his side facing the temple. The High Priestess of Xoutha then swept out through the temple doors. She was wearing a high-collared purple cloak, elaborately embroidered with green and golden threads and a tall headdress adorned with abundant leaves and flowers. She stepped forwards into the space under the arch of the gateway and stood facing the couple.

The spoken part of the ceremony was quite familiar to Kesh, after having been through it so many times with Ahbrem and Kesh's thoughts strayed constantly to Maina, standing so close to him after all those moons apart. When it was time to hand Ahbrem the gold marriage cuff he woke quickly from his reverie and held his hand out for Ahbrem to take it.

> *"As this cuff is clasped, I hold you to me.*
> *May the gods of Nature never free me."*

Ahbrem spoke the lines quietly with his newly modified pronunciation, sounding neither Xouthan nor Morthern to Kesh, who was soon wrapped up in his own thoughts again, thinking that Harg would never free him of his attachment to Maina even if they remained unmarried for ever. So close. They would almost certainly be obliged to speak. What could he say? How to condense the thoughts from two rounds of separation into a few sentences? How could he convey all that he felt in the presence of so many?

Ahbrem and Wyn were declared married and the trainee priestesses launched into a fast paced and powerfully voiced celebratory anthem. The guests parted and a path was opened leading down to the roadway that took them away from the temple and back into the heart of Zoradetra. Wyn and Ahbrem led the procession, arm in arm, closely followed by Salwell, Wyn's mother and Kesh, then the emperor and his company, then the High Priestess, priestesses and trainees, still singing heartily, and finally all of the other guests.

At Wyn's home, the doors opened as they arrived and Wyn led Ahbrem into the large dining room. They found it decked out with flowers and greenery, bows and ribbons and there were tables set against the side walls piled high with food and drink. Against the far wall a table was laid out for the newly-weds and their principal guests, the emperor and the high priestess and also Kesh and Maina, placed at opposite ends.

Before they took their seats, however, there were the presentations. Maina stood in for consort, standing next to her father, while first Ahbrem was introduced.

"May I present my husband, Ahbrem of Khoulan?" Wyn said.

"Congratulations, my boy," said the emperor. "You have yourself a fine wife. Take good care of her."

Ahbrem bowed low.

"I will, Your Majesty."

"And may I present Kesh of Khoulan?" asked Wyn.

Kesh bowed.

"Pleased to meet you," said the emperor. "Are you brothers, then, you two?"

"No, Your Majesty."

"So where is this Khoulan? The name sounds familiar but I can't quite place it."

"A little way away, Your Majesty."

"Indeed. I judged by your accents that you were not from Zoradetra."

"No, Your Majesty."

Maina held out her hand and smiled playfully. Kesh was keen to move on from the emperor. He took the hand and lifted it gently to his lips, taking just a moment too long to brush his mouth against her skin. The emperor watched with one eyebrow starting to lift as Kesh bowed deeply and stepped away from her without speaking.

Once the formalities were over, the festivities started in earnest. The food and drink began to be consumed. After a while, the emperor took it on himself to make a speech to his subjects, thanking his hostess, wishing the newly-weds a long and happy marriage and so on. Then a band of musicians who had set up in a corner of the room began to play dance tunes. Wyn had taught Ahbrem some of the traditional Xouthan dances and they confidently led the other guests around the room but, before Kesh dared to ask Maina to dance, he had to spend a good while watching in order to pick up the steps.

Then, just when he thought he had got it and had stepped towards Maina, lifting his hand to ask for hers, Salwell stepped in front of him and he and Maina swept off into the throng of moving bodies. There were other dances and he watched the patterns of steps until he thought he could make an attempt to follow them himself, but just as this happened the music would stop and another rhythm would be struck up and there was yet another new set of steps to be absorbed. At last, with a repeat of the first dance he had tried to follow, Kesh was able to go straight away to Maina and claim her for a partner.

As she stepped along by his side, spinning into turns at arms length, promenading on his arm, side stepping in front of him, he caught breaths of her smell, intertwined with the aroma of herbs from her soap or the flowers in her hair. They danced face to face for a few steps, and his hand was on her side. He felt the sparsely covered bone, the rise and fall of her ribs as she sucked in the air to fire her steps, the muscle tensing in her back as she arched into another spin. He had never been this close to a woman before, at least not so far as his memory would admit. His eyes followed her every move. At the end of the dance he walked Maina back to her place. She was laughing breathlessly. He would have asked her to dance again, never mind whether he knew how or not, but Salwell stepped between them, giving Kesh an ugly look, and spinning Maina in amongst the dancers once again.

Maina was tiring. She made her excuses to Salwell at the end of the dance and sought out her friend.

"So how does it feel, Mrs Ahbrem of Khoulan?"

"A little strange," Wyn said. "But good. Everyone keeps coming up to me and saying what a nice young man he seems to be, how handsome he is, how lucky I am."

"Does your mother like him?"

"She is besotted! She came to me a little while after I had introduced him to her. She told me approvingly that he looks seensible and that she thinks I've made an excellent choice. Now she can't stop talking about him. She is going round all the guests just to hear their admiring comments, telling them that we waited two years for the wedding for her sake, because of her loss, and what a lucky woman she is to have such a considerate son-in-law and so on and so on."

"Oh, I'm so glad," Maina said, genuinely relieved. "So you have had nobody commenting on his foreign accent or asking awkward questions about where he comes from?"

"Nothing so far."

At that point Kesh came up and stood at Maina's side.

"May I offer you my congratulations, Mrs Ahbrem?"

"Thank you, Kesh."

"Where is he, anyway?" Maina asked her.

"Over in the corner, with those three trainee priestesses," Wyn told her. "I think they're trying to get him to dance with them. I'd better go and rescue him."

"He looks like he's enjoying the attention," Maina said.

"Hmmph!" was Wyn's only reply as she left them.

"Perhaps we can dance again, if I can work out the steps," Kesh suggested. "I should have asked Hannala for dancing lessons along with the language tuition."

"You're actually very good," Maina assured him. "This tune's just finishing. Let's see what the next one's going to be."

Maina led him in amongst the dancers and offered prompts to help with the upcoming steps. She thought back to the first time they had danced together. She could only remember that there had been dancing and that they had danced. She couldn't remember the details. How had they managed to dance the unusual Enaha dances to those unfamiliar tunes, she wondered. Perhaps they had already been so drunk they had not worried about whether they were getting the steps right. It had felt so magical that it had all seemed to go wonderfully well at the time.

When the band paused between tunes, Salwell appeared again and asked her to dance.

"I'm sorry. I don't think I could dance another step just now," she told him. "I must sit down and catch my breath. But first I must find something to drink."

"Allow me to fetch you a beverage of some kind," Salwell said and started towards one of the side tables."What would you like?"

Maina followed him, looking over her shoulder to check that Kesh was following too.

The afternoon had become evening, the windows showing black in contrast to the brightly lit interior. Wyn's mother organised the closing of curtains. The emperor came up to Maina by the table where the wines and juices were displayed.

"My dear, I will be returning to the palace shortly. I am about to take my leave of the bride's mother."

"Oh! I suppose I'd better get my cloak."

"No, don't you come with me. You should remain here and enjoy the party. You seem to have one or two admirers. Stay and make the most of it."

Any other woman might have been insulted by the implication in his tone that having admirers was an unusual situation for her. Maina, however, was only too happy to receive such a comment when it was accompanied by this permission to outstay her father.

A few moments later, she saw Wyn's mother crossing the room to the musician's corner. They struck up 'Conquering Emperor' and the guests moved aside to make an aisle so that her father and some of his company could make a small but dignified procession out of the room. They passed through the entrance hall and away into the street.

Chapter 16

Once her father had gone, Maina was a little taken aback at how the mood of the remaining company changed. They had seemed to be enjoying themselves before but now, suddenly, the band got noisier, the dancing more flamboyant, the conversation entirely more raucous. She danced once more with Salwell and was jostled by the energetic revellers cavorting all around her. When Kesh, shouting to be heard above the crowd, asked her to dance, she shook her head and took his hand. She led him out of the room and through the kitchens to the garden at the back of the house.

"I need to cool down for a bit," she said once they had stepped out into the night air. "Things are getting a bit wild in there. Let me show you one of my favourite places. I hope they haven't changed it. I used to come out here as a child. Even when I was living at the palace with my father, I used to come back here to be alone if ever I felt upset."

They passed through an archway in an old stone wall and then Maina led Kesh to the right where, behind the wall, there was a little arbour and an old wooden bench.

"Good. It's still here. You can't really see it in the dark but this is an ancient kutzim bush. It drapes over the seat so gracefully, and when it is in flower the scent fills the arbour."

They sat down side by side on the bench. A rustling was heard in the branches of a tall tree somewhere above them.

"What was that?" asked Kesh.

"A bird, I think. Look there's a dark shape in the branches."

"Then it is a mighty bird."

"Could be a seacrow. They seem to be getting awfully cheeky lately. Hardly bother to fly off when they're approached."

"Is that all it was? I find it hard to relax, knowing I am in Xouthan territory."

"I think you are safe enough now that my father has gone back to the palace. I thought he would expect me to go with him. I didn't think we'd get a chance to speak properly, yet here we are, quite alone."

"I have been dreaming of a moment like this for two long rounds - a moment when I can look into your eyes and tell you my innermost thoughts - but now it has happened, I am lost for words."

"There's plenty of time. I don't think anyone will miss us while the party's in full swing."

"That is good."

"First, tell me about Calim Bradmutt. How is he? What's he like now?"

"He is adorable. He is beginning to speak quite fluently but he still calls Ahbrem 'Brebbum'. He walks, but more slowly than a grown-up, of course, so he prefers to be carried whenever he can persuade one of us to pick him up. I am sorry to say that I have missed one or two of his visits lately but I am sure Ahbrem has been looking after him well enough. They are quite fond of one another."

Kesh stopped. He thought he saw moonlight glinting off tears on Maina's cheek.

"I am sorry," he said. "Perhaps that is not what you wanted to hear."

"No, no. It sounds wonderful. I am glad that he has such good people to care for him. I do so regret abandoning him. The one person in the world who should have given him the most has given nothing."

"That is not true. In your sacrifice you have given much. You stopped the war, Maina. That is something that none of the rest of us could, or would, have done. I often think of all the lives that could have been wasted in the rounds of conflict that would have ensued if we had both acted on our instincts for revenge. You saved all those lives."

"In theory, perhaps, but we can't be sure that any one else would have died. What if the war could have ended without me doing anything?"

"I know that it would not have ended, not for many rounds, not until one side or the other ran out of soldiers to die, or food to feed them, or weapons to fight with. The war would have gone on until one or other of our countries was completely broken. There are many men from both our countries who owe their lives to you, even if they will never know it. Your sacrifice has not been in vain, and you must never suspect that it has."

Maina smiled weakly, grateful for his words.

"Thank you. You are the only person I can discuss this with. I know that, at the time, you didn't want me to carry out my plan. To hear you say, now, that you think I did the right thing means a great deal to me."

"I am sorry for trying to persuade you to do otherwise. I am glad now that you took no notice of me."

"Oh, I took notice Kesh. It was so tempting, just to run away with you and hide somewhere. We could have had such a wonderful life, couldn't we, you and I and little Calim?"

"I think so."

"But it was not to be. And here we are, still hiding, seeking out dark corners so that we can spend a little time together. If hostilities were truly over, you and Ahbrem would not have to conceal your true identities and Wyn and I could have organised a double wedding. That is, if you'd still have me?"

"Maina, you do not have to ask me that. I dream about being with you every spare moment that I have."

Maina looked at his dimly lit face and smiled. The curve of the cheekbone, the firm mouth, the expressive eyes, were just as she remembered from two rounds before and she loved them just as much.

"So, how have you been these last two rounds?" she asked. "What have you been doing with yourself all this time?"

"Let me see. Where do I begin? Quite a good deal of my time was taken up in helping to run the monastery, teaching the students and so on. My life was becoming rather mundane, until a messenger came to call me to Chief Ackhart's funeral. Do you remember that Hernst's father, chief of the Ahn Dehar, had said he wanted me to sing the Morthern lament at his funeral?"

"I remember."

"Well, I went to Ahn Dehar and I performed the lament, but then I foolishly let slip to Hernst something I had overheard when I was with Ship and King Nathan on the Sacred Mountain about what the Four Kings had done to Ackhart."

Kesh related the sorry tale of the slow poisoning and Hernst's subsequent murder attempt and how he himself had promised to help the Four Kings in order to save Hernst's life but then had ended up betraying them.

"So now I have made a complete mess of everything. The Four Kings can't have their coal unless I betray the Anh Dehar and the economy of the Ahn Dehar will collapse unless I can find an acceptable alternative to the mining of coal on their land. I wish with all my heart that I could turn back time and 'untell' Hernst about his father."

"I think Hernst deserved to know the truth. Deceiving Hernst would not make things right."

"But now there is an innocent man imprisoned by the Ahn Dehar at my suggestion. That cannot be right either. I abandoned him to come here. I have been dancing to joyous music, talking intimately with the woman I love, while he is held captive by strangers and kept far from his loved ones. He looked so broken and betrayed and I just left him there to suffer. I must be a uniquely evil person to have caused such a thing to happen."

"Not so uniquely," Maina told him. "Strangely, I have done much the same thing recently. Worse, in fact, for I have imprisoned not one, but four, innocent men and kept them away from their loved ones. Mardek province borders on the Wildlands and I discovered that both Wildlanders and Xouthans were regularly losing their lives in trespass skirmishes. I suggested that we send some Xouthans over the border so that we could learn something of their culture and find out why the Wildlanders keep attacking us. That idea was rejected by the military commander. He said it would be too dangerous, so my second suggestion was to capture the next group of Wildlanders who attacked the boundary wall and then employ a linguist to attend the gaol in order to learn their language, study their customs and perhaps discover the motivation behind the attacks. I had hoped that eventually we could negotiate an end to them. Unfortunately, the prisoners are not being very cooperative, so their incarceration is achieving very little."

"Your intentions were good. You should not be too hard on yourself."

"Ah, but there lies the difficulty, you see. I cannot use good intentions to justify what I am doing to those men. The Xouthan book of Sacred Texts has a verse that clearly states:

'Measure not your deeds by the goals you seek
Judge each action on its merit
The goal cannot be declared as just
If evil is done while achieving it.'

"Ah, yes. I remember Ship has a saying: 'The road to Hell is paved with good intentions'. You are right. I cannot use the greater good which I hope to achieve as an excuse for encouraging the imprisonment of Applad. I must tell the Ahn Dehar to release him."

"And I must have the Wildlanders released as soon as I get back. I must think of a new way to learn how to communicate with them."

"But the Wildlanders have done something wrong, at least. They attacked the border wall. Their detention has prevented them from making further attacks. Indeed it may have saved their lives."

"But what of the families waiting back in the Wildlands? Their wives and mothers must be suffering. They probably think their husbands and sons are dead. It is an awful thing I am doing to those women, yet they have done nothing wrong. I must thank you, Kesh, for making me see it this way. I needed this conversation to change my perspective."

"No, wait. I think you are misunderstanding me. I believe imprisonment is necessary sometimes. I would dearly love Hernst to be free but I do not think it would be wise for the kings to free him. He has no remorse about attempting the murder. I know because I asked him. I think he would try it again if he were freed in the present circumstances. Imprisonment seems to be the only option. How do you know your Wildlanders will not attack again if you free them?"

"I fully expect them to attack again. Unless we find out what motivates the attacks and remove that motivation, they will go on attacking. But I was too quick to take away their liberty. I have become callous during my time in office."

"On the contrary, you seem, as ever, to see the best in people all the time. The Wildlanders attack your walls and kill your soldiers and yet you seek a way to communicate with them and worry about how their wives and mothers are suffering. I would hardly describe that as callous. I think it is that sweet nature of yours – the one I came to love so deeply – that is threatening to interfere with your good judgement."

"Wyn says I have a reputation for being a harsh employer. How did my sweet nature produce that, I wonder?"

"I find that hard to believe."

"The old governor told me to be strict right from the outset. He warned me that it would be so much harder to rein things in later on and I believed him. He told me I must on no account appear lax at the start of my governorship."

"Ah, there is precious little pleasure to be gained from being in charge. Shouldering the responsibility of running Khoulan is bad enough, where all the monks aspire to the same ambitions as the mattouk, but taking charge of the Ahn Dehar is a different matter all together. I do not feel at all confident that I will be able to do it. I should confess that to the Four Kings. I misled them when I consented to do their bidding. I have got myself into a tangled mess. I will end up letting everyone down and making the situation worse. Harg knows, I am the last person our own king should choose as his heir. All good institutions in this world seem to crumble at my touch."

"Kesh, you are exaggerating. Khoulan is not crumbling, is it? You are a good mattouk. I am sure, if the king has chosen you as his heir, it is because he sees in you the qualities all the rest of us see: a kind heart and a desire to do good. You will make an excellent king."

"I do not think so. I keep hoping that something, or someone, will come along to take that burden away." He sighed. "Anyway, the king is in good health and he is not yet old enough to need an heir. That problem is not going to be upon me for a little while yet."

Kesh fell silent and they listened to the sounds of the night. A thin high-pitched squeaking from somewhere in the undergrowth, the call of a cliff-owl from further away, voices spilling out from the house, feint, broken melodies from the band, the occasional raucous laugh.

"The party is going well," Kesh commented. "Ahbrem deceived me. He led me to believe that it was going to be a small family affair."

"So it was, until my father expressed disappointment at not being invited. Then it became a grand occasion and everyone in Zoradetra wanted to come. Plenty of friends and relatives from further afield, as well."

"It has perhaps been all to the good. Ahbrem and I seem to have been able to merge into the crowd to some extent. I do not feel that we have been as conspicuous as I expected us to be."

"No," agreed Maina. "So far, so good. It all seems to have gone rather well, though I don't know when Wyn and Ahbrem will get to the marriage bed. The revellers seem to be showing no signs of letting up."

"Ah, the marriage bed! Ahbrem was having anxious thoughts about that, you know. He was worrying about the 'closeness', as he put it. As a father, I should have been able to offer him some advice, but I could say nothing."

"No. I suspect that the night of the Hittan festival might have been the most wonderful night of my life but I don't remember anything of it."

"I hope ... that we may get a chance to relive it, one day."

"I dream of that, too. But I don't see how. We have had to go to such lengths to conceal Ahbrem's nationality. How much more difficult it would be to conceal yours, if you and I were to marry? And I have been training to take my father's place. I can't just leave my country and live at Khoulan, like Wyn is going to do. If I gave up my claim to the monarchy, my uncle would take charge after my father, and he has a reputation for brutality. In Wyn's opinion the whole empire would suffer if he took power. Just like you, I need to find someone with a good heart to take my place before I can be free."

"We cannot be together as Ahbrem and Wyn can now be, but perhaps we could try to relive just a little part of our time in Hittan. When we danced together, we were re-enacting a part, I think."

"Yes." Maina closed her eyes momentarily, remembering the warmth of Kesh's hand against her ribs when they had danced, a warmth that melted through the fabric of her dress and found an answering warmth in her own body.

"Would it be so wrong to hold one another again?" Kesh asked. "We do not have to be married in order to embrace, do we?"

"No, I believe an occasional embrace is acceptable before marriage."

"I am very glad to hear it."

Kesh held out his arms, the moonlight picking out the folds in the fabric of his sleeves. He smiled a shy invitation but did not move any closer. Maina shifted towards him and slid one arm between Kesh's back and the seat and the other around his chest. Her hands easily met at the other side of his slim body. In response, Kesh leaned forwards and touched his lips briefly to hers, but he pulled back again straight away.

"I apologise," he said. "I did not mean to do that. It was very presumptuous of me."

"No, don't apologise. It was nice."

"I have imagined kissing those lips many times. They have always been long miles away. Now you are here. Right here, next to me."

Maina tilted her face up and his mouth found hers again. He gently kissed first one side, then the other. Finally, their lips met in a full embrace, kindling a response in Maina's body that she had not expected.

She let out a little sound, half groan, half moan, as she said,

"I think I see at last. I think I finally understand how it happened. I believe, if I had drunk one more mouthful of wine this evening, I would never want you to stop kissing me, and I would not be able to stop myself from wanting ... more than just kisses."

"More than kisses? You will have to explain."

"No, Kesh. I don't think I need to explain."

"Perhaps you could show me, then."

"I could not show you without ... Kesh, I think we should stop now before we go too far."

"Do we have to stop?" Kesh asked. He spaced out his words meaningfully, "Whatever we did, it would not be anything we had not done before."

He kissed her again, pulling her closer to him, all shyness gone.

For a few moments Maina relished the delicious feel of his body against hers. She pulled away reluctantly. "Kesh, we can't let it happen again. We could forgive ourselves the last time because we didn't know what we were doing. This time we would know exactly what we were doing. And I can hardly go back to my governorship carrying Calim's brother in my belly. I think it might be noticed."

Kesh released her slowly, leaned his head back, sucked in a great gulp of air with his face turned up to the moon.

"Ahh, you are right, of course. What was I thinking? Forgive me!"

"No, forgive me. I am equally to blame."

Maina leaned her head on Kesh's chest. His heart was beating so very fast. Could she have done that to him? She hugged him tightly and sat still for a while, reliving the kiss in her head, trying to fix it in her memory, enjoying the closeness of his beating heart.

"I wish," she began. "I wish I could make this moment last forever. I thought I had lost the ability to feel happiness, but no, this is it. I am completely, blissfully happy. I wish I could remember every detail precisely so that I could relive it, again and again, when we are apart. I have yearned for your company for so long, and now I have you here, it is so wonderful, but our time is too short. If we sat here the whole night, it would not be long enough."

"Oh, Maina, we have suffered so ... " Kesh's voice diminished to silence.

They sat not moving, each denying their desire yet drinking in the joy of the other's closeness. After a while, voices floated to their ears above the general noise of the party.

"Is that someone coming?" Kesh asked, tensing and straightening up.

Maina listened, waiting for closer sounds.

"No, I don't think so."

He relaxed again, leaning back and closing his eyes. Maina wrapped her arms around him and put her cheek against his chest once more. His chin rested gently on her hair and they clung to one another, defying intrusion, defying the passage of time, defying the circumstances that would inevitably pull them asunder in so short a while.

"Maina, I want to make you a promise," Kesh spoke quietly. "I want to promise you that one day I will hold you in my arms like this again. No matter how long it takes. Even if I have to wait for you to become empress, or for this world to come to an end and Harg's Realm to descend, I promise that this will not be the last time I hold you like this. I will travel the miles and bide the long rounds through, do whatever is required of me, but I promise I will come back to you."

"Dearest Kesh. I will be waiting."

They held each other for a little while longer but soon voices drifted to them over the garden wall. Some of the guests were starting to leave. They were at the front door bidding farewell to Wyn and Ahbrem. From their hiding place Kesh and Maina listened to their footsteps fading as they passed along the shadowy streets.

"Look, there is a glow in the east," Maina said. "I think the night is over."

"I suppose we had better go indoors."

"I'll go first. You follow in a few minutes. I don't want everyone to know we've spent the night together."

"Alright. I will see you again before you go, I hope?"

"I should get back to the palace. The party's finished."

"Perhaps tomorrow?"

"The coach is ordered to start the journey back to Mardek at noon. That's only a few hours away."

"One last kiss, then."

They kissed goodbye. Kesh wondered if his memory of it would have to last him a lifetime. He tasted salt and realised that he was kissing Maina's tears.

"Goodbye, my love," she whispered to him.

"Peace and long life, searer of my soul."

***

Maina arrived at the breakfast table a little while later, looking not quite her best.

"I see you enjoyed yourself last night," her father said.

"Yes."

"You should drink plenty of water this morning. Water washes down the wine, you know."

"A cup of tea would be very welcome."

A servant immediately stepped forwards and poured tea from a large pot into her cup.

"I notice you still draw the attention of young men. You have lost none of your appeal. Like viper-wasps to a pot of jultie jam. Salwell certainly paid you a great deal of attention and that friend of Wyn's husband, too."

'Oh, dear,' Maina thought. 'He saw us!'

"Why can't you choose one of those for a husband? Salwell, for instance. Wouldn't he make a good enough husband?"

"Salwell is like a brother to me," said Maina and gave a little shudder. "It would seem quite wrong."

"Ahbrem's friend, then. He seemed alright. Didn't you like him?"

"Oh, yes, I like ... liked him very much."

"Well, then," said the emperor. "Mind you, this Khoulan must be a tiny place. It sounds familiar but it's not marked on my map of the empire. I looked. Do you know where it is?"

"Geography never was my strong point."

"You have travelled farther than most women of your age. You should have a good grasp of geography by now. So you've never been to this Khoulan?"

"No."

"Well, I'm going to send out one of my men to find it."

"No! Please don't." Maina said a little too suddenly. "I mean, it would look so obvious. I don't want to seem desperate. Let him come to me if he's interested. After all, he is Ahbrem's best friend. He will know where to find me."

"Oh," her father said with a hint of disappointment. "Very well."

Chapter 17

Kesh went back to the inn to pack his belongings and also those few of Ahbrem's things that he had not taken with him. He had to get to Khoulan to prepare for the Morthern marriage ceremony, due to take place in two days time, but there was someone he had to speak to on the way.

As he led his horse up the path to the Sacred Mountain he was trying to plan what he would say once he came face to face with King Doug again. The first thing was to apologise, both for his rudeness in walking straight past him two days before and for not being with the Ahn Dehar, as the Four Kings had requested. Presumably, they had expected him to stay at least until the negotiations for the coal contract were completed. Both misdemeanours were unforgivable. He could imagine excuses but none of them were valid justifications. He could only beg forgiveness and hope that Doug was feeling magnanimous. He did not feel as though he deserved to be forgiven. He had enjoyed the previous evening so much that he now felt he should be paying for it in some way. He suspected that his great joy was about to be balanced by great sorrow.

He arrived at the Xouthan gate and one of the maidens came down to open it for him. He enquired about King Doug's whereabouts, and was told that he was taking tea with the other two humans in Ship's study. The trainee offered to take a cup up for him, assuming he would join them, but he didn't feel able to face them all at once. He said he would wait. The trainee invited him to take tea with her in the kitchen, but he turned that offer down too.

"I'll just go and wait on the balcony," Kesh told her.

"But it is starting to rain," she said, perplexed.

Kesh shrugged in reply and turned to make for the Great Hall.

A little while later, Hannala came on to the balcony followed by the trainee carrying a tray with two cups. She set it on the table amongst the beads of rain. Occasional spots of water were augmenting the tea in the cups as she withdrew.

"The temple maiden said you refused to take tea with them," Hannala said, obviously concerned. "Is something wrong? Was there a problem at the wedding?"

"No, no," said Kesh. "It went very well."

"The emperor did not catch wind of your being Morthern?"

"Not as far as I know."

"I will feel happier when Ahbrem is back here safely."

"He should be here soon. I have business to attend to, so I came on ahead."

"And this business is what is causing you to refuse company?"

"Partly, yes."

"Only partly? Did you not enjoy the wedding then?"

"I enjoyed it very much. It is coming back to reality that has drained all the joy from my heart."

"Tell me."

"I saw her, Hannala. I saw Maina. She was so ... beautiful. We sat together in the garden. We were together until the eastern sky began to pale. But I do not know when I will see her again. It could be many rounds before we meet once more."

"So she still has feelings for you?"

"It would seem so, yes."

"Then you must rejoice in that and put any misgivings about the future out of your head. You have already borne many moons of parting. The future waiting cannot be any worse than the separation which you have already endured."

"No, I suppose not."

"Now drink your tea and gather your energy to tackle this 'business' that you mentioned," Hannala commanded. "Do you want to tell me about that too?"

So Kesh told Hannala the story of Hernst and his broken pact with the Four Kings.

"I see," said Hannala at the end of it. "Well, if I can offer any encouragement it would be to tell you that the two kings we have here on the mountain are in quite good spirits at the moment. Doug dived down to Ship's old vessel yesterday and he is full of talk of diving down again and trying to get inside it. Nathan was annoyed at being held up because Ahbrem has not been here to help with the translation work but I have been doing a bit for him now and then, when I can spare the time, and that seems to have improved his mood. Moreover, he has just had a set of tools and some timber delivered so that he can now start building his etherium. He will want to ask you if you can send some monks to help with it. So I don't think either of them will be very cross about the Ahn Dehar. They both have other things on their minds."

"Oh, Hannala, thank you." said Kesh. "You have given me just the right kind of news. You always know how to cheer me up."

"I do?"

Kesh drained his cup and stood up.

"You do," he said and stooped to kiss her on the cheek. "I will go now and seek out the humans. You do not need to sit in the rain any longer."

***

In Ship's study, Doug was describing what he had seen on his dive.

"The water was quite clear. I could see the outline of the hull and, despite a generous coating of marine life, I could just make out a hatch. I may need to clean it a little in order to free up the door but I think it will still be possible to get inside."

"How will you do that?" Ship asked, "The opening mechanism isn't going to work after all this time."

"I'll give it a try and, if it doesn't work, I'll use a crowbar or something."

"What about the air lock? If you use a crowbar you won't be able to reseal it. Even if the door works, I told you the pump was really struggling the last time I used it. You could drown down there just waiting for the chamber to empty."

"One step at a time. I'll rig up some sort of air supply from the surface, maybe, if I need to."

"It all sounds too risky to me. Why is it so important to you?"

"I would have thought it was pretty important to all of us," Doug looked to Nathan for support but his colleague said nothing.

"I don't see why," Ship said.

"Just think about it, old man. You told me there were frozen embryos on the ship. Female embryos. They could be the last human females in existence and they are certainly the only hope the five of us will ever have of seeing a woman, a human woman that is, again."

"They've been down there years and years. They'll have gone to mush by now."

"Was the cryo-system still working when you last went down?"

"Yes, as far as I could tell."

"So it might be working now."

"After all this time? I doubt it."

"It's worth a try. It's our only chance. For all we know, it could be the last chance for the survival of the human race. I've got to give it a go."

"You say some of these embryos were from eggs donated by his wife's sister?" Nathan spoke at last. "I wouldn't be happy with incubating those. He wasn't married to her."

"What's that got to do with anything?" Doug asked.

"It's all unnatural, but using Diane's sister – that was immoral as well as unnatural."

"Okay, we'll chuck those ones in the bin, then, shall we? Is that moral enough for you?"

"No," Nathan sounded shocked. "That would be murder."

"Well, not giving them the chance of life is the same thing, isn't it?"

Nathan turned away without speaking.

"Nathan, I don't think Diane's sisters' embryos were fertilised with Brannan's semen, if that's what's bothering you." Ship said. "As far as I know, they were going to be her own husband's offspring." He turned to his other crewman. "How do you propose to incubate them, Doug? There were no facilities on the ship to take them to full term. I don't know if such facilities were ever fully developed, were they?"

"I think the first approach would surely be to try implanting them into Penethellan women."

"What?" Nathan exclaimed.

"Kevin told me that you were all convinced that humans and Penethellans are entirely incompatible," Ship said.

"We can't seem to get them pregnant but that's not to say a ready-fertilised embryo would not implant," Doug told him. "It's got to be worth a try."

"And who would carry out such a procedure? None of us are doctors."

"Ted's a biologist."

"An exo-biologist, yes."

"Exactly. He could act as advisor even if he doesn't want to actually do the operation. He could supervise a Penethellan doctor."

"And how are you going to persuade the Penethellan women to take part?" asked Ship. "Pay them?"

"Perhaps. Maybe they'll just volunteer. Ted has a way with Penethellan women, you know," Nathan grinned. "Some of them seem ready to do anything for him, even getting shaved and marrying him."

"Oh, don't remind me," groaned Nathan. "That poor woman."

"Thing was, Ted preferred her the way she was before, fur and all."

"Yes, so Kevin told me," said Ship.

A tentative tapping on the study door caused the humans to suddenly fall silent.

"Come in," Ship called out.

Kesh entered hesitantly and bowed low to each human in turn.

"Hello, Kesh. How did the wedding go?" Ship asked.

"Very well, thank you."

"All set for the Morthern ceremony? I'm getting there by horseback, I've been told, even though I haven't ridden a horse since I was six."

"The mounts here are very placid," Kesh assured him. "I am sure you will find it easy enough."

"So it was you I saw!" Doug broke in. "I thought you were meant to be with the Ahn Dehar."

"My humblest apologies," Kesh said. "Once Wanhild had been sent away with the message about Applad, I could no longer communicate with the Ahn Dehar."

"So you came home?"

"Um ... "

"Never mind the Ahn Dehar," Ship said. "He is booked to conduct a marriage ceremony in two days time and it's his best friend getting married."

"I am very sorry for leaving my appointed post," Kesh said.

"You could have told us, at least," Doug complained.

"At the time I undertook the task, I was resigned to missing the wedding. It was only when Wanhild left and it became obvious that I could do nothing until he returned that I thought I may as well come back here. I will go back to the Ahn Dehar straight after the wedding, I assure you. However, I should point out that I am not altogether happy with the idea of destroying their beautiful homeland by mining it for coal. I would rather they found an alternative form of trade."

"I thought that was the deal," Doug said. "We spare Hernst, you get the coal."

Kesh hung his head. "Will you execute Hernst if I do not fulfil my promise?"

"Who's talking about executing anyone?" asked Ship. "You have the guy locked up, don't you? Isn't that enough?"

"I think he should be executed," said Nathan. "We should set an example to deter other potential trouble makers."

"I'm not quite so bothered about him now. I don't feel so traumatised now I'm over here," said Doug. "Back at the palace, with my murderer living in the same building, pretty much just underneath my feet, I couldn't sleep for thinking about it. I guess while I'm away he can stay where he is."

"Seems to me, you need to move him out of the palace," suggested Ship.

"Perhaps, but that might make it worse. How would I know for sure, then, where he was? He could escape and the next thing I'd know I'd wake up with a knife in my back again. While he's still alive, the only other place I feel safe is on the other side of the sea from him."

"Well, you're welcome to stay here as long as you like," said Ship.

"In exile, you mean?"

Ship shrugged. "What's this about a coal mine, anyway?"

"Our seam is running out. It's already producing less coal per shift because it's getting more difficult to get at what remains. The Ahn Dehar have coal really close to the surface and yet they're not using it. They seem to prefer to burn wood."

"And can't you burn wood?"

"I don't think we'd get a high enough temperature in the boilers to turn the turbine. I'm afraid my generator design is a bit on the primitive side."

"So this is for your electricity supply?"

"Yes, and for the heating system."

"So why don't you use a different energy source - wind or solar, perhaps?"

"I wouldn't have the foggiest how to make a solar cell. A coal-fired steam turbine was relatively straight forward to construct and the coal was already there, poking up out of the ground."

"Wind turbines wouldn't be too difficult to make, would they?" Ship asked the engineer.

"I suppose not. We'd still need coal for the smiths to make the components, of course."

"Well, I'll buy one from you, if you do start making them."

"I'd give you one, if I could come up with a design that our smiths could put together with their primitive equipment. We'd need a good supply of copper, as well as coal and iron, though."

"The Xouthans have copper."

"So do we," said Kesh. "These mountains have gold and copper seams running from the Morthern side right through to Xoutha."

"The Ahn Dehar have copper, too," said Doug bitterly. "But I don't suppose they would want to sell us that, either."

"It is the destruction of their farmland which I fear," said Kesh.

"The copper is up in the mountains, mainly," Doug told him. "It isn't near any farmland."

"Then I will be happy to negotiate with them to sell you their copper mining rights."

"Okay," said Doug.

"Would that mean that Hernst can live?" Kesh asked.

"I tell you what," said Doug. "If you can get me copper from the Ahn Dehar, I'll forgive you for going back on your word. Hey, why don't you take the murderous Hernst back with you to Morth? If you could promise to keep him there under lock and key for the rest of his life, I'd overlook the little matter of you abandoning your post.'"

Kesh's face broke into a broad smile, "Really?"

"Yeah, really."

Kesh could not believe his luck. Here was a proposal that would see Hernst's life assured and provide the Ahn Dehar with income.

"I cannot thank you enough," he told Doug. "This is an extremely generous proposal."

"Perhaps too generous," said Nathan, holding up his hand to interrupt the proceedings. "You do realise that it was precisely this Penethellan before us that caused all this trouble in the first place? He was the one who told Hernst about the power unit."

"I realise that."

"And you would trust him to keep Hernst locked up? He's already broken his word to you once."

"I think he cares enough about this Hernst to keep him out of our way," said Doug. He turned to Kesh. "We'd make it a provision of the deal that, should Hernst escape, we'd sentence him to execution once again. You would have no problem with that proviso, I take it?"

"I understand," Kesh said solemnly.

"I'll vouch for Kesh's trustworthiness," Ship put in. "I've always found him a very reliable sort. He is the mattouk of a monastery, after all. We're not dealing with some irresponsible young delinquent."

Nathan drew in a breath to say something but Kesh broke in.

"I understand you may be ready for our carpenters to help you build your etherium platform, now," he said to him.

"Ah!" Nathan was cut short. "Yes, I have the materials. The project could begin."

"Very well," said Kesh. "I will ask the volunteers to pack and be ready to travel the day after the wedding." He turned to Ship. "Some of the men may not have been here before. Could I please request that arrangements are made for them to climb the waterfall?"

"I am sure that would not be a problem. Let me know how many monks it will involve and I will make sure the appropriate preparations are carried out. Now, Kesh, you have a very important event coming up but are you resting with us here before you go on to Khoulan?"

"I think I'd better be on my way, if I can borrow a fresh horse."

"I am sure they'll find one for you in the stables. One of those placid mounts, perhaps? Or had you better choose the fastest?"

"I will be happy to take whichever mount the stable mistress offers."

"I look forward to seeing you at the wedding, then."

"I hope I can do the betrothed couple justice. It will be my first, you know, and I am feeling a little apprehensive."

"Really? Well, I am sure you will carry out the task magnificently. Good luck, anyway."

"Thank you. I will take my leave of you now then, if I may. Peace and long life, Ship. Peace and long life, to you, King Nathan and to you, King Doug."

The kings returned Kesh's good wishes and the mattouk left the study.

"So he's conducting the service for my translator's wedding, is he?" Nathan asked. "I declined Ahbrem's invitation but now I rather wish I'd accepted. I'm curious as to how Kesh will handle it."

"Why don't you both come?" Ship suggested. "I'm sure they would be honoured to have two kings at the ceremony!"

"Sounds like fun to me," said Doug.

"Fun? I'm not so sure about that. It's rather sad for Kesh, actually. He arranged the dispensation that enables Khoulan monks to get married because he wanted to marry the mother of his son."

"He has a son?" asked Doug.

"Yes. Maina - the lady he was travelling with when they first visited you - she was already carrying his child when they first found you but their two countries were at war, so their marriage never went ahead. I have been paying for the child's upkeep since then but he's been living with a foster family in Morth. I feel rather sad that the parents aren't together. I think they would have made rather a nice family."

"Sounds to me as though they had already behaved very irresponsibly, indulging in the pleasures of the flesh without waiting for God's blessing." Nathan said. "It doesn't sound to me as though they would make particularly good parents."

"The story they tell is that their Enahet hosts made them both drink a potion that put them to sleep. Neither of them remembers anything after going to bed. When they woke up they didn't realise anything had happened. It was only when Maina discovered that she was pregnant that she began to put two and two together."

"A likely story!" scoffed Nathan. "Surely they just made it up as an excuse for their indiscretions. It doesn't improve my assessment of Kesh's character one bit. It's very good of you to support the child but don't let them dupe you with any more of their tall tales."

"As I told Kevin, the birth was partly my fault. I was the one who sent them away together. I should have foreseen that possibility."

"I think the mattouk of a monastery should have known better."

"Perhaps. Of course, he wasn't a mattouk then, just a young man who'd led a rather sheltered life. I doubt he'd seen a woman for several years before he came here and met the priestesses."

"Make excuses for him, if you like. His friend Ahbrem has told me stories of what he was like as a child. A bit of a wild one, apparently. Escaping over the monastery walls and so on."

"Just an ordinary boy, then," smiled Ship. "Was that the bell for dinner?"

Chapter 18

Ahbrem arrived at Khoulan with his bride, accompanied by Ship and the two human kings, on the evening of the following day. An extra two primers had to be asked to vacate their rooms and sleep in the student's dormitory so that the extra guests could have their beds. Wyn took up residence in the newly appointed married quarters, but Ahbrem went back to his own room. Kesh went to see him there to discuss last minute arrangements.

"Were you afraid that the community would disapprove if you went to the married quarters tonight?" he asked Ahbrem.

"I told Wyn that this is what would be expected. I think she understands."

"I am sure all the monks know that you are actually already married. They all know about the ceremony in Xoutha."

"I have told Wyn that I will not feel married, that I do not regard myself as properly married, until there has been a Morthern ceremony and a declaration before Harg."

"Oh," said Kesh. "That puts a rather large responsibility on my shoulders. I was telling myself that it was just going to be a formality."

"Kesh, I have something to confess."

"But you are perfect, Ahbrem," Kesh teased, his humour tinged with a little latent jealousy. "What actions of yours would ever cause you to have to make confessions?"

"This is serious, Kesh. It is difficult enough, without you making fun of me."

"Sorry," Kesh's expression became sombre. "What is it you want to confess?"

"We did not ... I could not ... On our wedding night, I was unable ... I told Wyn that I had decided to wait but that was just an excuse. Tomorrow night I will have no more excuses. Kesh, what am I going to do? She is going to have expectations that I may not be able to fulfil."

"Um ..." Kesh could not think of anything helpful to say. He had certainly felt 'able' himself when he had been sitting in the garden with Maina but he had no memories of his own abilities beyond that stage of the proceedings.

"Perhaps, if I just leave now and hide at another monastery... you could explain to her."

"No, no, no!" Kesh exclaimed "That is definitely not an option. The Prophet of the Burning Ship is here together with two human kings. The king and queen of Morth will be here by tomorrow, as well. Your wedding is the biggest social event this monastery has ever seen. If you have to run away, it cannot be until after the ceremony."

Ahbrem closed his eyes and swallowed.

"Alright. The ceremony takes place, but after that ..."

"Listen, Ahbrem. When you are properly married, in the sight of Harg, you may feel differently. Perhaps it is not just an excuse. Perhaps Harg really did not want you to ... perform until you were properly married. Once the ceremony is out of the way and you can relax and enjoy one another's company, the problem might just disappear. There is no rush. Give yourself time. Wyn is a lovely woman, handsome, earnest and devout. Enjoy her loveliness, and her love for you, and everything else will surely follow."

Ahbrem took a breath and blew it out between pursed lips.

"Alright. Yes. I must not pressurise myself. Relax, enjoy. You are right. I will try."

"No, do not 'try'. Stop 'trying', merely ... allow. Perhaps, tomorrow night, you should just tell her that you are very tired, that you just want to lie in her arms and enjoy being beside her. That way there will be no expectations. Ahbrem, we have both spent a life time denying ourselves the pleasure of the company of women. We cannot expect to change our ways of behaving overnight. I tell you what: if you still have problems after tomorrow's ceremony, I know of a certain magic potion they produce in Enaha that is bound to help. I will go and fetch you a bottle."

"I do hope I will not have to resort to magic potions. I do not approve of magic."

"Well, I am certain that you will have no need of it once you feel properly married."

***

The Morthern royal entourage arrived at Khoulan the following morning, bringing with them a cart piled high with food prepared in the royal kitchens together with several casks of wine. Khoulan's modest offerings would pale into insignificance once the monarch's gifts were laid on the table but the king's generosity meant that a feast was now available that would be fit for the most discerning of their royal guests.

As soon as the king and queen of Morth had alighted from their coach in the courtyard of Khoulan they were introduced to the humans. The Morthern king impressed Ahbrem by remembering to thank King Nathan for the bible he had been sent.

"Did you find it inspirational?" asked Nathan hopefully.

"Well, I haven't read it all yet," said the king.

"Ah, you must persevere with it. There are some very important concepts explained in its pages."

"Yes, I am sure."

"You worship one god, I understand, as we do. I am sure that you will find that you can relate to it quite easily. More easily than the Xouthans, say."

The king did not like his people being compared to the Xouthans and he was not altogether sure that being expected to relate to King Nathan's religion more easily was a very great compliment.

"Quite possibly," he said.

"Once you have had a chance to read it all, I would like to ask for your permission to preach in Morth."

"To preach?" the king was a little taken aback that a king would want to take up preaching.

"Yes. The purpose of translating the bible into the common tongue was to make it accessible to the whole of your people. I observe that you speak what you call the Sacred Language perfectly well yourself but I understand that there are many people in Morth who do not."

"Ah well, permission to preach is a matter for the Council of the Clergy. I am not the right authority to consult on such matters."

"I see. So how would I go about contacting them?"

"You should speak to Mattouk Kesh," the king told him.

"Ah!" Nathan was not happy to learn that his prospects would depend on Kesh's intercessions. "Thank you. I will."

Ahbrem had stood by patiently waiting to introduce Wyn. Now he stepped forwards, bowed and greeted the king. Holding out his hand towards Wyn he said:

"It is my honour to present to you my bride, Wyn of Khoulan."

"Aha! A local lass," the king said. "I am pleased to find that someone as well travelled as you still recognises the excellent qualities of our beautiful Morthern ladies."

Wyn bowed low while Ahbrem coloured noticeably.

"Um ... K ... Kesh is the well-travelled man amongst us," he finally stammered.

"Indeed," the king agreed and turned to Wyn. "I am very pleased to meet you, my dear. I wish you a long and happy marriage."

"Thank you," Wyn said quietly in her best imitation of a Morthern accent, bowing her head again.

Kesh had been standing to one side while the introductions had been made. He coughed nervously.

"If everyone is ready?" he said and turned to lead the way in through the door of the main chapel.

Grenholt ushered the royal guests into their places while the choir sang a gentle hymn of praise. They started into a robust celebratory anthem during which Ahbrem led his bride to the front of the chapel where Kesh waited, facing the central aisle. Nathan had been uneasy about entering the holy place of another religion. He felt that he was committing a sin, betraying his beliefs. However, he now noted that, although the monks' singing sounded very strange, the chapel layout and the couple standing before the celebrant (he could not bring himself to call Kesh a priest) looked comfortingly familiar.

Once the couple were standing before him, Kesh caught his friend's eye and smiled as warmly as his own anxiety would allow. The singing stopped. The chapel was silent. This was it. Kesh looked at his own king and queen and told himself: 'Uncle and aunt, uncle and aunt.' He looked at the three humans, pale and freshly alien in this setting. 'Dear friends, just dear friends.' Well, Ship was a dear friend anyway, one of several rounds standing now. He looked beyond them at the courtiers of the royal entourage, grand military men and noblemen, a few of whom were known to him. 'What was it that great uncle Calim had once said to him? "Think of them as rows of gourde-cabbage." Yes, rows of cabbages, rows of cabbages.' Someone coughed and the sound elongated through the silence, echoing around the stone pillars. 'Just pretend it is another rehearsal before the mirror.' He took a breath.

"Ahbrem of Khoulan and Wyn of Khoulan, you have summoned these chosen guests here today to witness the promises you are about to make to Harg and to each other. Once these promises are made, you are bound by Harg to honour them, and the witnesses here present have a duty to remind you of your promises, should you appear to falter, and to seek to encourage you in your efforts to maintain them."

'The worst is over with', Kesh told himself. 'The opening section recited with not a single stutter.'

A seacrow squawked from the chapel roof as if to prompt him to continue. Kesh felt sure the tiles were not as good at soundproofing as the thatch that they had so recently replaced.

"Ahbrem of Khoulan, please repeat the words I utter. I, Ahbrem of Khoulan, hereby vow before Harg to bind myself to Wyn of Khoulan, to care for and support her, and to care for and support all the children she may bear me, for all my life."

Ahbem repeated. Then, it was:

"I, Wyn of Khoulan, hereby vow before Harg to bind myself to Ahbrem of Khoulan, to care for and support him and to care for and support all the children he may give me, for all my life."

Wyn answered quietly but seemed to remember most of the changes to her pronunciation that Ahbrem had suggested. Kesh's anxieties diminished. Further traditional Morthern vows and promises followed and then it was time for the exchange of tokens. Grenholt passed Ahbrem's token to him and he pinned it carefully to Wyn's cape. Mittan had been elected to stand in for Wyn's seconder and he fumbled in the folds of his habit searching for the token. After a few moments, Kesh pulled a spare token out of his own pocket and thrust it towards Mittan, who handed it to Wyn. She pinned it onto Ahbrem's habit but looked distressed. It wasn't the token she had chosen for him. Kesh nodded, trying to convey reassurance with his smile, trying to let her know that it was alright, that they would replace it with the right one later. The seacrow cried again and Wyn looked up anxiously. Kesh wondered if the bird's calls were upsetting her. Perhaps she was prone to superstition and was reading this calling as an inauspicious omen. Kesh caught her eye, nodded encouragingly and smiled again.

"I hereby declare you Mr and Mrs Ahbrem of Khoulan," he announced and slowly raised his hands and eyes heavenwards. "Almighty Harg, god of all things, bless this marriage made here today, we pray. Guide these your servants with your love so that they may show love and mercy to each other, to be quick to praise and slow to chide, to cherish happiness and forgive mistakes, to use their love to soothe away pain and welcome pleasure, to serve you every day and in all ways better, dedicating their love and their lives to your praise and honour. Hear our prayers, almighty Harg."

Most of the congregation then responded "Hear our Prayers."

Once the chapel was silent again, the choir master raised his arms and the choir burst into a sudden and vigorous song of celebration, voices soaring and cascading in multiple harmonies, filling the chapel with a sound that set the rafters ringing. They had been practicing, Kesh could tell. Ahbrem offered his arm to Wyn. They turned and walked in time to the music along the aisle and out of the chapel. Congratulations began as soon as the congregation began to spill out behind them. As the harmonies of the choir reached a crescendo and then fell silent, a faint whirring sound began to build in the air and shadows flickered across the faces of the guests. Ahbrem looked up and saw a flock of seacrows circling directly above them. They began to swoop and a few birds dipped right into the quadrangle before circling high again. One bird in particular swooped down right in front of Ahbrem. Wyn surpressed a cry of alarm and clung tightly to him, hiding her face on his shoulder. He put his arm around her, hugging her to him, and chuckled as he recognised Sakki dipping his flight in front of him. The birds were calling softly to one another, not the usual raucous squawk, but a more musical cooing that Ahbrem had never heard them make before. They circled lower, winding into a tighter spiral, turning above the chapel roof and skimming through the courtyard, all the while calling softly, filling the air with the rush of wings and the hum of their voices.

"Ha! They're saluting us!" he told Wyn.

She still winced at every close swoop of feathers, but Ahbrem was filled with joy. It made him feel elated, justified, energised, powerful. He raised his arm and lifted his face, wanting to reach in and become part of the swirling celebration.

Nathan was observing the scene from the edge of the courtyard. He thought the monks' singing had sounded alien enough but this was far stranger. As the birds rose and fell through the air, so their eerie calls rose and fell in discordant arpeggios, making a sound that cast his mind back to childhood when a high wind would sometimes set the old electricity cables into a melancholy wailing all along the length of the road that linked their settlement to the next. Then again, perhaps it was more like the sound that had come from the antique humming top his grandfather had once shown him. That old metal toy had created strange harmonies rising and falling according to how fast the handle had been pumped, another memory from childhood that he had not thought about for many years. The strange song was accompanied by a yet stranger sight. Nathan had never experienced anything like it. One bird kept dipping down right in front of Ahbrem. He could see that it was always the same bird. He followed it round with his eyes. This was surely not natural behaviour for these creatures. Some other force was operating here. There were people in his old church who would have assumed that this was the devil's work, this whirling mass of dark feathered birds, but Ahbrem was smiling, and that monk was no demon, or Nathan was no judge of character. Ahbrem could be stubbornly unreceptive to the Christian message but his heart was true.

He was a good man, Nathan was sure of that, therefore he had to conclude that it must be the hand of God guiding these flying creatures, and if God was acknowledging Ahbrem's goodness, then so would he. His regard for Ahbrem doubled from that moment on.

After circling twenty times or more the seacrows flew high into the sky and dispersed in different directions and the guests, discussing the event appreciatively, as if it had been planned like a display of fireworks, made their way towards the dining hall. Wyn was still trembling. Ahbrem grinned, kissed her forehead, and hugging her tight, lifted her off the ground and swung her around. He was, he told her, the happiest man alive. After looking into his shining eyes she was reassured. She smiled back at him.

Towards the end of the feasting, Kesh approached the King of Morth and requested an armed guard, perhaps four good men, he suggested, to be allocated to him in order to accompany him to the Land of the Four Kings to fetch Hernst. He explained about the attempted murder, how he was partly to blame and how Doug now wanted him to keep Hernst in exile at Khoulan. He took the king to where Doug and Ship were sitting together. Doug confirmed Kesh's story and told the king that he would be very grateful if they could take charge of Hernst, as having him at the palace was giving him nightmares. The king agreed and Kesh thanked him, heartily relieved. Kesh asked Doug to provide an official letter for him to take to the Land of the Four Kings explaining the situation to Kings Kevin and Ted and asking them to release Hernst to Kesh. He suggested that he should return the prisoner to Khoulan via Ahn Dehar, in order to reassure Hernst's mother as to his health and well being and that, while he was there, he would begin the negotiations for rights to mine for copper in place of coal.

A little while later Ahbrem and Wyn took a turn round the hall, thanking their guests for attending and wishing them all goodnight. When they reached Kesh, he attempted to give Ahbrem a sympathetically reassuring smile, expecting him to be apprehensive about going with Wyn to the married quarters but Ahbrem gave him an altogether cheerful embrace and seemed to have forgotten his concerns. He had been grinning from ear to ear since walking out of the chapel door.

The King of Morth declined Kesh's invitation to sleep at the monastery. There were about twenty nobles in the entourage. He could not foresee there being enough space at Khoulan to accommodate them all and they had not brought sufficient kit to camp. He and the queen withdrew a short while later, followed by the humans who were to spend a second night in the primers' rooms. Kesh helped with the clearing away. Although the guests had eaten and drunk their fill, there was going to be plenty to eat up the following day. Kesh stacked the remains on the shelves in the cool underground pantry, all the while worrying about Ahbrem. He hoped that he was sleeping peacefully in Wyn's arms by now. He sympathised with the problem Ahbrem had confided to him and yet could not help wishing that it was *he* who was in the married quarters, sleeping in Maina's arms, that the seacrows had sung for him instead of for Wyn and his best friend. When he climbed the stone steps back to the kitchens he found that the other monks were leaving, wishing one another a good night.

"You had best to bed, my Lord," Grenholt told him, wiping his hands on a tea-towel. "Your first wedding and, indeed, Khoulan's first wedding, is now over. Your work is done."

"Do you think it went alright, Grenholt?"

"I think it went excellent well, my Lord. You should be very proud."

"Thank you, Grenholt. Your support is much appreciated. I will go to my bed then. Goodnight to you."

"Good night, my Lord."

Chapter 19

"I hardly slept at all," Doug said to Nathan, reining in his horse before they started up the mountain, giving Ship a chance to catch them up. "How those monks can sleep on those hard mattresses every night I'll never know."

"I have every respect for how they live. I think God approves of them. We all saw a little miracle yesterday, don't you think? The way those birds flew round Ahbrem after the service. You can't tell me that was natural behaviour."

"It was a little weird," Doug conceded.

"But beautiful, too. Like a host of black angels descending from the skies."

"Could angels actually be black?"

"Before yesterday, I would have said no, but now I think I'm reassessing my evaluations. It didn't feel in any way bad, what happened, you know? I didn't sense any presence of evil, no fear or foreboding. I just felt like I was witnessing something really special, like we were truly privileged to be there."

"Mmm ... Maybe."

"I believe it was a message, a sign, telling us that Ahbrem is very special and we must heed his words."

"You don't think he's ... I know you are hoping for a Second Coming, but Ahbrem doesn't seem ... "

"No, it's not him, but I think he has a purpose. I think Ahbrem is here to prepare the way. He told me months ago about a special child they have the care of. A child born to a virgin mother, a child with no Penethellan father. He is the one we have to find."

Doug frowned.

"Really?"

Ship was getting closer.

"You alright?" Doug called out.

"Fine, fine," Ship called back. "I'm still a little stiff from the journey there, that's all. I'll be glad to get back home."

Doug cast a final glance at Nathan but knew he would have to move on to a different subject.

"I've been thinking," he announced, once Ship had caught up. "I reckon I'm going to organise a dive on the ship in the next day or two. It's autumn here already, and the weather will be deteriorating pretty soon. I'm going to pick a low tide and see if I can get inside. I reckon one dive to clean round the door, maybe two. Then I'll try the opening mechanism. If it doesn't work, I'll have to rig up some sort of system to pump air down there, but I won't waste my time fiddling around making a pump unless I know it's going to be absolutely necessary." He turned to Nathan "Will you be my man topside? You up for that?"

"It was Nathan's turn to shrug, "I suppose. Don't go taking any risks, though. I don't fancy having to go down to retrieve your soggy corpse."

"No," Ship joined in. "Don't go pushing your luck. What you are likely to find down there just isn't worth it."

"But what if you're wrong? I'm willing to bet that I'll find the ship's in better shape than you think."

"I can understand that you have to go inside and see for yourself," said Ship. "So I suppose the sooner you get it out of your system, the better."

Doug shook his head. "I may surprise you yet. Anyway, I have been more cheerful since I've had something else to think about, you have to admit. At least diving down to the ship has taken my mind off being murdered in my bed."

"Poor Doug," said Ship.

"Come on," said Nathan. "I can see that church we passed, through the trees. Time to start the climb up the mountain."

***

The morning sun was shining into Kesh's room by the time he woke. A second knock made him realise that he had been woken deliberately. The door was pushed open a little way.

"Kesh? Are you there?" asked Ahbrem.

"Yes, I am here. Are you unwell? You have come away from the married quarters rather early, I observe. Is everything alright?"

"Everything is very alright, Kesh, and it is not early in any sense of the word. The sun is not far short of its zenith."

"Oh," said Kesh, wrestling himself to a sitting position. "So ... um ... did you sleep well?"

"Very well, thank you."

"And did you tell Wyn that you were tired, as I suggested?"

"No. Not exactly."

"Oh. So did you ... ?"

Ahbrem beamed.

"And ... how was it?"

"It was ... mm ... ah ... indescribable," Ahbrem laughed. "As you should know."

"I do not remember," Kesh said, shaking his head sadly.

"Then you cannot be Calim's father!" Ahbrem wheeled himself around, his face upturned, as if he was about to dance round the room. "Kesh if you had ever done what I have just done with a woman you loved as much as I love Wyn, then you would remember. There is no chance that you would not be aware of what you were doing, or that you could be aware and then forget."

"Oh," said Kesh glumly. "I am very happy for you."

Kesh was a monk, and duty bound to utter only truth, yet he had just told an outright lie, for Ahbrem had just wrenched one of his most precious possessions from him and he was not at all 'happy'. The relationship he cherished most dearly, that gave most meaning to his life at Khoulan, had been challenged. The person he loved the most in the world after Maina was being denied a connection to him. Kesh knew that Ahbrem had not made his comment deliberately to hurt him but to step ahead of him into love and married bliss and then to deny the validity of the only other loving relationship in Kesh's life would have been unforgivably cruel of Ahbrem, had he had the slightest inkling that he was doing it.

"Oh, here is the marriage token you gave to Mittan," Ahbrem was saying. "He discovered that he had left the one Wyn had chosen for me on the table in his room, so I have it now. Look!"

He proudly held out the cloth of his habit to display the new pin.

"Very nice," said Kesh.

"So how come you had a spare?"

"It was my grandfather's, Mattouk Calim's brother's. It came to me when he died. I put it in my pocket before the ceremony on an impulse. I do not know why."

"I am so glad you did. Thank you for the loan of it, anyway."

"You are welcome."

"Come to breakfast," Ahbrem entreated him. "Or, rather, come to lunch. My wife is preparing food and she sent me here to fetch you."

"What about the humans? Should we not be saying goodbye?"

"The humans left long ago, before even I was up. Grenholt says he offered to wake us, but they told him to let us sleep. We needed time to recover from the pressures of the last few days, Ship told him, apparently. He must have meant the Xouthan wedding, I suppose."

Kesh remembered his missed night of sleep in Xoutha and realised that, although he had not been aware of tiredness, it must have finally caught up with him.

"Ah, well, we had better not keep your wife waiting, I suppose."

Kesh went with Ahbrem and ate at the little table with its crisp checkered cloth laid in the newly whitewashed room with its little stove and sink. Wyn seemed flushed with the same exuberance that had taken over his old friend, normally so restrained. She did not seem to mind the restricted space or sparse furnishings. The scene sparked a deep memory in Kesh, one that belonged to a time before his present life, a time he had tried not to think about for so many rounds. It was as though she were playing at tea parties, as Kesh's sister had once done, making Kesh sit at a little table with her toys and pretend to drink out of tiny cups and eat off tiny plates, at a time when Kesh had been part of a family and had felt loved and cared for, before he had been abandoned at the monastery.

Kesh drank the tea gratefully and ate a little, but he did not stay long. He thanked the newly-weds but said that he would leave them to it and take the afternoon to visit Calim.

It was an unscheduled visit but he was doing it for Maina. If he was to keep a proper check on Calim's foster family, he should make occasional unscheduled visits. He told himself this as he rode the horse at a steady pace westwards from Khoulan. Even if he were not his son, Calim was Maina's child and Maina was his love, the woman who had pressed herself to him only three days beforehand, returning his kisses with such a mix of tenderness and passion that he had become intoxicated, befuddled to the extent that his powers of reason seemed briefly to abandon him. He would visit the child on her behalf.

He questioned himself afresh about his relationship to the boy. Maina had seemed so sure that he, Kesh, was the father. Hannala had told Kesh at the birth that Calim had his eyes. That had helped to convince him for, although he might have doubted Maina at the start, what cause had he ever had to doubt the word of Principal Hannala? He owed so much to her. That woman had gone so far out of her way to help him, concealing him during the war, devoting hours of her time, not to mention the considerable effort expended in teaching him the Xouthan language. He could never believe that she would ever have endeavoured to deceive him.

When he reached the small farm where Calim's nurse family lived, Kesh tied his horse to a fence and pushed open the gate into the yard. Garden-fowl clucked and complained as they bustled out from under his feet. He knocked on the door. He could hear muffled sounds from the other side. A smell of baking stole through the cracks in the woodwork.

"Well, well," said the man who opened it, speaking in Morthern. "Marda, look who it is!"

"Oh, Goodness me. Mattouk Kesh! We are honoured. Do come in. Oh dear, you'll have to excuse the mess," Marda cleared two used baking tins off the table. She tucked a stray strand of her hair back in place, only to leave it feathered with flour. "There, you sit down, and I'll get you some tea. Calim?" she called out. "Calim, come and see who's here. Now, where's he got to? I can't take my eyes off him for a moment. He's always into something. Calim, where have you gone?"

She pulled back a curtain over a doorway and there stood the child, wide eyed, sucking one finger, his face decorated with smears of jam. Behind him three other children looked up from their activities, the youngest being Calim's nurse-sister. A grey haired man dozed beyond them in a fireside chair.

"Matty Keth! Matty Keth!" Calim Bradmutt pointed, his face breaking into a broad smile, but he was quickly swept up and carried to the sink to have it scrubbed off him.

A moment later he was set down on the floor and he ran to Kesh, arms outstretched. Kesh bent to pick him up, his small body taught and easy to lift. The little arms wrapped around Kesh's neck and the mattouk buried his face in Calim's diminutive shoulder, breathing in his smell, boiled cotton and kitchen soap, feeling loved and loving in return. Yes, they loved each other, that was the important thing, was it not? What did biological technicalities matter to this tiny child? Kesh rubbed his tears into the child's clothes, hoping to conceal his upwelling of emotion.

"Now then, tea," Marda said, turning away and busying herself, filling a kettle at the tap.

Kesh sat at the table with Calim on his knee for the rest of the afternoon. He was given tea and cake and, those parts which he did not give to Calim, he ate so hungrily that he was quickly offered a second portion. He told them all about the wedding and how it was the first one at Khoulan. It felt strange to have to express himself in the Morthern language again. He found himself having to search for the right word now and then, struggling as he might do if he were speaking Enahet. He told them also about the seacrows and their strange song.

"Ah, yes," said Calim's foster father sitting at the other end of the table. "I've heard of them doing that before. Swarming, I've heard it called, but I don't rightly know what causes it. All the juveniles and parents flying round and round together, like a gathering of the tribe. It doesn't happen often, though. I've never witnessed it myself."

"Well, what goings on!" Marda exclaimed. "No wonder you needed to take a breather."

"I did," Kesh agreed. "And I feel better for it. Thank you so much for your hospitality."

"Well, you're welcome anytime, Mattouk Kesh, you know you are."

He asked if their payments came through regularly, and they assured him that they did. He apologised for not having anything to offer them himself.

"No, no, not at all. You monks make sacrifices the rest of us couldn't contemplate," Marda told him.

'That is true,' thought Kesh. 'But it is not the money that I miss.'

Out loud he said, "I would have liked to bring something for little Calim. It was his second birthday half a moon ago, was it not? Wait, what do I have?"

He slipped his hand into his pocket and pulled out his grandfather's marriage token.

"Perhaps a strange gift for a child, but I will call it a memento of the wedding."

Kesh told them the story of Mittan leaving the real one in his room.

"It may be a little sharp," he warned as he passed the pin to Marda. "You'd better keep it for him until he's older."

He took his leave a short while later, feeling refreshed and reassured.

'Ahbrem is wrong,' he told himself as the horse stepped briskly back to Khoulan. 'If not I, then who? The Enahet have potions, but I cannot imagine any of those good people drugging Maina in order to take advantage of her. Besides, I was with her nearly every moment. The woodsman, yes, but Maina did not meet him until after she had been experiencing symptoms. There was no-one else. On other hand, we were both a little drunk and, if we had begun to kiss as we did three nights ago then, as Maina implied, our inhibitions might have loosed their normal hold, and our reason may well have escaped us. I still think I could be Calim's father. I was feeling guilty at having given my grandfather's marriage token away on an impulse but now I am sure it has gone to the right person. It is only proper that it should pass to Calim.'

Chapter 20

Cleaning the hull was harder than Doug expected and he wasn't that good at holding his breath. It had taken half a dozen dives just to locate the remains of the ship in the bay and another two to find a hatchway. Then it had taken him several more to clean around the outline of the door. He had spent what little time each breath gave him working away at barnacle-like encrustations with one of the chisels that had been delivered for Nathan's carpenters. He had a problem finding the control panel. It wasn't on the right, where it logically should have been, but on the left. It was dead, of course. In frustration he punched it with his fist as hard as the viscosity of the water would allow. To his amazement a light flickered under the green slime. He went back to the surface to get air. Nathan was reading now instead of looking out for him over the side of the boat, as he had done for the first couple of dives.

"Anything?" he asked in a voice that expected little.

"Got a light on the control panel," Doug gasped between gulps of air.

"Really?"

Doug nodded and grinned.

"Be careful. One light doesn't mean the whole mechanism is in good order."

"I will be."

Doug took another deep breath and dived again.

He plugged in the opening sequence on the control panel. Nothing. He tried again. Still nothing. Another surfacing for air and down again. Third time lucky. The hatch opened about a quarter of its full span. Doug tried helping it. In fits and starts, it opened some more until it had cleared about three quarters of its span. Good enough. Doug headed for the surface.

"Okay, I need you now," he told Nathan as he trod water. "Dive down and I'll show you where the hatch is. Do you remember how to operate it?"

"Remind me."

Doug reminded him. "Then I want you to dive down about two minutes behind me to see if the airlock is emptying, because if it doesn't I will need to get out but I'm worried that it might stick and I'll get trapped inside."

"And what happens if I can't shift it?"

"Then you come back to the surface and fetch the crowbar."

"So that I can get your body out? Can't we just bury you at sea? Come on, Doug. It's too dangerous. It's crazy. Just leave it."

"I'm doing it whether you help or not. Two dives, that's all I'm asking. Two dives to save the human race."

"Yeah, yeah, like that's ever going to happen. It's just a dream. It's never going to work."

"Maybe not, but I'm going to try. You coming or not?"

"It looks cold."

"Actually, it isn't. Well, for the first minute or two, perhaps, but it's really quite warm. Best time of year for a swim. Just come down and see the old girl, at least."

"Okay, okay. One dive, and then I'll decide, okay?"

"Good man. Come on then."

Nathan rolled into the water and gasped, flailing his arms.

"It's freezing!"

"You'll soon warm up. Ready?"

Nathan followed Doug down and saw the vessel's hull looming out of the green gloom. Memories flooded back. The day they arrived at the orbiting space station and saw the newly constructed ship still attached to it, like a baby before the cord is cut, that was the only time he had seen the outside of the ship in full before today. It looked smaller now, less impressive. Doug showed him where the hatch was, where the control panel was, but Nathan was bursting for air and had to surface.

"Well?" Doug asked, waiting for him to get his breath back.

"I guess, if you're determined to go in, I'm going to feel obliged to come and check on you but I still think it's too dangerous. I wish I could persuade you not to try."

"Great!" said Doug, ignoring his last comment. "Right, count to two hundred, then come down and check."

"Doug!" Nathan protested but Doug had dived.

Nathan counted and went down. At first he couldn't see the ship in the gloom. Had he veered off course? Then it was there ahead of him. What would he find? He imagined having to resurface for tools and wished he'd taken something with him. He pictured having to go back and then diving again, too late, and fetching Doug out, and trying, and failing, to revive him, lifting, dragging him, limp and lifeless, into the boat.

He got to the hatchway. Doug was inside, lit by a yellowish light but not easy to make out because of all the growth on the window. Nathan just caught the grin on his face and a hand held up against the window making the okay sign, the water level halfway down the hatchway. He resurfaced and gulped the air in gratefully.

He sat shivering in the boat with a blanket around him for what seemed an age. He was just beginning to think that he would have to go down again to look for Doug when he saw bubbles, and a moment later Doug's head in the water.

"Never thought I could feel so pleased to see you!" he told him.

"I've re-pressurised the system and guess what."

"What?"

"Ship was wrong. There's no problem with the ship's power. The cryo-unit is still functioning and the contents are still frozen solid!"

***

Maina sat dozing in the carriage as it rattled and swayed over the rough roads to Mardek province. Occasionally she would open her eyes and watch the landscape passing but most of the journey was spent in reliving the previous evening. If it had been dark outside, her reflection in the window might have shown that her lips spread into a blissful half-smile whenever she thought about Kesh. She remembered him hesitating before asking her to dance and discovering that it was because he was unsure of the steps. Of course, he had managed admirably with a little help and guidance. Salwell, on the other hand, had no such inhibitions. He had asked her to dance many times. She hoped he had not forgotten her telling him that a relationship between them was impossible. Did he still harbour hopes? But she could not have refused to dance with her best friend's brother on her wedding day. That would have seemed too churlish. He had been a bit short with Kesh, though, she felt, and had constantly pushed in whenever Kesh had hesitated. He should have been a little more polite to the mattouk, his sister's only Mortherm guest. Or was that it? Perhaps Salwell was no better than other Xouthans. Perhaps he still regarded Mortherners as the enemy.

She wondered, as she studied the silhouette of a dead tree set against a bright white sky, how far Salwell's enmity had gone. As her father had pointed out, Salwell was responsible for sorting any written correspondence arriving at the palace. He would surely have realised that the letter addressed to her from Morth would be from Kesh. Did he deliberately put it in with the letters addressed to her father? Did he mean to ruin them, to betray her secret to the emperor? If so, was it general anti-Morthern feeling that had motivated him, or did he hope that she might still turn to him once Kesh was out of the way?

Maina was fully awake now and frowning. Perhaps she should no longer trust Salwell with her correspondence. More importantly, she should warn Kesh not to send correspondence through him and most certainly not via the palace. She decided that she had better write to him as soon as she got to the governor's residence and send the letter by messenger direct to Morth from Mardek.

Maina sent for the colonel the day after she arrived back. She asked him how the linguists were getting on with the prisoners from the Wildlands.

"They are not making very much progress, I am afraid," he told her. "I have chided them for their lack of success, but they complain that the Wildlanders are still refusing to cooperate and pretend to understand nothing that does not pertain to food and drink."

"I am reconsidering the validity of our current approach," she said. "Perhaps we are feeding them for nothing. I think we should send them back over the wall, perhaps with a few gifts to make sure they understand that we mean to do them no further harm."

"I think giving them gifts would just encourage them to attack again. You can't train a hound not to come into your bedchamber by giving it titbits every time it does so."

"Perhaps," agreed Maina. "What about if we gave them gifts specifically for women and children? Toys, dresses, strings of beads, and so on. That surely wouldn't encourage the young men to come back for more?"

"Why give them any gifts at all?"

"We have held them prisoner for too long. I wanted to be able to communicate with them but all we have communicated to them so far is that we are good at keeping people captive. I want to try to demonstrate our good will."

The colonel turned away from Maina and she imagined that he was rolling his eyes in exasperation. She couldn't even communicate with him, let alone with the Wildlanders.

"I would like to send a Xouthan explorer into the Wildlands after we have released the prisoners, if there is some way of keeping them safe," she went on. "I wondered if we might try sending a soldier dressed as a traveller together with his wife. I have heard that a young couple can seem less threatening than, say, two young men would be. Would you be willing to seek volunteers for such a journey? The man must be someone fresh, not anyone who would be recognised as a soldier or guard from previous encounters."

Maina was sure the pause before the colonel spoke contained a smothered sigh.

"I will request volunteers," he said.

Maina wished she could have volunteered herself. After the colonel had left, she fell into a reverie in which she and Kesh went off into the Wildlands to get to know its people and to escape the world where Morthener and Xouthan could not be seen openly together. It was a delicious dream but only that, a dream, and reality still had to be engaged with.

***

"Okay, so if it worked, although I can't see it ever working," Ship was talking to Doug. "But if it did and you got girl children, how long would you boys wait? Until they were sixteen? You got that much self-control? Or are you going to decide that they'll be old enough at twelve. Some cultures count them old enough at twelve, I seem to remember."

"Christ, not twelve!" exclaimed Doug. "They'd still be children!"

"And how are you going to determine their proper age, anyhow? Will you wait sixteen rounds? Maybe give it a little longer because the years pass by so quickly here?"

"You make it sound like they're going to be sold in a cattle market. They're not going to be our slaves."

"Aren't they? You see, that's just what I think it will be like for them. You are only trying to give them life because you want partners. They aren't going to have much choice when it comes to it. And, as well as being your partners, you'll want them to produce the next generation. That's all they're going to be born for. Sex and reproduction. What kind of a life is that?"

Doug had no answer. In desperation he turned to Nathan.

"You don't feel that way about it, do you?"

"You know I'm very unsure about the morality of this whole endeavour. I can see that you think of it as a way to save the human race, but this frozen embryo business is problematical all round."

Doug gave up trying to convince them he was right but the conversation did get him thinking. By the time he saw Ship and Nathan the next day he'd had time to come up with an idea.

"What if we each adopt some of the embryo children? Then we would undertake to limit ourselves to pairing off only with the female children of someone else's 'family' and not with our own. That way each child would have an adopted human father who could help to bring them up and who could protect them from exploitation."

"It sounds like an improvement on the original plan," Ship conceded. "You're still going to have the age difference, though. You are all middle-aged men and you're expecting to partner teenage girls."

"That's the way it was always going to be. That's what Brannan planned for, wasn't it?"

"I suppose so, but you're all a lot older now than you were when we first arrived. It's a pity you didn't come and find me and the ship straight away."

"I agree, but time is being very kind to all of us. You said yourself, the four of us have hardly aged since we arrived."

"True," Ship conceded. "Let's hope you can hold out another twenty years or so."

"I'm sure we'll manage," said Doug. "Right. Step one: get Ted to make the journey over so that he can thaw out the embryos and supervise the implantations."

"Step one should surely be to find Penethellan women who are willing to undergo the procedure and become, potentially, mothers of human children," said Ship.

"Well, Ted can deal with that, too," said Doug. "Penethellan women seem to adore him. He'll have no problem finding volunteers."

"We'll have to make sure they understand exactly what they are doing," said Nathan. "Having a human child will change their lives, especially if they're going to help bring them up."

"Have you thought about how we're going to feed them?" asked Ship. "There was a supply of formula on the ship but I've no idea if it would be okay to feed it to babies after all this time."

"Perhaps the Penethellan mothers will be willing to nurse them," suggested Doug.

"Then you might get compatibility problems all over again," Nathan put in.

"First things first," said Doug. "We have no idea that the implantations are going to work. I think it's a little too early to be worrying about how we're going to feed them."

"Yeah, let them be born only to starve to death, why don't you?" Nathan said cuttingly.

"At least let's wait and see what Ted says about it. He's the astrobiologist."

"Astrobiologist! What we need is a gynaecologist and a paediatrician. It will be a miracle if Ted's know-how is going to be sufficient to get your plan to work."

"Then pray for us, Nathan," Doug said, and turned to leave. From the study doorway he said, "I'm going to write a note to Ted. Can we send a messenger there, Ship?"

"Sure," he answered. "I'll ask Hannala to send for one to come here from Zoradetra."

The door closed.

Nathan sighed. "I'd like it to work, really I would, but I think Doug will have to prepare for disappointment."

"Let's see what Ted says, shall we? Doug will listen to him, I think." Ship decided it was time to change the subject. "How's the etherium coming on?"

"Not bad. Not bad at all. The supporting framework's all in place and they've started boarding over the floor."

"Good," Ship said. "Got any converts yet?"

"No, but I'm looking forwards to talking to Ahbrem when he comes back off his honeymoon."

"Honeymoon? Half a moon at his old monastery? Doesn't sound like much of a honeymoon to me."

"It's a half a moon when he's not doing the translation work he promised to carry out."

"As an unpaid volunteer. I think you expect too much."

"I offered to pay him. He says he can't accept because he's a monk, so he suggested I donate something to the monastery."

"And will you?"

"I gave some Wadderhick gold to the chief administrator after the wedding."

"Ah, good."

"I keep thinking about those seacrows singing. That was magical, wasn't it, the birds circling round and round and humming?"

"Very eerie, yes, and very beautiful."

"I can't help feeling there was more to that than meets the eye. There must be something very special about Ahbrem for the Lord to cause the birds to pay him homage, don't you think? I think we should listen to him more carefully, pay more attention to what he says."

"He is a good man, right enough, but I always get the impression that it all comes naturally to him, almost too easily. Kesh, now, he's a character I can have sympathy with. He's more human, if you like, more prone to mishaps. His heart's in the right place but things never go quite to plan for him."

"Ahbrem holds Kesh in high regard, and I respect his opinion, but even Ahbrem knows Kesh has his limitations."

"Isn't Kesh going to your palace to fetch his murderous friend? He could perhaps take Doug's note to Ted for him."

"As you have just admitted, Kesh has a habit of getting into mishaps. It might be better to send it by messenger. Anyway, maybe it would be better for him to wait until Doug goes back before fetching Hernst. We don't want him at Khoulan while Doug is still here."

"And when will that be, do you think? I'm very happy to have the company but you have your translation and Doug has his save-the-human-race project. I don't see either of you going back any time soon, and now Ted is being fetched over. Why don't you all just make your homes over here?"

"Hmm. Poor Kevin. He's going to be on his own. I hadn't thought of that till now. Perhaps you're right. On the other hand, I thought Doug was going to mine copper and make wind turbines. He might want to go back for that once Ted starts over here."

"And do you think Ted will come? He might just tell Doug that the embryos have no chance and not bother setting off."

"I think he'll come. He's the only one who hasn't visited you yet. He'll come over to see you, even if he sees no possibilities in Doug's big plan."

A messenger set off for the Land of the Four Kings two days later and Doug sent one of the carpenters back to Khoulan to tell Kesh that he did not want him to fetch Hernst until he was due to return home himself.

Chapter 21

Kesh was not altogether happy to receive Doug's message. It was difficult to accept that he was not going to be allowed to fetch Hernst to Khoulan straight away, and he was concerned about the Ahn Dehar. Afterall, when he had left them, he had only intended to come back to Morth for the wedding. By now, his translator, Wanhild, would be back with the tribe, so it was time for Kesh to go back himself to see if he could do anything to help. He had good news to give them, after all. He hoped they would be pleased to hear that Hernst was soon going to be released into his charge, as he was pretty sure that they trusted him enough to know that Hernst's life would no longer be under threat once at Khoulan. He hoped that they would then be happy enough to let Applad go home. Moreover, the prospect of selling copper mining rights in place of coal was good news for their economy. The problem was that some Ahn Dehar would be against selling anything to the Four Kings. Kesh decided he would seek out a mineral mining company in Wadderhick. If he could find a mining concern based in neutral territory and offer to put the company in touch with both potential supplier and eager customer, he hoped that the mountain tribe's copper might seem an attractive proposition to them.

Even if he couldn't bring Hernst back, it still seemed a good time to visit the Ahn Dehar. Ahbrem and Wyn were still at Khoulan and, once they returned to the Sacred Mountain, Grenholt could take over. It no longer mattered if both mattouk and mattouk designate were away at the same time.

It was too late in the season to use the Dinash pass and the sea route from Odout, so Kesh went south, called in at the Sacred Mountain to see his friends, and then set off down the Xouthan road to Larkat. This was his first time travelling alone and he was still nervous about passing through Xouthan territory, despite having a better grasp of the language now. He appreciated the company of the seacrow that seemed to watch his every step. On the long trek through Anthrakat, Sakki was there to beg crumbs at each meal and to drink next to Kesh's horse at each watering place.

The sea passage was not so easy this time. Winter storms blew the ship forwards at a great pace one day, and then drove it far off course the next. Kesh had many extra days to play dice and learn more songs on the pig-lute while the sailors struggled with slippery wet decks and unruly, flapping sails. He was glad when he caught sight of land at last and could look forward to a night in a bed that was not constantly moving beneath him.

He disembarked at the port and led his horse up to the palace of the Four Kings. He wanted to see Hernst and find out how he would feel about moving to Khoulan. Kesh hoped that Hernst would see it as an improvement on being held in the dungeon at the palace but had begun to fear that he might view it as being forced into exile across the sea. Would Hernst, in fact, regard detention in Morth as worse than being held closer to home?

But before seeing Hernst, Kesh looked forward to spending an evening with the kings, especially his old friend, King Kevin. By the time he arrived he found that Ted was already on his way to the Sacred Mountain – their ships must have passed at sea – and that King Kevin was ruling the land alone. He was pleased to have a visitor.

"It must be difficult, having to run things on your own." Kesh suggested as they sat down to a meal in the palace kitchens soon after his arrival.

"No, not really. Things pretty much run themselves here now but it is very quiet without any of the others. I hope they come back soon."

Kesh nodded. "You will gather from Doug's letter that he is going to allow me to take Hernst to Khoulan once he returns to the palace."

"I'm all for that," said Kevin. "I rather suspect that Hernst would be happy to murder me as a stand in for Doug, if he were given half a chance."

"How is he?"

"Hernst? He seems just fine. Not very talkative but still vigorously resentful."

"But you never wanted him executed."

"I don't think that makes me immune from his hatred. I'm still a human. And he's right to be resentful. I went along with that plan to kill his father. Never said a word against it. Ted was the only one who voiced an objection."

Kesh took advantage of the fact that he was speaking to King Kevin without any of the other humans present. Even so, it was with some trepidation that he said:

"You sound as if you feel some remorse for that inaction. Have you ever thought of apologising?"

"Apologising? For what? Not speaking against it?"

"Yes."

"I don't see how that would change anything."

"Perhaps you might like to suggest to Doug that he apologises, as well."

"Oh, that would go down really well! Tell Doug to apologise to the guy who tried to murder him? I can't ever see that happening, I'm afraid."

"Well, it was just a thought. I would like to stop Hernst's pain somehow. It is a pain that I caused him in part, of course, by telling him about the poisoning. I know I am at least partly to blame for the present situation. I feel I must continue to make efforts to put things right, if I can. I thought that, if we all apologised, some of the resentment he feels might be assuaged."

"Well, I'll think about it, I suppose. I guess apologising for my own part wouldn't do me any harm."

"No, I am certain that it would not."

"Humph!"

King Kevin took him down to the dungeon and told the guard to let Kesh in to see Hernst. This time Kesh went right into Hernst's cell. Hernst wasn't in shackles but the cell had very little furniture, the floor was dirty and the walls looked damp. Kesh was used to sparse furnishings but at least the rooms at Khoulan were clean and dry.

'This is no place for a man to spend his life,' Kesh said to himself. Then out loud he said, "The kings are going to let me take you to Khoulan as soon as King Doug comes back from the Sacred Mountain. Would you like to go to Khoulan? You would still be a prisoner, officially, but you will be able to roam around the monastery. I think you would find it more comfortable there."

"I would be very happy to see your home," Hernst answered. "But I would rather see my own."

"We may be able to visit Ahn Dehar on the way but you would not be able to stay, I am afraid. I understand the kings have sentenced you to life-long imprisonment?"

Hernst nodded.

"I will continue to make efforts to change their minds," said Kesh. "But, for now, I can only hope to make your imprisonment a little more bearable by taking you with me to Khoulan as soon as they will allow it."

Hernst nodded again and then asked, "What news is there regarding the coal? Have you been able to find my people an alternative income?"

"Possibly. I hear that there is copper in the mountains of the Ahn Dehar. I am going to see if there is a mining company in Wadderhick that would be interested in it. How would you feel if they then sold the copper to the Four Kings? Would you want to control who the copper was sold on to?"

"I suppose not. As long as the Ahn Dehar do not have to do business directly with the Four Kings, I don't think the eventual fate of the copper will matter much."

"Good. You see, I have heard that the kings might want to purchase certain quantities of copper in the near future. I hoped that mentioning a potential customer to the Wadderhick mining company might encourage them to buy from you."

"I thought you told me that you were no business man. It seems to me that you might have quite a good nose for business."

"Other peoples' business, perhaps. I hope that I may be able to put one particular business in touch with a potential customer who has certain needs but I would not want to be the one handling the ensuing negotiations."

"Let Wanhild take charge of the negotiations. He will act for my mother. I trust him to act in the interest of all the Ahn Dehar."

"Very well," said Kesh. "I must now get to Ahn Dehar as soon as possible. Now that I can stop worrying about the possibility of the Four Kings executing you, I have to arrange for Applad to be released."

Kesh told Hernst the story of what had happened on his last visit to the Ahn Dehar and how he had regretted, afterwards, that an innocent man was being held captive and kept from his family."

"And I am not an innocent man!" Hernst exclaimed disconsolately.

"You were the victim of a very evil deed. Of that I have no doubt, but you are not innocent of bad intentions. For all I know, you would still gladly murder any human that happened across your path."

"I am not like you, Kesh. My hand will do what my heart decrees, not what some higher power defines as 'right'. Your god leads you towards righteousness. Our gods are happy for us to follow our instincts and my instinct tells me that the Four Kings should pay for what they did and that I should be the instrument of that retribution."

"Most worshipers of Harg would accept revenge as a justification for acts of war, but not for personal recrimination. I must admit that I do not really understand their reasoning. My great uncle, the previous mattouk of Khoulan, solved the conundrum by interpreting Harg's scriptures as calling for peaceful reconciliation to avoid all acts of war. I try to follow where he led but often find it difficult to ignore the temptation to seek revenge."

"You aspire to a level of self control which I could never hope to attain."

Kesh sighed. As on the previous occasion when he had broached this subject, although he detected a slight softening of Hernst's anger, his friend still displayed no sense of remorse.

Nevertheless, Kesh came away with Hernst's permission to arrange for the sale of their copper.

The next day Kesh mounted his horse and wished peace and long life to King Kevin, expressing his regret that he could not keep him company for longer. Sakki saw that Kesh was leaving and watched like a coiled spring, ready for the moment when he should take flight.

Kesh urged his horse northwards through the streets and once, out of the city, he started along the road towards the distant line of mountains in an optimistic frame of mind. He was looking forward to releasing Applad and offering Hernst's mother the possibility of profitable trade. This mood held despite the chill winds and driving rain that beat against his face for much of the journey. He wrapped Ship's cloak tightly around his body only to find that some of the stitching was giving way. The tighter he pulled it, the larger the split became. Nevertheless, he refused to be downhearted, and spent the miles dreaming of the warm hearths and hot tea that might be enjoyed at the next inn or, on the third day, within the walls of the mountain fortress of the Ahn Dehar.

Once he reached their territory, Kesh left his horse in the barn and his crow in the trees and climbed up the path on foot. He soon gained admittance to the fort and Hernst's family all greeted him with welcoming smiles but Hernst's mother looked harassed and anxious. Wanhild translated her first question, which was an enquiry after Hernst's well-being. Kesh told her that he was well and that he hoped to bring him to visit her en route to Khoulan. He explained about the arrangement he had made with the kings to take him there. She began to look a little more cheerful. Kesh told her briefly about his plans for their copper and she said that, in principal, she did not oppose the plan but that she would need to know exactly where the mine would be and what kind of disturbance it would entail. Kesh was pleased that she seemed to share his concerns about the beauty of their lands. She did not want to make money regardless of the disadvantages, as her son had seemed inclined to do. Finally, Kesh broached the subject of Applad, and respectfully requested that he be allowed to go back to his family now that they could be confident that Hernst's life was no longer threatened. Hernst's mother's face grew serious. He had been ill, Wanhild told him. For a moment, Kesh was afraid that they was about to inform him of his death but instead Wanhild offered to take Kesh to see him.

He was led to a solitary hut at the back of the community. Wanhild turned a large key in rusty lock and pulled the door open. He lit a lamp and held it aloft. Kesh was shocked by what he saw. Applad was sitting on a bunk against one wall, staring at the floor. The monk could hardly believe there could be such a rapid change in a man. Barely a moon ago he had been vigorous, proud and portly gentleman. Now he was thin, stooped, besmirched with grime, his hair and beard untrimmed and streaked with extra strands of grey. Kesh felt an almost tangible blow as he realised that he himself was to blame for the deterioration he saw in this man. This was not what he had intended.

"Applad!" Kesh knelt before him. "Forgive me!"

The old man did not respond but continued to stare at some point on the floor a little distance in front of him.

"What have they done to you?" Kesh looked in horror at the disheveled hair, the gaunt figure, the sunken eyes "Oh, this is all my doing!"

The old man started to mutter something but his eyes were on the floor still, not on Kesh. The monk leaned in closer but could not make out what Applad was saying. He did not seem to be making any sense, raving aimlessly.

"Merciful Harg, how could I leave an innocent man captive of a tribe he could not communicate with?" Kesh gently took hold of the man's hand and pushed up the sleeve, looking for bruises, afraid that the Ahn Dehar had been taking their grief out on him. He checked the other arm. He could see no marks. The mouth was still moving but little more than a moaning sound was coming out.

"Applad, it is I, Kesh of Khoulan. Do you remember me?" Kesh took hold of both his shoulders. "Look at me. Do you remember me? I am here to release you, to take you back to your family. You remember your family, do you not? They will be waiting for you."

The old man's eyes slowly lifted and he seemed to be struggling to focus on Kesh's face.

"It is I, Kesh of Khoulan, here to take you back to freedom," the mattouk repeated. Then he muttered bitterly to himself. "Kesh of Khoulan, who so wrongly robbed you of it in the first place."

"Freedom?" the old man's thin voice wavered. "Family?"

"Yes, yes, that is right. I will take you out of here, to freedom and your family."

It was obvious to Kesh, by now, that the man would need to be taken home by cart, or escorted on a steady mount, at least, and Kesh knew he would have to be the man to do it, if he was ever going to repay the wrong that he had wrought him.

"Wanhild, fetch me a blanket, will you, please? Let us get this old man out into the fresh air for a while. Then we should get him some hot tea and a meal. We need to build up his strength if we are going to get him down the mountain."

***

When Kesh arrived back at the palace of the Four Kings with a rather worn looking Applad he asked Kevin if he could borrow some money so that he could pay a doctor to attend Applad at his home. Kevin generously gave him enough money to cover any likely medical bills for a whole round of seasons and told him not to worry about paying it back. He knew, he said, that Morthern monks did not actually have any money of their own. A few days later, when Kesh had gone north again, making for Wadderhick this time, to try to interest a mining company in the Ahn Dehar's copper, Kevin went down to the dungeon to see Hernst.

"May I speak with you?" he asked the prisoner with sudden deference.

Hernst shrugged. "How would I be able to stop you?"

"If I speak, I would request that you be prepared to listen."

Hernst wondered what could be coming. "I am listening," he said.

Kevin spoke slowly and with many hesitations. "I want to apologise for what we did - for my own part, at least. I now feel very ashamed at what happened - at what I allowed to happen without even raising an objection. We accepted the argument too easily - that taking the life of one Penethellan - namely, your father, the one who stood in our way over mining your coal - might save the many lives that could be lost if we went to war with your people. I now see we had neither the right to take that life nor the right to take the coal by force. We should have respected your ownership and respected your father's decision. I am sorry that we did not."

Hernst said nothing and, for a long while, stood looking at the damp wall of his cell.

"Well, that's all I had to say," Kevin finished. "I guess I'll be going now. Kesh should be back in a moon or so to take you to Khoulan. I hope that you'll be more comfortable there."

"Yes," Hernst said eventually. "Thank you."

Kevin nodded, and made to go. Then he turned back and said, "I'll send down some warmer bedding and get the kitchen staff to improve your diet. I don't want you getting sick like Applad."

"Thank you," Hernst said again. "But what I really want to know is how much of my sentence I am expected to serve. How long will I be exiled at Khoulan?"

"We'll see," Kevin answered. "That's not up to me. It must be decided between us. The decision will have to wait until the other kings get back."

And with that he left the dungeon.

Chapter 22

Ted's arrival on the Sacred Mountain came suddenly and unexpectedly to his hostesses, as, unlike Doug, he had sent no message on ahead to warn them. Nevertheless, he was greeted warmly by his old shipmates and Hannala smiled sweetly, declining his offer to seek rooms somewhere in Xoutha, telling him that, of course, they would be able to find him a room within the community. Doug was absolutely delighted to see Ted. When he arrived at the gate, he greeted him with almost childlike excitement, eager to tell him all about the sunken ship and his plan for some of its contents. When Ship joined the group of welcomers, Ted's demeanour became more formal.

"Sir," Ted straightened and gave a deferential nod, half raising his hand as if to salute.

The old man reached for his hand and shook it.

"You must call me Ship from now on," he told him.

"Yes, sir," said Ted, not quite managing to obey.

"Have you been offered tea?" asked Ship.

"Oh yes, of course, we must have tea," said Hannala, waving off one of the trainee priestesses towards the kitchens.

The group slowly made their way up to the balcony of the great hall. The table was too small to accommodate Hannala and all four humans, even after they had pulled it away from the wall and brought out extra chairs. Hannala offered to take her tea in the kitchens, but Ship suggested that they find an extra table from somewhere to make enough space. A second table was duly brought and pushed up against the first. Ship sat at one end and Hannala at the other, while the other humans arranged themselves along the sides with Ted and Doug facing out to sea. Pots of hot teas of several varieties arrived on trays together with freshly baked savouries and cakes. Soon after they had started eating, Ahbrem arrived from his room in the north tower and, behind him, pulled along by the hand, trailed Wyn, who had taken over the majority of the Xouthan translation task in order to be with him. More chairs and tea were sent for. Ted listened dutifully to tales of how the translation was progressing and how quickly the etherium was coming along and then it was Doug's turn to speak again of his plans to retrieve the embryos from the ship at the bottom of the bay.

"You mustn't get your hopes up," Ted warned. "There are going to be problems at all stages. Even if the embryos prove to be viable and we actually manage to get some to implant, assuming we can find willing Penethellan mothers, and then we manage to feed them successfully and raise them up so that we could eventually make them our wives, the human race still might not be saved. Our children would all be very closely related. The mothers would all be Brannan's daughters so our offspring would all be cousins. There would be too much risk of heritable diseases building up."

Doug looked glum. "You're saying there's no point in trying? I thought cousins used to marry all the time. I don't see why Brannon would send his offspring off into space if there was no chance of them marrying when they grew up."

"Yes, they could marry, but it isn't ideal. Future generations could become dangerously inbred, because the offspring of the cousins will only have each other to take as partners. It really isn't advisable."

"Surely we should at least give them the choice. A human cousin for a partner has got to be a better prospect than no humans at all, which is what we are currently facing, gentlemen. What do you think, Nathan?"

"That's not an easy question for me," said Nathan. "I have been giving it a lot of thought since you went down to the ship. I don't think we should bring these children into the world just because we have no partners. On the other hand, leaving human embryos on the bottom of the sea until they rot isn't very ethical either. I suppose," Nathan took a breath before making his final pronouncement "Overall, I suppose we should try to save them, if Ted's willing to give it a go."

Doug looked pleased. Nathan was declaring his support in front of the other two humans, but Ted wasn't showing much enthusiasm.

"Do you have any volunteers?" he asked.

"We thought we'd leave that one to you, Ted," said Doug. "You're the one the Penethellan ladies like."

"I don't want them to do it because they like me. In fact, I can't see why they would want to do it. Why would they care? What's the human race to them? What are the embryos to them? Childbearing is a big undertaking and motherhood is usually a lifelong commitment."

"I'd do it," said Hannala suddenly.

The humans all turned to stare at her.

She coloured a little and said, "You humans are very important to us. If there was anything I could do to help, I would. Unfortunately, I am a little too old for childbearing but I would do it if I could."

"So would I," said Wyn. "If my husband didn't mind."

She looked at Ahbrem, whose expression made her add, "But perhaps we should have one or two of our own before I volunteer."

"There you are, you see," said Doug. "We would easily get willing volunteers."

"Be careful," said Nathan to the women. "We're not what you think, you know. You Penethellans seem to think Ship has some religious significance but he doesn't. He's been misleading you, I'm afraid. He's just a man. He's no more important than any one of you."

"You are entitled to an opinion," Hannala told him. "But so are we. We understand the significance of the Prophet of the Sunken Ship more with every passing round. His friends are our friends. We humbly offer you our service."

"You've got your head in the sand," Nathan told her, suddenly showing his frustration. He lifted the book, which he now carried everywhere with him, in front of Hannala's face. "Open your eyes to the truth. I offer it to you but you refuse to even consider it."

"Your truth is alien to us," Hannala said simply, and turned her gaze to the most senior of the humans. "Ship, why don't you set this service as the task for this year's maidens?"

"Oh no!" Ship said quickly and emphatically. "No. That would be like giving them an order. If any Xouthan women want to volunteer to carry human babies, the offer must come from the women themselves. I really should have nothing to do with this proposal. I'm too old. I will be gone by the time these girls have grown if, indeed, they are ever born."

Hannala smiled and did not argue. She looked at Nathan as if to imply that Ship had just proved her point.

"So will you dive with me tomorrow?" Doug asked Ted.

***

Maina looked out some gifts that she thought might be suitable to give to the Wildlanders to take to their women folk. There was a favourite dress she had worn to attend palace events when she was younger. It was tight fitting and, although she was lean enough for her ribs to show through her fur, she had never regained her original narrowness of waist after Calim Bradmutt's birth. In her jewel box there were strings of beads and silver necklaces set with coloured glass which she never wore, and a scarf of Anthrakat silk which was such a garish colour that it did not match any of her gowns. Maina packed all the items into a box and tied it up with string. The colonel had already told her with regret that, unfortunately, no soldier had volunteered to venture with his wife into the Wildlands, so that, unless she gave an order for someone to be picked for the task, it would be impossible to carry out. Maina had decided to release the captives anyway and a date was set. Arrangements were made for her to watch from the safety of the guard tower above the gates as the Wildlanders were taken through the wall and presented with their gifts.

She looked down on the group of soldiers below as they unshackled the captives. Their captain handed over the box with as much ceremony as he could muster and held his open hand out to the south, a display that Maina easily understood as indicating that they should take the box away with them. However, the Wildlander who took the container turned it over in his hands and pulled one end of the string so that the box fell open and spilled some of its contents onto the ground. The young man picked up the dress, at first by the hem then, turning it the right way up, held it up against his chest and frowned. One of the others picked up some of the silver and crammed it into his pocket, while a third pointed southwards towards open country and shouted something. It was as though they had not realised until that moment that they were being freed but that, now they found themselves released, they must run away as quickly as they could before their captors changed their minds. The dress was dropped amongst the spilled beads and all four men took off at a brisk pace, moving towards a tree-covered knoll a little way off. There they paused briefly to look back before moving off again and disappearing into the distance.

A messenger was sent up the stairs to Maina to ask if the guards should leave the gifts on the ground or collect them up. Maina asked for them to be retrieved. If the Wildlanders didn't want her cast-offs, then she might as well keep them as reminders of more innocent times. So much for her efforts to befriend the neighbours! She would have to think of another plan. She had achieved one short term ambition though. She had sent the captives back to their families.

***

Ted spent long hours on the sunken ship gleaning information from its database on embryo handling and implantation. He then asked to be taken to consult both Xouthan and Morthern doctors on the biology of Penethellan reproduction. One of that round's priestess trainees, Cestra of Ghaba Head, was given the task of accompanying him to Zoradetra and introducing him to doctors and midwives and also translating Xouthan medical texts for him in the city's library.

On their return to the Sacred Mountain, the trainee expressed a desire to learn more about all things human. Ted went into Morth, accompanied by Ahbrem and Wyn, to consult medical tomes in the Khoulan and Ahbresk libraries and Cestra, having completed her task very early in the round, had some free time. She attached herself to Nathan and began to attempt a passage of translation into Xouthan. Afterwards, she showed it to Hannala who complimented her on her efforts, pointing out just one or two phrases that could be reworded. Cestra went back to Nathan to start work on a second passage, but she was more interested in listening to what Nathan had to say. She took to reading ahead in the Sacred Language far beyond the sections she might have time to translate. She asked many questions. 'Did all humans have the same religion?' Nathan admitted that, unfortunately, many did not believe in this religion. 'Did King Ted follow this religion?' As far as he knew, said Nathan, he did, although he did not recall having many conversations about religion with King Ted. She expressed an interest in seeing the etherium, complete now apart from furnishing it with an altar. Nathan took her up the steep steps onto the new platform. He found the fresh scent of newly sawn timber and the magnificent view of the Xouthan coast a heady mix. He knelt to praise God for his good fortune. Cestra gently sank to her knees at his side. Nathan turned to look at her, kneeling with him in this Christian space. A blissful smile began to stretch across his lips and he thanked God anew for sending him, at long last, a potential convert to the faith.

Still on his knees, he took her hands into his.

"Cestra, if you are going to pray to God - to 'my' God – then you must tell Hannala that this is what you want to do. You cannot continue to pray to the Xouthan gods as well. It is not allowed. You must choose between them and the one true God. Perhaps you should take a few days to think about it before you commit yourself."

"I don't think I need time to think. If He is the true God, then it is to Him that I must pray."

"Very well, my dear. You have made a wise decision but you must realise that it will destroy your career as a priestess. I advise you to go to Hannala straight away. Explain that you want to convert. Ask her what you must do. Ask for permission to remain on the Sacred Mountain so that you can work with me. I am not Hannala's favourite human being, I fear, yet I rely on her good will. I do not wish to annoy her, so you must do as she commands".

"I will," Cestra's face was flushed with the thrill of making such a profound change to her life. "I'll go to her study now."

Hannala was not happy that Cestra was abandoning her training but decided that the young woman would have the best chance of changing her mind and picking up the threads if she remained on the Sacred Mountain. Hannala gave Cestra permission to work for Nathan full-time and to be excused all temple duties while retaining her rights to board and lodgings. Nathan thanked Hannala personally, later that day, for her exceptional generosity.

When Ted returned from Morth, Cestra sought him out.

"I have converted!" she said excitedly.

"How do you mean?"

"I have converted to your religion. I have become a Christian."

"Really?" asked Ted. "So Nathan's convinced you?"

"Yes. Aren't you pleased?"

"I am pleased for you, if you're sure it's what you want."

"Oh, I am."

"Well, good," Ted said, nodding.

After a moment of hesitation, suspecting that her efforts to impress Ted had not quite hit their target, Cestra rallied.

"How did your medical studies go in Morth?"

"They went well, thank you. The Mortherners are a little more reticent, somehow, but very thorough and methodical. I learned a few extra facts."

"Are you ready to proceed?"

"I don't know," Ted sighed. "As ready as I'll ever be, perhaps."

"I want to be the first!" she exclaimed.

"What?"

"The first to bear a human child."

"No," he told her quickly.

"No? Why not?"

Ted hesitated, questioning his own motives. Why not? Was it just because he knew her, or was it because he had actually begun to care about her?

He certainly didn't want to let Cestra think that he had feelings for her.

"Because I'd like you to be my assistant."

"Oh."

"I need someone who understands what we're trying to do but can see things from the Penethellan perspective. It would also be good to have a female assistant present to reassure the Penethellan volunteers during the procedure. I need a nurse, if you like, to assist the doctor that I will have to pretend to be."

"You will make a wonderful doctor."

"Thank you. I'm not so sure but I'm the best hope, apparently."

"Be sure," Cestra said and smiled with the authority that only a female Penethellan could have offered him.

Over the next few moons, Hannala arranged to visit several of the nearest Xouthan temples and there she gave inspirational talks to both priestesses and lay women. With her help, ninety five married Xouthan women volunteers of childbearing age were recruited. Their details and medical histories were registered by Cestra, together with a document signed by their husbands giving permission for the procedure to take place. They all came from either Ghaba or Zoradetra and so lived relatively close to the Sacred Mountain. That meant they could be easily monitored during any resulting pregnancy. Each of the four kings was initially allocated a roughly equal number of women and financial support was to be provided by them for any human children born to the women, although there was an agreement that it would be the children who would eventually be shared equally between them, rather than the women, in order to reduce the possibility of unfair differences in the sizes of any resulting 'families'.

In the initial batch of procedures, Ted and Cestra implanted five of the embryos from the ship, one for each human 'father' and, as Ship refused to get involved, one for luck. They monitored the women for any signs of success. One woman began a pregnancy. There was great excitement amongst those involved, although Ted was convinced that she was simply carrying her husband's child. She miscarried after seven moons, an event that was traumatic for both the mother and for Ted. He rushed down to Ghaba as soon as he heard that something was wrong and found the midwife carrying a sacking bundle out to the garden for burial, as was the accepted custom for stillborns, and the husband with a spadeful of soil ready to throw into the hole he had just dug. Ted begged to be allowed to take the foetus away for examination. The parents hesitated. Ted offered money. They refused, but then relented and gave their permission. Although they still refused to take the money, Ted left it anyway, piling the gold coins on the top of a cupboard that stood against the wall in the hallway of their modest dwelling.

Alone in his room on the Sacred Mountain, Ted cautiously unwrapped the little bundle. It was covered in blood and slime and had a very strange smell. He studied it closely. It was hairless and the genital arrangement confirmed that it was human, a little boy. Ted stepped away from it and could not bring himself to touch it again for quite some time. Although the mother had been allocated to Nathan, Ted felt that it was somehow his child and that he had horribly failed the boy. Nathan knocked on the door at dusk.

"Well, what's the verdict?"

Ted could not answer. He pulled the sacking aside for Nathan to see.

"It's human!" Nathan breathed in wonder "Isn't it?"

Ted nodded.

Nathan let out a whistle but said nothing more. He could see Ted's distress.

The next day he led a funeral service for the baby in the etherium, attended by Doug and Ship and Cestra as well as Ted. They buried him in a small cemetery on the mountain. The funeral helped to soothe Ted's disquiet - it went some way towards displaying a recognition of the human origins of the child - but he absolutely refused to make any further attempts at implantation. Doug was angry at Ted's stubbornness but it seemed as though nothing would change his mind. Since the season's weather was now rapidly deteriorating, making dives more difficult, Doug saw little point in remaining on the Sacred Mountain for a second consecutive winter. At the palace, he would be able to organise delivery of some copper and devote a little time to the design of turbines. He sent a message to Kesh asking him to fetch Hernst from the palace as soon as was convenient. Although time had healed the wound, inside and out, the thought of Hernst haunting the palace was still a little unsettling.

Chapter 23

It was a full round since Wyn's wedding and Maina was nearing the end of her term as governor. The deputy governor, who had taken over perfectly competently while she was away at Wyn's wedding, suggested that Maina should take a holiday before deciding whether to stay on in Mardek province. Maina would have loved to travel to Morth to see Kesh but Morth was still a focus of hatred for her father and, it seemed, to most other Xouthans. She decided to visit Enaha instead. Enaha held many happy memories for her and she spoke the language reasonably well. Furthermore, she had long ago told herself that she would study their religion and, if invited, attend their winter solstice ceremony. She hoped that it might bring her some certainty about her own faith. She wrote to Wyn at the Sacred Mountain, enclosing a letter to be forwarded to Kesh, asking him to meet her in Enaha. However, by the date of her departure, no reply had come. The morning she was due to leave a letter arrived from Wyn, in which she said that she thought that Kesh was overseas, collecting Hernst and visiting Applad and the Ahn Dehar.

Maina was disappointed but did not cancel her trip. She travelled to Enaha with a female companion, Nenya, an unmarried administrator from the governor's office, still dreaming that Kesh would somehow know where she was going and would come to visit her on his way back from Ahn Dehar. It was early winter but the weather was unusually mild and no snow had fallen as yet in Enaha.

They arrived at Odout after a long journey by cart and rested the first night at an inn. The next day, Maina took Nenya to the little village of Hittan. She showed her the tiny house where she had stayed, carefully omitting to say that a young monk had lived there with her, and then she took her to seek out Bim and his wife. The couple were surprised, but claimed to be absolutely delighted, to see her. Both their daughters were married now, the youngest to Ginn Gilleth, and so were not at the house. Bim immediately asked Maina about Kesh and she told him that he had seemed well the last time she had seen him.

"And the baby?" asked Bim's wife. "Do tell me there was a baby."

"Yes, there was a baby," Maina smiled and blushed, glancing in Nenya's direction, hoping she had not suddenly developed an understanding of Enahet. "But please do not say anything to anyone. Kesh and I were not married. The baby is with foster parents."

"Oh," said Bim's wife, obviously disappointed. "But you were a perfect couple. You should be married. You should be a family."

"Believe me, I would love to be married to Kesh but I am Xouthan and we were at war with Morth. It was impossible."

"Ah," she said as if some understanding was dawning.

"I'm so sorry that we did not explain at the time," Maina continued. "Our grasp of Enahet was not all it should have been."

"I knew there was something different about you."

"Well, if the child is well, that's all that matters," Bim said reassuringly.

"He was well, the last time I had any news, but he's in Morth. Sadly I have not been able to see him."

"Oh, how awful for you!" Bim's wife exclaimed. "I'll get you some tea."

Tea, the answer to all problems, was served on the table that Maina remembered from the time of her first lesson in Enahet. While they were drinking it, Maina explained how she intended to make a study of different religions and would be interested in witnessing the dawn celebration of the winter solstice that she had missed the last time around.

"Would it be possible for us to attend the event, do you think?"

Bim's face grew serious.

"We've had a very poor harvest this round," he said.

"Oh, I'm sorry," Maina said. "Does that mean the celebration will be cancelled?"

"On the contrary, it means that the celebration will be more ... intense than usual. The more we need the help of the Sun, the more we must do to please him."

"I see," said Maina, wondering why it made him look so glum.

"Well, you will see, perhaps, at the ceremony. Why don't you bring your things here and stay with us until then. You can both sleep in our daughters' old room."

Maina thanked them gratefully and sent for their baggage from the inn at Odout.

On the day of the winter solstice Maina and Nenya were woken well before dawn. There were stars still shining in the sky. Bim said that this was a good sign. It meant the disc of the rising sun would be visible and the ceremony could be timed precisely. They joined a procession of Hittan people who walked almost silently through the darkened streets and out of the village to the south-west. They followed a narrow track that lead round a hill and up a little rise to a mound near the river, around which were planted a circle of tall stones, each set upright in the ground. The nearest stones were only waist height but the furthest stones were higher than a man's shoulders. From a distance the tops of the stones seemed to be rounded but, on closer inspection, it could be seen that each stone had been carved into a narrow wing at the top, decorated with a curved tail leading down diagonally from the highest point to a groove that ran all around the neck. Each groove contained a line of twine encircling the stone. Between the two tallest stones on the far side of the circle lay an enormous rectangular block of rock in line with the circle. The villagers spread out a little as they neared the stones but most stayed near the side where the smaller ones stood, where they were likely to get the best view over the top of them. As the black of night thinned, Maina could see that there were already figures standing beside each stone. Each held a tethered animal. The nearest had yard fowl, then there were grass-geese and, finally, sheep. Maina frowned as she began to wonder what the animals were for.

A cloaked and hooded man at the far side of the circle by the largest rock began to sing. He had a powerful voice but the sound of it was sometimes lost in the air across the space. The song seemed to be the signal for all faces to turn to the east and, within a few moments, a dazzling crescent appeared on the horizon. At a shout from the hooded man, the figures holding the yard fowl lifted them above the smallest standing stones and brought their necks down hard on the sharp top edges. The curved tails proved to be carved runnels and, at their ends, tied by the strings going around the neck of each menhir, Maina now saw that there were cups which collected the blood drained from the neck of each slaughtered beast. By the time she had worked out the function of all these parts, the animals had all been slaughtered in turn until only the sheep remained. It took two men to lift each sheep aloft and the beasts struggled and bleated in terror. Maina turned her face away. Her attention was caught by a young woman walking slowly towards the stone circle accompanied by a robed man on either side of her, making for the largest rock. Maina was pleased for a moment, thinking that this must be a priestess who would now draw the slaughtering ceremony to a close but, after the young woman had been helped up onto the top of the large rock, instead of standing on it to use it as a pulpit, she lay down on it as though it were a bed. The hooded singer now climbed onto some sort of platform on the far side of the rock and drew a large sword, raising it above the recumbent woman in line with her breast. Maina screamed in horror, turned on her heel and ran.

Looking back, she wondered why she had not tried to do something to stop the murder. Why had she simply run away? What weakness of spirit had taken over at that crucial point? But, at the time, Maina had not thought at all, only felt. She ran and ran, shocked and sobbing, half way back to Odout. It was only after she had run out of breath and was forced to stop, gasping for air, that she realised that she would be obliged to return to Hittan. Nenya was still there and spoke no Enahet. All their luggage was at Bim's house. Reluctantly Maina turned and walked slowly back.

It was full daylight now and the sun was shining down on the pale winter fields through the leafless branches of the roadside trees, but it brought her no cheer. Her disappointment was profound. So much for seeking renewal of her faith with the Enahet! They were nothing more than savages. She would choose the Xouthan gods over theirs any day. At least the gods she had been brought up to worship demanded no more than flowers or petals as offerings. If the Xouthan gods could bring them good harvests with such modest offerings, why did the Enahet gods need the blood of slaughtered creatures? The Enahet had always seemed such a kind and homely people, peace loving and hard working. Maina had enjoyed the happiest time of her life, living as an equal in their midst. Now those memories were destroyed, ripped from her, forever tainted by the knowledge of the disgusting religious practices that were hiding behind a front of living by honest toil and taking joy from innocent pleasures.

Nenya met her a little way out of Hittan. Bim and Ginn Gilleth were with her and they looked concerned. They said that two men set off on the road north to look for her, in case she had gone that way. Ginn was despatched to fetch them back.

"Where were you?" Nenya asked in Xouthan.

"I'm so sorry," said Bim in Enahet before she could answer her friend. "If I could have known that it would upset you like this, I would never have let you see the ceremony. I did try to warn you."

Maina nodded but could not bring herself to speak to him.

"I think we should go back to Odout," she told Nenya as they followed Bim back to his house.

"And miss the party?" asked Nenya.

"I don't think I feel like going to any party."

"You do realise that everything will be closed in Odout, don't you?" Nenya asked her. "Everyone there will be at a party, too. There's no point in going anywhere until tomorrow or maybe even the next day, to be on the safe side."

'Ugh!' Maina thought. 'Two more days to endure of this nightmare!', but she agreed that they would have to stay where they were for the time being.

"I will stay here with you," Nenya said later, when they stood alone in the bedroom at Bim's house.

Maina realised with some surprise that Nenya actually still wanted to attend the evening festivities.

"No, no. You go along without me."

"But I don't speak the language."

"I'm sure Bim and his wife will look after you. Ginn Gilleth is a good man too. You managed to communicate before, when they came with you to look for me."

"I think they saw my alarm, noticed your absence and put two and two together."

"Well, I didn't speak any Enahet the first time I went to their winter festival and I managed to survive."

"Very well. If you're sure you don't mind, I will go."

Maina sat alone in the bedroom at the front of Bim's house. She had listened to the muffled fragments of cheerful conversation between Bim and his wife floating up from the living room as evening fell. She imagined they were decorating Nenya's hair with berries and ears of corn as they had done with hers four rounds before. Then Nenya put her head round the door to say goodbye and the house fell silent. With only memories to keep her company, Maina asked herself how she had arrived at this miserable state of affairs. It wasn't merely her disappointment with the Enahet that plagued her but all the misery that seemed to have threaded itself into the tapestry of her life. Why had she not taken her chances when she had them? Kesh had wanted to marry her when Calim was first born. Why hadn't she clung to him? She could have had the love of a good man and kept her child. She could have known happiness. Instead, here she was, disillusioned and disappointed, alienated in the very place she had thought of as being the wellspring of her happiest memories.

The stub of her candle flickered, the wick reaching up heroically from a pool of molten wax. She opened the window for some air and heard music from the village hall. At least she would not be asked to perform tonight. She wondered what Nenya would choose to sing, or whether she might refuse to perform altogether. Maina felt a twinge of guilt for not warning her about that part of the proceedings.

She looked up at the dark sky and wondered when the first snow would come. The weather had been unusually mild. She realised, however, that the ship that crossed from Wadderhick to Odout would not be operating in the depths of winter, even if there was no ice, so there was, in reality, no chance of Kesh travelling via Enahet on his way back with Hernst. She might just as well have stayed in Mardek. In fact, Mardek seemed quite appealing from this distance. At least there she had a function and seemed able to fulfil it tolerably well. 'Ah, there is nothing like a miserable excursion,' she sighed to herself, 'to make you appreciate the benefits of home.'

After lighting a second candle and gloomily watching it burn halfway down its length, Maina heard the revellers return from the festival. There were footsteps on the stair and a knock came at the door.

"Come in," she said.

She was surprised to see that it was Bim's head that pushed hesitantly in through the opening, lit by the candle he was holding out in front of him.

"Are you alright?" he asked.

"Yes, perfectly, thank you."

"May I speak with you a moment?"

"Of course. Sit down, won't you?"

"It's chilly in here. You should come down and warm yourself by the fire."

"There's no need. I will be going to bed very shortly. What is it you wanted to speak about?"

"I just thought I should confess that I rather took a liberty this morning with certain personal information about you that I am privy to. I hope I have not damaged your good name."

Maina said nothing and so Bim continued.

"Being chosen as the solstice maiden is a great honour, of course, and great honour is bestowed on the family that gives its daughter for the solstice, but the parents came to me late last night in great distress and suggested that we might use one of our guests instead. There have been occasions in the past when advantage has been taken of the mistimed visits of strangers and the solstice maiden has consequently originated from out-with the community. So, although we now know that you were not Kesh's wife, I am afraid I told them that I happened to know that you have borne a child, that you cannot therefore be a maiden and that you would not therefore make a suitable sacrifice. Of course, their second choice was Nenya, so I told them that I could not be sure of her status in that respect, either, and that the only maiden that could be relied upon was their daughter. Eventually, they acquiesced, and I carried out my duties on the original chosen one."

"*You* carried out ... ?" Maina repeated, horrified.

"Yes. I am Head of the Council now. The solstice ceremony is one of my duties."

"Great Tarn!" Maina muttered under her breath. She swallowed hard, shrinking in her seat in an effort to move further away from the murderer.

What a poor judge of character she was, she told herself. She had thought of Bim as a homely, fatherly figure. Her fondness for him had ranked almost as high as her fondness for her nurse-father, Bradmutt. How misplaced that fondness had been.

Despite her shock, she realised that a great good fortune had been bestowed upon her by way of her mistimed motherhood. What a lucky escape, what a close shave! Then she felt the guilt for, although she had escaped, another young woman's life had been suddenly terminated.

'In effect, that woman died for me,' she told herself.

She forced herself to speak to the executioner. "I must go to the ... what is the name for it in Enahet? ...the burial ceremony, to pay my respects."

"Ah, yes," said Bim. "I will go at first light to the circle to see if the sacred birds have done their work. Once the soul has been released, we can arrange a burial."

Chapter 24

All winter, Cestra worked hard at trying to cheer Ted up. She also made a further study of medical texts, frequently asking Ted to explain passages that weren't clear to her. She wanted to become a midwife, she said, if Ted had no further use for her. He told her that it probably would be a good career for her but that he would miss her if she left. She stayed. Eventually, she made him see what a breakthrough it had been to have one of the embryo's successfully implant and that it was surely worthwhile trying to implant some more.

"You said there were some frozen ovules on your ship, I mean, unfertilised eggs?"

"Yes, a few," said Ted.

"So why don't you try fertilising them and implanting them? Perhaps freshly fertilised eggs would have a better chance of implanting."

"Possibly," Ted reluctantly allowed.

"Ted, I want to have your child."

Ted looked at her blankly.

"Why don't you try fertilising one of the eggs yourself, then you could implant it into me."

Ted was still silent. She had obviously been picking things up quickly. He turned his head on one side and frowned.

"Why would you want me to do that?"

"Perhaps because I am in love with you," she said, and dropped her eyes.

"Are you?" he asked, abrupt because of his surprise.

"A little, I think," she said.

"I would have to marry you. I mean, you would have to marry me."

"I don't mind," she said.

"But you wouldn't be the first," he said, then quickly added, "Sorry, I didn't mean to point out that you would not be my first wife. What I meant to say was that I wouldn't want you to go through the procedure until we've had at least one successful implantation with one of the volunteers. I don't want you to become part of the experiment."

"Alright," Cestra agreed.

And, with that, the implantation programme was resumed. Ted did not relish the prospect of requesting sperm donations from his colleagues, so he embarked on a last-ditch attempt at using prefertilised embryos from the ship. Another five women were treated. Two implantations resulted in pregnancies. One miscarried at three and a half moons. The remaining one survived.

Four moons passed, then five. At seven moons, Ted visited the woman daily, often demanding that he be accompanied by a Xouthan doctor. He was dreading a repeat of the trauma of the previous miscarriage but the foetus continued to grow. Ted even allowed himself a little smile as the Penethellan mother invited him to feel the baby kick. Eight moons passed, then nine.

At ten moons, in the autumn of the sixth round after Kesh and Maina's first visit to the Sacred Mountain, which was therefore close to the date of Calim Bradmutt's fifth birthday, the first human child on Penethella was born. It was a little girl.

***

News of the birth soon arrived at Khoulan. Hersnt was sitting next to Kesh at the dining table when it was first discussed. He could not understand why the arrival of a human baby was a cause for celebration amongst the Morthern monks.

"The child is human? Born to a Penethellan mother? Then it is an abomination!" he declared. "These humans do not belong here. They corrupt and contaminate. They destroyed their own world and now they have come to destroy ours. They are evil. They are monsters. How can you contemplate encouraging human multiplication?"

"I know you do not see them in the same light as we do," Kesh admitted. "But the Ship Prophet is very important to us. You must understand: that what gives joy to him gives joy to us also."

"How can you let your women be used in this way?"

"The Xouthan women are all volunteers. They are quite happy to do this for the Ship Prophet and his friends."

"And if it was your woman, if it was Maina? Would you be happy if she chose to do this?"

"Um," Kesh hesitated.

"No! You would not, because deep in your heart you know this subjugation is wrong."

"If Maina was willing and in a position to volunteer, then I would not object."

"You are blind! Your religious beliefs have blinded you to the truth, to the real nature of these aliens!"

"I'm sorry that you feel like that," said Kesh. "I know you have had a terrible experience with the Four Kings but Ship is a good man and he had nothing to do with the murder of your father. Please try to keep an open mind about him. I hope you will get a chance to see a better side of all our human visitors before too long."

The humans waited anxiously to see if the baby would survive. She was nursed attentively by her Penethellan mother and seemed to thrive. Doug had returned to the Sacred Mountain as soon as he heard that the pregnancy had outlasted the sevens moons at which the previous one had ended. As soon as news of the birth reached Kevin, he also came to see the baby, leaving the Land of the Four Kings in the hands of Penethellan administrators for the first time since their arrival. Once they were all present and the baby had survived a moon and a half of life, the humans felt confident enough to hold a naming ceremony. The humans all felt very strongly about the significance of the birth and they'd had heated discussions about names. In the end, they had decided to vote anonymously. There was one vote for Una, one for Prima, one for Mary and two for Eve.

As the mother had been one of those allocated to Nathan, he was allowed to choose the nature of the ceremony and he arranged a christening service which he would lead in the etherium. All five humans were to attend, together with Cestra and the surrogate parents. They also invited several other Penethellan friends. Maina had accepted with alacrity, hoping to see Kesh there.

Kesh, however, was in a quandary, for he now had Hernst to supervise. He didn't want to lock his friend up and there was no dungeon at Khoulan in which to lock him, anyway. Hernst was bound only by honour and his high regard for Kesh's friendship. Kesh trusted him to remain at the monastery while he was there with him but did not quite trust him to stay put if he wasn't. The only way to attend the naming ceremony was to take Hernst with him.

"It is very important that you promise not to say anything against the humans while we are on the Sacred Mountain," he told him "I am going to have a hard enough time smuggling you in as it is. No man is supposed to go there unless he has taken vows. I am going to have to dress you up as a priestess in one of their hooded robes and hide you in the guest quarters. I do not expect that you will want to attend the ceremony but I will have to ask you to stay quiet while it is taking place and not to let anyone know who you really are. Please appreciate that I am risking breaking several of my vows by allowing you to accompany me."

***

Hernst peered cautiously through the narrow window of his guest room on the Sacred Mountain and watched as the humans led a small procession up to the high wooden platform, their so-called etherium. A Penethellan woman was part of the cortege, carrying something wrapped in a shawl of Anthrakati silk. She stepped carefully, as though she was conveying a precious treasure but Hernst knew that this was the abomination. He was curious as to what it might look like. Strangely drawn, he pulled up the hood of the borrowed robe and slipped out. Once in the open, he gazed up at the platform which stood defiantly above the roof of the tallest building, silhouetted against the morning sky. Above it, a lone seacrow was circling majestically. Hernst crept up to the base of the wooden staircase and saw a space beneath it where he would be hidden. The human Nathan was speaking slowly, as though chanting or reciting. The other humans and the Penethellan woman spoke occasionally, giving formal responses in the pauses. It created the most evil-sounding supernatural incantation.

Hernst had a sick feeling in his stomach, as though it was slowly twisting around, and his heart was beating wildly against the sides of his ribcage. He remembered the last time he had experienced this sensation. It was when he had held the knife above the sleeping king. All the injustices perpetrated against him now flashed through his mind: his father's assassination, his detention in the palace expecting execution and his forced separation from his home and his family. All this was the fault of the humans, alien creatures that had somehow found their way to this world and were slowly corrupting it. Hernst began to tremble with rage and fear, but he knew he must use his anger wisely this time. There would not be another chance as clear as this.